# For Better . . .
# For Worse

December 2020

Time at home allowed me
to complete Book 2. Best
wishes for a healthy and
happy 2021!

Life Is Good!

Elaine

PARLIAMENT SQUARE SERIES

BOOK TWO

# For Better . . . For Worse

*a sara jennings novel*

Elaine C. Baumbach

SPANGLER PRESS

FOR BETTER . . . FOR WORSE

*Parliament Square Series*

*Book Two*

*A Sara Jennings Novel*



Email: Elaine@ElaineBaumbach.com

Facebook: Elaine Montchal Baumbach

Spangler Press



ISBN 978-0-578-81856-6

Printed in the United States of America.

# Dedication

This book is dedicated to special friends I have lost since the publication of my first book, *You Can't Get There From Here*.

Jean Jama was one of my "friend book editors" for my first book. She was so excited to see it published. Although Jean and I met later in life (she was one of my diamond-in-the-rough friends), our friendship grew and we became close. We met for dinner soon after she was diagnosed with cancer and I spent time with her over the next twelve months, through her many ups and downs, before she was taken from us. Jean remained optimistic and upbeat through her treatments and their debilitating side effects. During that time, I never once heard her complain. I like to think that she's smiling down on us, giving a thumbs-up to my second Parliament Square book.

Herb Shoffner was the father of my younger son's buddy during their teen years. He was one of my diamond friends and he was always there for the boys. At a skateboarding event many years ago, Herb showed them how it was done, and he broke a few bones in the process. He was a kind and gentle man with a heart of gold. The community, his friends, and his family miss him every day. I was blessed to reconnect with his family after his passing, as our communication had been limited for decades after the boys graduated from high school and went their separate ways.

In the obituaries I sometimes recognize the names of high school classmates, friends, and others I have known. Life is temporary and death will come knocking for us all. Sometimes we need to be reminded that we should be thankful for each day that our name doesn't appear on those pages. Understand and accept that it will, but today is not that day.

# Table of Contents

The Best Is Yet to Come
Chapter One

# Acknowledgments

Since writing and publishing my first novel, *You Can't Get There From Here*, in 2018, I have slowly authored the second book in the *Parliament Square* series, *For Better . . . For Worse*. In the process, I needed feedback to inspire and assist me in my journey. Most of my friend editors for the first novel signed up to read, review, and provide feedback for each chapter in my second book. Sadly, one of them was taken before her time. She is sadly missed.

Here are the friends who donated their time and energy to edit each chapter as it was written. Each review was greatly appreciated and provided the encouragement I needed to continue writing. After publishing the first book, their enthusiasm for me to write a second book in the series was overwhelming.

Barbara D'Agostino
Barbara Dashiell
Betsy Wray DeStefano
Deb Bolls
Diane Calhoon
Jan Stahlman
Veronica Miller
James Mitchell
Melanie Davis
Pam Wirt
Ray Protzman
Sue Clausen
Susan Straub

With the assistance of my editor, Jason Liller of Liller Creative, LLC, the goal of having a second book published came to fruition. Chapter by chapter, he reviewed and polished my original manuscript, creating the best possible product prior to publication. His numerous years of experience in the literary field enabled our author/editor relationship to grow and flourish through the process.

Be advised that the aging process takes no prisoners. Procedures are available to improve physical appearance by camouflaging the side effects of increasing chronological age, but they do not alter actual age. Those lucky enough to live into their seventies, eighties, nineties, and beyond must learn to accept the fact that happiness cannot be given by others, it comes from within and is truly a personal choice.

# Preface

For *Better . . . For Worse* is the second book in the Parliament Square series. Book one is *You Can't Get There From Here*. Those who have read that book may skip this recap and go directly to chapter one. If you read it but your memory's a little fuzzy, this recap may help. If you haven't read it, go pick up a copy!

Regardless, here is a brief synopsis of book one, along with the last several paragraphs, to help lay the groundwork for the new book . . .

> *When a woman of advanced age, previously independent and purposeful, is required to transition to a senior community against her will, she initially isolates herself, unaccepting of the changes. She experiences "What If" moments reflecting alternative life choices, until she accepts the reality that with age comes the need to compromise, to accept dependence on others, to learn how to redirect purpose and to assume responsibility for one's own happiness.*

Sara Jennings is a senior citizen who characterizes and experiences first-hand the many facets of life in later years. Although youth and middle age are often taken for granted, with the assumption they will last forever, those fortunate enough to live into their seventies and beyond soon realize the playing field has drastically changed. Independence and mobility are often replaced with dependence and immobility. Being healthy is no longer a given but a gift to be embraced. Every day is a present to be unwrapped with sincere gratitude and promise.

Sara refused to accept her nephew's decision to move her from her lovely cottage by the sea to the Parliament Square Retirement Village. She felt she was being robbed of her independence and forced to live in a community of strangers. Fortunately, she was able to take her best friend, Penelope the cat, with her in addition to some of her favorite personal belongings. Her apartment was spacious and nice, but it was not her home.

Her seven daily dining companions became her new friends and, over time, Sara transitioned from fear and sadness to acceptance, involvement, and active participation. Numerous activities at Parliament Square were anticipated and attended as the months passed and Sara developed a friendship with Joseph, who was recently widowed. Sara's college roommate moved to Parliament Square, brightening her spirit.

While at Parliament Square, Sara experienced "What If" moments, reliving decisions or events in her life as they might have happened had she chosen a different path. Life offers many choices; some are made for the wrong reason, some for the right reason, and others are made without any reason at all. Everyone at some point questions the decisions they made. We seldom get do-overs, but if we did, what would we change? What variables would be altered? What results would be achieved? All of these questions played through Sara's mind as she reviewed the years of her life.

The world of Parliament Square is interesting, colorful, and lively. As the average lifespan increases, our aging population grows in numbers. People of advanced age have much to offer.

The following is an excerpt from the end of the last chapter of book one of the Parliament Square series, You Can't Get There From Here:

She noticed that Joseph was perspiring in spite of the fact that the room was a bit on the cool side. "Joseph, are you feeling all right? You seem to be a little nervous and there's sweat on your forehead, although the room feels rather chilly to me. Maybe we should sit out a couple of dances?"

"I'm fine, Sara. Maybe I shouldn't have worn this blazer or maybe being close to you is causing my engine to overheat!" They returned to their seats after the first two songs played. Jim announced that he was going to turn the microphone over to Joseph for a moment before he dispersed his next round of humor. Joseph approached the makeshift stage and took the microphone in his visibly trembling hands. The room became dead (for lack of a better word) silent and...

Joseph cleared his throat and started to speak but no words came out. He cleared his throat again and put the microphone closer to his mouth. "May I have your attention please? After moving here a year ago I struggled with loneliness, sadness and depression. I thought my life was without purpose. I felt I had no reason to get up each day, no reason to live. Family and friends tried desperately to comfort and console me but to no avail. When I had all but given up, I met someone who brought a ray of sunshine into my dismal, gloomy life. As the months passed, I felt the darkness slowly lift. I questioned it at first but soon accepted the fact that at my ripe old age, I had been hit by Cupid's arrow and was lucky enough to feel genuine love again. Never in my wildest dreams did I ever imagine it would happen.

"So in front of my new friends and family at Parliament

Square and my daughter, Allison, I am asking Sara Jennings if she will accept this proposal of marriage. I hope that she will do me the honor of being my bride."

The room was silent as Sara rose from her chair. For a moment she thought that she was having a what if moment but no. This was real. She walked up to the stage on legs of Jell-O and took the microphone into her unsteady hands. She looked into Joseph's beautiful blue eyes and said, "What took you so long?"

The guests were on their feet cheering and clapping. There was going to be a wedding at Parliament Square!

For Better . . . For Worse invites readers to join Sara and Joseph with the wedding planning. There are invitations to address, a dress to buy, floral arrangements to make, a cake to design, reception plans to be made, and of course the honeymoon agenda. Along the way, we'll get reacquainted with the residents of Parliament Square and make a few new friends, too.

The Parliament Square series presents life in a retirement community through the eyes and ears of those who reside there. Life changes as we age, and not always for the better. Moving from life in a private residence of many years to live in very close proximity to many others can be difficult at best. Adjustments must be made, both in attitude and in lifestyle. It's not an easy task and some never learn to adapt. Parliament Square becomes home to those who learn to embrace their new surroundings and friendships, and a prison to those who are too inflexible or unwilling to adjust.

Life in senior communities is often thought of as dull and uneventful, but the world of women in housedresses and men padding around in bedroom slippers all day is a thing of the past. There is a new generation of what used to be called "the elderly," and they are keeping a bounce in their step, a song in their heart, and a smile on their face. They are winning the battle against advanced age being synonymous with being at death's door. As it has been said, eighty is the new sixty.

Enjoy your time with Sara, Joseph, and their friends. Reflect on life for these over-the-hill adults and remember that, one day soon, you or someone you love may be living at Parliament Square.

# Chapter One

## Cupid, Draw Back Your Bow

The initial shock of Joseph's proposal at the Valentine's Day Party lessened as many of the residents stopped before leaving to offer their congratulations and good wishes to Sara and Joseph. In her wildest dreams this was certainly nothing Sara envisioned happening as Joseph was such a private and reserved gentleman. It seemed more like one of her *what if* moments. She had to pinch herself to guarantee that it was really happening. *Ouch, that hurt.* Yes, she was really awake. Joseph proposed to her . . . she was going to get married. She was going to be Mrs. Joseph Jennings Zimmerman.

It WAS Allison she saw out of the corner of her eye when the evening began. Joseph's daughter was there to witness her father propose to Sara, and she was overjoyed to see her father so happy again. He had mourned the loss of Theresa, his wife and her mother, to the point of self-destruction. She feared for his life at times. Now, he was enamored with Sara and eager to author new chapters in their book of life together. The affection and friendship we feel for others can significantly alter our lives for the better as we age. We don't stop enjoying life when we get old; we get old because we stop enjoying life. Never underestimate the power of the mind. Our physical strength and abilities may diminish with the aging process, but mind over matter can be a powerful motivator. If you think strongly enough that you can do something, it may just be possible.

When Sara and Joseph were alone later that evening after the party ended, Joseph confessed, "Sara, I didn't want to put you on the spot in front of everyone like I did. My biggest fear was that you would decline my proposal and I thought if I asked you in front of everyone, there was less chance that you would say no. I realize that in doing so I put you in the hot seat and if you said 'yes' just to be polite and not embarrass me in front of everyone, you still have time to reverse your decision. I would be so disappointed, but I would understand, or I would at least make every effort to understand. You're a very special lady, and although I understand marriage at our ages will be challenging and life-changing, it's what I want. I hope it's what you want, too."

"Joseph, you big lummox, of course I want to marry you. I must admit that I never imagined you proposing in a group setting. You've always been so reserved and quiet. I think everybody else was as surprised as I was. That being said, I am flattered and honored that you feel two octogenarians have a chance to begin married life together. It may prove to be a very interesting and difficult journey. So many of our personal details are uncharted waters. The thought of a man seeing me naked again at my age terrifies me. Even more frightening is the possibility of intimacy. I'm actually afraid to visualize that or ask if it's even possible."

Joseph smiled. "We just need to take it one step at a time. When you met David and I met Theresa we had the same hurdles to deal with as a newly married couple. They only seemed less challenging because of our youthful appearance, our strong physical condition, and our I-can't-keep-my-hands-off-you desires. We're just older versions of those young lovers. Our minds may applaud one thought or activity while our bodies protest the same things. It'll be a balancing act between what our geriatric minds think we can do and what our seasoned physical bodies will allow us to do. I'm not saying this will be a turnkey operation, but I truly believe that we're up to making this work. Are you with me young lady?"

Sara hugged Joseph and said, "This may sound crazy, but I want a wedding here at Parliament Square with all our friends and family. I want it to be a big affair followed by one of those tropical paradise honeymoons. I see *Sandals* destinations advertised as luxury all-included resorts. Of course, the people in the ads are young, tanned, and in great shape. We could break the mold there. I think going to a resort would be perfect for us. I must admit that I am afraid to fly, but we'll work on that. Maybe we could set a record for the oldest newlywed couple to reserve their honeymoon suite.

"They have a bar in the pool that you can swim up to and order a glass of wine while in your bathing suit. I could even wear a two-piece . . . no, no, no, just kidding. I don't want to give those younger folks a new visual to associate with the phrase *beached whale*. But we'll make lots of memories, most of which, *wink, wink,* we'll share with our family and friends. If we're going to do this, we're going to do it right. Being past your prime doesn't mean you can't enjoy life. It just means you might have to experience it at a slower pace, or a lower altitude."

The time passed quickly as they discussed plans for the wedding and honeymoon. It was exciting. It would be the talk of the town. It provided something to look forward to in this often-mundane over-the-hill community. Weddings didn't happen very often. Funerals, 911 calls, and hospital visits? Yes. Weddings, bridal showers, and honeymoons? No. It would be an event the residents of Parliament Square would remember for a long, long time.

Joseph escorted Sara to her room. He embraced her tightly and gently pressed his lips to hers. This was the beginning of a new chapter for both of them. No one knows how their final chapter in life will end. Some hope for good health and longevity, others feel money is the answer, but truth be known, companionship is the real secret to happiness.

There is truth in the saying, "money can't buy happiness." Having a significant other by your side at night, to share meals and conversation, and to be there in the morning when you awaken, provides a true sense of security and an inner peace. Being married later in life is underrated. It can make all the difference in the world.

Sara chatted with Penelope, her cat. "We are going to expand our family. You'll like Joseph. I am not sure if he's a cat person, but we'll convert him if he's not. You're like family to me and your companionship has been a big help. Now Joseph is going to join us and make our lives even better. I am once again going to be someone's wife. I never thought I'd have feelings again for another man. I thought David was my one and only after I lost Andrew. It turns out I was wrong."

It was late and Sara was very tired. She nestled into bed with Penelope at her side. She expected a moment from the past to surface, but nothing did. She cuddled her pillow and fell into a deep sleep. Soon Joseph would be there to replace the pillow. Soon she would have someone to hold her at night, something she dearly missed since losing David. This was not a dream. This was really happening.

The morning sun illuminated the room and cast dancing shadows on the wall. The cold winter wind blew and bent the tree branches outside the window. Inside her heart it was warm, the kind of warmth that comes from a fire burning deep within the soul. It would be a wonderful day. The birds sang outside, and Penelope was curled in a ball, purring loudly, on the pillow.

Sara felt a bit overwhelmed thinking about all that had to be done before there could be a wedding. She didn't want a civil ceremony. She wanted to marry Joseph in the Parliament Square chapel with their friends and family present. She wanted to walk down the aisle as the wedding march played. She wanted Michael to be her escort. *Michael!* He didn't know about the proposal. She had to call him to tell him the good news. He just had to attend the wedding. She would plan it around his schedule if needed. She wouldn't get married without him. He was her closest relative.

They needed to select invitations and plan a reception. She needed to decide who would be in her wedding party—definitely Michele and possibly Allison. She remembered the gowns Jan and Betsy wore in her *what if* moment when she imagined that Jean was Joseph's bride. She shook the image from her mind. There would be no gaudy bridesmaid dresses and head pieces in *her* wedding party. Maybe two attendants would be sufficient. She didn't want to go overboard. She and Joseph needed to pick a date. First, she had to talk with Michael to determine what date would work for him. Yes, she would start there. Her head started to spin as the realization of the wedding gelled in her brain. This was really going to happen, and sooner rather than later. They weren't getting any younger.

After a quick shower, Sara went to the dining room for breakfast. She was starving. As she walked toward her table Linda almost ran over her. "Sara, Sara, I have great news. I was chatting with a friend at the local news channel this morning and mentioned the good news about Joseph proposing to you last evening. She talked to her superior and they want to interview you and Joseph for their evening news program. My friend said they might request to attend the wedding and broadcast it on their station. Isn't that great? Isn't that exciting? You, Joseph, and all the folks here at Parliament Square on television. How great would that be??"

This was a lot for Sara to process before her first cup of coffee. "I'll have to discuss it with Joseph. We're a couple now and we make our decisions together." As the words came out the reality of the situation slapped her in the face. She could no longer make a decision without consulting her "other half." She was once again part of a couple. She liked that. She missed

David, but she didn't realize until this very moment that what she missed even more was being someone's wife. That was all about to change.

The dining room was abuzz with conversation about the upcoming wedding. All eyes were on Sara as she took her seat. Joseph was already there and he glanced at her with his beautiful blue eyes. My, how different this morning was from yesterday. The players were the same, but the stakes had changed drastically. Their table would soon include a married couple. She would no longer be Sara Jennings. She would be Sara Jennings Zimmerman.

Jan insisted on giving Sara one of her over-the-top hugs to congratulate her on her upcoming nuptials. As nice as this seemed, Jan's hugs caused Sara to gasp for air and fight to regain normal breathing. Jan certainly was a strong hugger. Joseph was relieved when Jan returned to her seat without offering one to him.

Sara had noticed that there were basically three categories of huggers: The limp-noodle hugger allows someone to hug them but basically provides little or no return of affection. If given a choice, they would definitely rather shake hands or high-five instead of hugging. The second category is the middle-of-the-road hugger. They respond based on the level of hug received. If hugged lightly, they return a light hug. If hugged firmly, they return a firm hug. They also rarely initiate the hug. The third and final category is the all-consuming hug-like-your-life-depends-upon-it hugger. They engage quickly, without warning, and squeeze with unwarranted strength and control. Their embrace lasts too long and the recipient struggles to get free and regain rhythmic breathing. Jan was definitely a member of category three.

The conversation quickly centered on the proposal and upcoming wedding. Deborah was quickly brought up to speed since she hadn't attended the Valentine's Day event. Pam asked Joseph, "Did you give Sara an engagement ring? I didn't see any ring last evening." Sara never even thought about that. Maybe a ring would be nice. She still wore her engagement and wedding rings as she felt in her heart she was still married to David, and she never stopped wearing them after his death. That would have to change. She needed to remove them permanently and she felt that David would understand. She had a new man in her life now.

Spouses are like pets. You may choose another after losing one, but that new one doesn't replace the one who came before. Each is special. Your life goes on with the new spouse or the new pet, but in your heart, there will always be a special place for the departed one. Remarriage can be a part of the healing process for the survivor. For some it happens quickly, for some it takes time, and for others it never happens.

Joseph replied to Pam, "I want Sara to select her engagement ring. I'm not good at such things and my daughter advised me to have Sara go with me to pick it out. Allison will take us shopping next week, and Sara can select the nicest ring in the store. I want to be able to see it shine on her finger from across the room. She deserves nothing but the best."

Sara remembered Allison telling her about the wealth Joseph and Theresa had accumulated over their lifetime. Sara was concerned because parental wealth can become a hot button when a parent remarries later in life. If something happened to Joseph (hopefully many years from now), Sara did not want to inherit money that should be passed on to his daughters and their families. She would ask Joseph for a prenuptial agreement stating that the majority of his wealth would go to Allison and her sisters. It was the right thing to do. She was certainly not a gold digger and didn't want what wasn't rightfully hers. It was one more item to be added to the list and checked off prior to saying their wedding vows.

After breakfast Sara excused herself and returned to her apartment. She was so anxious to call Michael and tell him the wonderful news. She definitely wanted him as her escort at the ceremony. He and Joseph would look so handsome in their wedding tuxedoes.

Michael answered the phone on the third ring. He asked if anything was wrong because Sara rarely called so early in the morning. She said, "Everything is fine. In fact, everything's much better than fine. Everything is wonderful. Joseph asked me to marry him last evening at the Valentine's Day dance and I accepted. Your old Aunt Sara is getting married!" There was a long silence at the other end of the line. Didn't Michael hear what she said? Was there a bad connection?

"Aunt Sara, I am so happy for you. I'm just a bit surprised. I didn't know you two were so far along in your relationship. Are you certain marriage is what you really want right now? It took a while for you to get accustomed to living at Parliament Square. This will be another major adjustment. Marriage isn't always a bed of roses, as you know. At your age, or *any*, age it can be quite challenging. I don't want to be a wet blanket and rain on your parade, but I also do not want to see you unhappy because you decided too soon to accept Joseph's proposal."

"Michael, I appreciate your honesty and concern, but at my age there may not be time to spend waiting to be sure I'm doing the right thing. Joseph and I may have years ahead of us; on the other hand, we may have only months, or even days. That's why I want it to start as soon as possible. We don't have the option of exploring our relationship during an engagement window. That's for younger couples. We need to enjoy each other's company starting yesterday, and pray that we'll have many tomorrows. Nothing in life is guaranteed. I lost Andrew less than a year after we married. For me, whatever time Joseph and I have together will be the buttercream icing on the cake of life."

Michael laughed. "You sound pretty certain. You convinced me. I'm really happy for you. So, when's the big event? I want to be there to see you as the beautiful bride. Maybe I could even have the honor of escorting you down the aisle? What do you think?"

"That's why I called you. Would do me the honor of walking me down the aisle? I can't imagine getting married without you there. Check your datebook and we'll set a date when you can fly back here for the wedding. What does your April look like?"

"Let me check my calendar. I think Saturday, April 14th looks good, but I want to make sure. Also, on a different subject, Marcy decided the West Coast wasn't for her. She left last week. I'm not sure when or if she'll be back. We have our issues, and maybe this is for the best. I am giving the situation some time before making any permanent decisions. I always felt that you and Mother didn't approve of Marcy. She isn't perfect, but neither am I."

"I am so sorry to hear that. I'll pray for you both. In the meantime, check your availability for April and call me by the end of the week. Your old aunt is going to be a bride again. I had to pinch myself to believe it was really happening."

When their conversation ended Sara felt a mix of emotions. It was wonderful that Michael would return for the wedding, but she was sad that his marriage had hit a rough patch. Although she didn't think Marcy was a good match for Michael, it's hard when any marriage ends. Hopefully, there would be a happy ending for Michael, with or without Marcy. He deserved to be happy.

Once Michael confirmed the date, the wheels would start turning to reserve the chapel and a reception hall, order the wedding invitations, decide on the bridal party . . . and the list went on and on. There would certainly be nothing boring or empty about life at Parliament Square for Sara or Joseph in the coming months. Life would be very busy indeed!

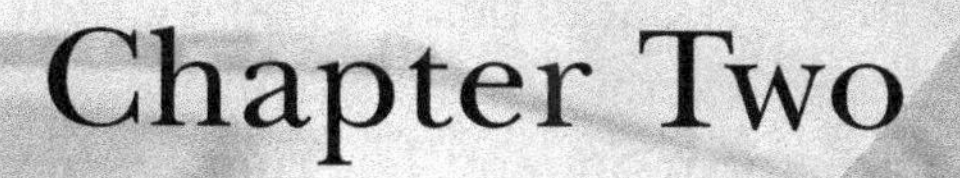

# Chapter Two

## Diamonds Are a Girl's Best Friend

Winter's grip tightened in late February, causing the snow to accumulate as the temperatures dipped to bone-chilling lows. This deferred a trip to the jewelry store to select Sara's perfect engagement ring. Joseph spoke with Allison several times insisting that she not drive in the snow to Parliament Square. The ring could wait until the roads were clear, the sun was shining, and the thermometer was back to double-digit readings.

Since the proposal, Joseph and Sara had been spending more "couple" time together in one or the other of their apartments. Sara encouraged Joseph to come to her place so Penelope wouldn't be alone. Once they were married, they'd have to choose which apartment would become their mutual home. Joseph's unit had two bedrooms while Sara's only had one. The two-bedroom apartment would allow them to accommodate overnight guests while also providing separate bedrooms for Sara and Joseph if needed. These were uncharted marital sleeping waters and it had yet to be determined if either one snored, talked in their sleep, hogged the covers, or had other annoying sleep activities.

As they cuddled watching *Jeopardy* under the New England Patriots fuzzy throw that Joseph got for Christmas, Sara said, "I talked with Michael this morning. he'll be able to fly home the weekend of April 14th. I think we should get married that Saturday. The weather will be nice and it doesn't conflict with Easter weekend. Spring is my favorite season so the timing is perfect. At my age, I don't want to wait to be a June bride. Let's leave that to the younger generation. What do you think? Does April sound good to you?"

Joseph gave Sara a squeeze. "This is your event. You tell me where to be and when to be there. The rest is up to you. I would take the bus tomorrow to city hall and marry you in front of two strangers we met on the street who agreed to be our witnesses. I'm glad you want a nice church wedding with our friends and families, but I'll leave the details up to you. I know Allison and Michele want to be involved with the planning and they'll be happy to help. I'll simply smile and say, 'Yes, Dear' on cue. I value and trust your judgement. I'm certain you'll plan a wedding the folks at Parliament Square won't soon forget. It could quite possibly be the event of the century."

"Joseph, are you sure you're on board with all this? I don't want to put you through a wedding that you feel is over the top and out of your comfort zone. I can't completely explain to you why I want this so much. I just do. Let's call it a woman's prerogative. So, should I start making lists and checking them twice?"

"Sara, I want you to be happy. If having an event here at Parliament Square is what you want, then let's do it. I'll try to stay in the background as much as possible, but please feel free to ask my opinion along the way. I want to know what's happening, but not at the florist and bakery level." He kissed her. "Let's get the ball rolling. April $14^{th}$ is only a couple of months away."

That evening the cuddling heated up a notch. Although younger people try not to think about their grandparents locking lips or, even worse, making love, it does happen. With new pharmaceutical advancements allowing physical intimacy into and beyond eighty years of age, lovemaking is for the young at heart of any age (health permitting, of course).

Sara started making lists and more lists. She wanted everything to be perfect. Michele was so excited to be able to help her longtime friend with the wedding plans. They reserved the chapel at Parliament Square for Saturday April $14^{th}$ at ten a.m. Sara wanted the wedding and reception to be early enough so no one would have to drive home after dark. Many older adults have impaired night vision, and not all of the guests lived on site, so better to be safe than sorry.

A late-morning ceremony followed by a lunchtime reception was the plan. Dancing and music don't have to wait for evening hours. While younger people would be in attendance, the entire event was planned by and structured for seniors.

Michele asked Cynthia to help with ordering the wedding invitations online. The winter weather still made travel treacherous, so shopping for some items via the computer made very good sense. They found beautiful quality invitations that could be delivered in less than a week. Sara compiled the guest list while Joseph reviewed and approved the names. There were friends and family from both sides and some residents of Parliament Square. Joseph's three daughters and their families were invited. Sara only knew Allison, but Joseph had two other daughters. They both lived on the West Coast and he had seldom seen them or their families since Theresa passed away. She was the one who planned all the trips. Joseph hoped they'd be able to have a family reunion of sorts. After checking and double checking, the final count came to just under a hundred names.

Since Joseph's proposal and Sara's acceptance, the conversation at their dinner table often focused on their upcoming wedding. Jim had what seemed like a never-ending repertoire of marriage jokes. This evening was no exception. "A therapist has a theory that couples who make love once a day are the happiest. So, he tests it at a seminar by asking those assembled, 'How many people here make love once a day?' Half the people raise their hands, each of them grinning widely. 'How many people here make love once a week?' A third of the audience members raise their hands, their grins a bit less vibrant. 'How many people here make love once a month?' A few hands reluctantly go up. Then he asks, 'Okay, how about once a year?' One man in the back of the room jumps up and down, ecstatically waving his hands in the air. The therapist is shocked—this disproves his theory. 'If you make love only once a year,' he asks, 'why are you so happy?' The man yells, 'Today's the day!'"

There was a burst of laughter. Jim always knew how to lighten up a moment. Jan spoke up. "I'm so fortunate to be seated at this table. It's the luck of the draw when moving here; I've never been able to determine how they decide the seating arrangements. I could've been assigned to a different table with seven others, but the powers-that-be decided I should be seated at this one. I am very grateful. Now, with the upcoming nuptials, I'm privy to all the details. I'm so excited for you both as you start this new chapter. Let's lift our glasses in a toast to the happy couple."

They clinked their glasses together and exchanged smiles and good wishes. Betsy toasted the soon-to-be newlyweds. "Here's to health and happiness in the coming years. Cupid's arrow targeted you both. As we get older, we often think we'll never again find love. You've disproven that. You make such a lovely couple and we all look forward to sharing stories of your life together in the years to come. I agree with Jan that we're all very lucky to be seated at this table. If you need any bridesmaids, please keep Jan and I in mind. We would love to be a part of your big day!"

Sara's mind flashed back to a *what if* moment in which Jean and Joseph were getting married. Betsy and Jan were the bridesmaids dressed in gowns that made them look like huge, colorful flowers. She shook her head to make the image go away. No, she would have two conservatively dressed bridesmaids, Michele and Allison. "Thank you for your kind offer, but I've decided to have Michele and Joseph's daughter, Allison, as my attendants. We're going to keep it small and low key. I'm sure some of you question our decision to have a wedding event at our age. Joseph would be content with a civil ceremony, but I want the church service and wedding reception. We hope you'll all be able to attend and share our special day."

Another round of clinking glasses signaled a unanimous yes. Although, with the exception of Michele, these friendships had all been recently acquired, Sara felt very close to these people. They were sincerely happy for her and Joseph, and they looked forward to the event with genuine anticipation. It was going to be a day to remember.

One dreary, cold winter afternoon, as the wind howled outside, Sara and Michele sat in the well-lit and warm activity room with a hundred invitations and one address book. Betsy and Jan offered to help and Sara accepted. Sara advised, "Penmanship is very important, so please take your time and be careful. The inside response envelope is preprinted with my name and address. You'll need to put a stamp on that envelope and also one on the outside envelope."

The process began. Each person was given a portion of the list. Jan began to quietly hum Mendelssohn's "Wedding March" as she worked. Betsy told the group that she got A's in penmanship when she was in school, although her hands weren't as steady as they used to be. The group worked quietly, each keeping their thoughts to themselves. Now and then, Jan's humming volume increased and Betsy reminded her to lower it. "Sara," Betsy said, "Jan and I were wondering, since we won't be in the wedding party, if we could possibly sing before the ceremony begins. We did quite well at karaoke night and we'd love to sing several songs before the 'Wedding March.' What do you think?"

"Betsy, I think that's a marvelous idea. Some music would be great while the guests find their seats. I was thinking just some organ music, but singing would be even better. You and

Jan have wonderful voices and maybe Pam would consider making it a trio. You three were the highlight of karaoke night with your wonderful, melodious voices. Let's discuss music choices and ask Pam if she's interested. Great Idea, Betsy! This is shaping up to be a wonderful day."

One night in her room, while getting ready for bed, Sara decided it was time for her to remove her engagement ring and wedding band. She always thought she'd wear them until her dying day. Now all that had changed. She was going to be married to Joseph. She was sad and happy at the same time. One door was closing but another was opening. It was a double-edged sword. She put the rings into her jewelry box and cried herself to sleep.

The first week of March came in like a lamb, not a lion, and the weather improved enough for Joseph to allow Allison to chauffeur them to the jewelry store. The trip was well overdue. Joseph was more excited about looking at engagement rings than Sara was. He wanted something perfect for his betrothed and money was no object. Sara actually felt that matching wedding bands with diamond chips would be perfect. No need for an engagement ring. She didn't need something gaudy or over-the-top expensive. People would think she was marrying Joseph for his money when nothing could be further from the truth. She loved him before she knew he was wealthy. It wasn't his money that drew her. It was his kindness, his gentlemanly manners, and his good looks, not his bank account.

Several younger couples were in the store holding hands and hugging as they shopped for engagement rings when they arrived. Love was definitely in the air. Cupid's arrows were almost visible when the young couples looked into each other's eyes.

Wouldn't it be wonderful to be that age again, with life's

journey stretched out ahead of you instead of memories visible only in the rear-view mirror? So many choices. So many possibilities. So many opportunities. Young love is so innocent, like a breath of fresh air. Life's milestones waiting to be encountered and embraced. The end of the road is nowhere in sight. Youth is invincible and the thought of getting older is nowhere to be found.

Sara returned to reality when the clerk asked if he can assist them. Joseph replied, "Yes, please bring out your best engagement ring for this lovely young lady to model for us. We are getting married in April and I have waited much too long to put a ring on her finger. Spare no expense. I want something special."

Sara interrupted. "Don't listen to him. I told him diamond-chipped matching wedding bands would be nice, but he refuses to listen. What am I going to do with him?"

The clerk said maybe they could compromise. He described a stunning piece with a platinum setting and a half-carat marquis-cut diamond surrounded by small emeralds. "I have the perfect ring for your betrothed. It's classy but not flashy. It's not bargain-basement, but neither is it the price of a small house. I think you'll both like it. Wait here; I'll be right back."

Sara and Joseph exchanged glances and, like the younger couples, shared a heartfelt hug. This ring was just a token of their new relationship. What they felt in their hearts was what held true meaning. They could get married with or without an engagement ring. It was nice, and a token of Joseph's affection, but nothing more.

Sara heard "Diamonds Are a Girl's Best Friend" playing in the background. For her fourteenth birthday her parents had taken her to New York City to see *Gentleman Prefer Blondes* on Broadway. She vividly remembered Carol Channing singing that song. It had been her first Broadway musical and it was the last time she traveled with her parents before their divorce. It was a bittersweet memory.

Some women are very impressed with diamonds and expensive jewelry. Those had never been of any interest to Sara. Most of her jewelry came from department stores. This ring would be special, but is was unnecessary. She agreed to let Joseph purchase it in return for him allowing her to have her fantasy wedding at Parliament Square.

The clerk reappeared with the "perfect" engagement ring. Sara had to admit it was nice. Not too big but certainly beautiful. "Let me slip it on the young lady's finger to see how it looks. We can resize the band, but I want to see how it looks on her finger. Oh my, it's not only gorgeous but a perfect fit. No modifications are needed. You can wear it home after I complete the paperwork with your husband-to-be."

"Joseph, what do you think? I'm not going to deny that it's a beautiful ring. It's one of a kind, just like you. The diamond is perfect. The setting is platinum. The emeralds are the finishing touch. I wasn't in favor of a ring, but this is hard to refuse."

Joseph asked the clerk to give them a private moment. He looked into Sara's eyes and said, "If you like the ring, then I love the ring. You have given me a reason to go on. You have transformed a sad and lonely old man into a happy man full of excitement and hope for the future. You are the best thing that has happened to me in a long, long time. You deserve this ring, and so much more."

Sara and Allison sat together admiring the ring. Sara confided to Allison, "I've told you many times that I fell in love with your father before I knew anything about his wealth. I tried to talk him out of buying this, but he insisted. I don't want you or your sisters to think I am in any way a gold digger looking to get my hands on your father's money. I'm going to insist upon a prenuptial agreement stating that the bulk of his estate goes to his children and their families. I want no hard feelings. And I hope many years pass before we have to worry about this. I'm looking forward to many years of wedded bliss. I can't tell you how long it's been since I felt so much happiness and optimism. Your father truly is a wonderful and caring man."

Allison wiped away a tear and gave Sara a hug. "I'm so glad you came into my father's life. You've made a very sad, depressed man suddenly vibrant and happy. I don't worry about him like I used to. You've given him a reason to care. You've given him purpose. I'm so happy for both of you. It's more than I could have hoped for. Welcome to the family."

Joseph returned to find Sara and Allison teary eyed. "I can't leave you two alone for ten minutes without this happening? Dry those eyes and freshen your makeup. I'm taking two of my favorite ladies out for lunch. We have so much to celebrate."

# Chapter Three

## *Just Say Yes to the Dress*

The day dawned sunny and bright, matching Sara's attitude even on the windy, coldest, New England February morning. Life was once again an adventure instead of a meaningless progression of hours until the next day arrived. She heard the songbirds chirp more sweetly, she appreciated the sunrise and sunsets more, and felt almost like a schoolgirl again in Joseph's presence. Life was good even though old man time was still ticking away her remaining days. She had a man in her life again which seemed almost like a dream or a *what if* moment. Those moments in time had stopped happening as abruptly as they had begun. She was going to get married!

In spite of her busy schedule with the wedding planning, Sara continued to spend two mornings a week in the child-care center. Being there had helped boost her spirits in those difficult transitional days, and she wanted to continue volunteering with the children as long as her health permitted her to do so. She would take a short break for the wedding and honeymoon, but being married wasn't going to change her weekly routine. The children were so cute and full of life. Their hugs were like magical fairy dust. Maybe they didn't allow her to fly, but they helped her return to a time when she was younger. Time spent there was more effective than anything on the market that was supposed to restore youth and vitality.

As she walked back to her apartment, she thought about the power of a hug. It changes over a lifetime. As a child, we hug our parents and relatives without giving it a thought. There is nothing that compares to the sweet, warm embrace of a small child. Then, as the child gets older, that hug transitions to a pat on the back, a handshake, a high five, or a fist bump. The affection is there, but the delivery has changed. Seasoned adults often return to that childlike hug, taking them full circle. Some people are lifelong huggers while others appear to endure the activity rather than actually enjoy it. Joseph's hugs and the children's hugs made Sara feel warm all over, something she hadn't felt in many years. Jan's hugs, on the other hand, made her feel oxygen deprived and overwhelmed.

Linda appeared out of nowhere when Sara arrived, as was often the case, and gave her a big hug. She was a member in good standing of the lifetime huggers association. "Sara, I just talked with my friend, Nancy, at the TV station. She wants to send a crew out to interview you and Joseph. This is so exciting. You'll be on *The Local Moment* portion of the evening news, not to mention the fact that Parliament Square will get some good PR. Nancy said they may want to tape in the dining area so they'll have the ability to interview the residents sitting at your table. This has never happened before. You and Joseph will be celebrities."

"Linda, slow down. Yes, we're honored that your friend is interested in our wedding, but we want it to be for all the *right* reasons, not as a novelty item. We're in love and we want that to be the focus of the segment, not the fact that we're an anomaly because we're so old. As for the others at our table, they'll have to give their permission to appear on camera. Some may not find this as exciting as you do. Joseph and I discussed this and we'll do the interview, but we have to discuss the details. We don't want our special day to be ruined by an overabundance of cameras and TV personnel."

"Sara, I totally understand your concerns and I will convey them to Nancy. Maybe she could chat with you and Joseph before they send a crew out. She's a very nice person and I'm sure you'll feel more comfortable once you meet her and talk. Does that sound like a good idea?"

"Yes, let's do that. I'll talk to Joseph about it today and I'll let you know tomorrow. Thanks for your help. Please don't feel that we're not excited about this or unappreciative of your involvement. We simply want to be certain that it's done tastefully and in a way that presents us as a loving older couple and not a page from *Ripley's Believe It or Not!*"

As the conversation ended, Joseph walked into the lobby. "Sara, would you like to join me in the dining room for lunch? I hear they're having grilled cheese. We can add bread-and-butter pickle slices to them. Then maybe a little cuddle time at my apartment? You must be tired from your morning at the childcare center. I'm very good at giving foot massages." He raised his eyebrows playfully.

"You had me at bread-and-butter pickles," she replied and gave his hand a firm squeeze.

The dining room was crowded. Grilled-cheese-and-tomato-soup day is very popular during the cold winter months. The only person missing at their table today was Pam. She had been under the weather for the past week and having her meals taken to her room. Hopefully it was just the flu or a bad cold. Maybe they would check on her after lunch.

Sara tapped her water glass with her knife to get everyone's attention. "Fellow diners, I have an announcement to make."

Jim jumped up and asked, "Are you pregnant and getting married because it's the right thing to do?" The table erupted in noisy, contagious laughter. Sometimes Sara wondered if those at other tables noticed their camaraderie and were jealous of it. Jim, with his endless repertoire of jokes, kept them laughing most days. If laughter is the best medicine, they should all be very healthy.

"No, Jim, I am not with child! That would certainly make the national news and all the record books." Then she addressed the table. "The local news station has offered to do a segment on our upcoming wedding. They'd like to tape a portion of the piece here at our table. They're hoping to get comments from those of you who sit with us each day and watched our relationship grow over the past six months. I want to be sure you're all okay with that. The taping will be shown on *The Local Moment* portion of the evening news. So, who's in?"

The hands of her tablemates went up enthusiastically with the exception of Deborah's. That was no surprise. Sometimes Sara wished that snooty Deborah would request a seating change so another fun person could join them. Unfortunately, she was still waiting for that to happen. Maybe her family would decide she should move to a more upscale facility. That would be perfect. Sara could refer to her as Debbie Downer but she only went by her formal name, Deborah. Not to worry, everyone else was excited and embraced the opportunity. Deborah could sit this one out as she did every other activity. It would be her loss.

Sara went on, "I'm going to meet with Nancy from the TV studio and I'll update you with specifics afterward. Hopefully, Pam will be better by then. I'm sure she'd want to be included. Joseph and I will stop in to visit her later today."

Lunch continued and the conversation centered on the TV taping. Jim shared that he would save some of his favorite jokes for that day to audible groans from the others. Some of his jokes, although clean and suitable for dinner-hour television, just weren't that funny. Maybe the group could screen the contenders and chose several of the best ones to be included?

After lunch, Joseph and Sara headed to his apartment. They decided to check in on Pam before dinner. Right now, they were looking forward to a little quiet time. Her feet were killing her after spending the morning at the daycare center and a foot rub, followed by some cuddling and an afternoon nap, sounded heavenly. Who says the young have cornered the market on happiness? She felt pretty spry for her age.

The afternoon passed quickly and it was soon time to depart for the dining room again. They would check on Pam after dinner if she didn't show up for supper. Michele joined them while they waited for the elevator. "Sara, we need to go dress shopping. You have to shop for the perfect wedding dress and Allison and I should accompany you because we need matching attendant's dresses. Since this is a spring wedding, I was thinking something pastel in color, street length in design, because it's a morning event, and flowing to mask any figure flaws; mine, not Allison's. Let's call Allison after dinner and set up a date to have her pick us up to go shopping. We can go bridal-store quality or chain-store off-the-rack fashion. Your call."

"That sounds like a plan. If we need alterations or special-order items we'll have to plan ahead. The wedding is less than two months away." Sara paused a moment. "Wow, saying that out loud makes my knees feel wobbly. This is really happening. Anyway, I have visualized a gown in my head. Nothing fancy. Nothing floor-length with a long train. Nothing with sequins and pearls. Nothing virgin white. A nice cream color, below the knee, tailored dress that accentuates my few remaining good body parts and camouflages the plentiful not so good ones. I wonder if such a dress exists? No way to find out but to go shopping. Come to my apartment after dinner and we'll call Allison."

"Agreed," Michele responded as the elevator doors opened. Jan and Betsy were already inside, their faces solemn and pale. "What's the matter?" Sara asked.

Jan replied, "We just saw paramedics wheel Pam out to an ambulance. We don't know what the problem is. We only caught a glimpse of Pam. Her eyes were closed. It was frightening." As they exited the elevator, they saw the ambulance, its lights flashing, outside the front entrance. This wasn't an uncommon sight at Parliament Square, as medical emergencies were frequent, but it was scary because it was Pam who was going to the hospital.

Betsy put her arm around Jan who was visibly shaken and upset. They walked silently to the dining room. The empty seat at dinner was unsettling. Jim, in his usual fashion, tried to offer humor to lighten the evening. The reality was that everyone seated at the table realized that they could be the one in the ambulance. Life is fragile at any age, but those in their senior years are as fragile as a crystal goblet or a bone-china plate. The years take their toll and no matter how healthy one feels and looks today, it could all be taken away tomorrow. Watching someone lose their health or mobility is eye-opening. Getting older is a privilege, not a given.

After dinner, everyone at the table except Deborah went to the lobby where they were told that Pam had been transported to the hospital because she was having difficulty breathing and that it was likely that she'd be admitted. There was nothing else they could tell them. The group sat together for a short time trying to find strength in each other and saying silent prayers for Pam's recovery.

Michele and Sara went to Sara's apartment to call Allison to discuss wedding dress shopping. Sara felt guilty for being so happy about her wedding while Pam was in the hospital. Michele told Sara that there was nothing they could do to help other than keeping Pam in their prayers and visiting her as soon as possible.

"Sara, you deserve to be happy. You and Joseph have found something very special and nothing happening around you should negatively impact that. Concern for Pam is natural and expected. I'll go with you tomorrow to visit her if we're allowed. Until then, we have to focus on you finding the perfect wedding dress. Please call Allison and find out when she can take us shopping."

Allison answered on the third ring. "Hi Allison, this is Sara. Michele and I were discussing the dresses for the wedding and wondered if you could take us shopping. I hope you know the best places to look for the perfect bride's and attendant's dresses. The forecast calls for dry weather this week, so if your schedule permits, maybe we can set a day and time to go shopping. We also have a friend who was taken to the hospital today and we were wondering if possibly we could stop to visit her while we're out."

"Sara, I think Wednesday is completely open for me. That's the day after tomorrow. Does that work for you and Michele? I could pick you up around ten. I have a couple of shops in mind. After dress shopping, we could go to lunch and check in on your friend afterward. How does that sound?"

"Allison, that sounds great. We really appreciate you taking us. The Parliament Square van could take us, but we need you to be there because you and Michele have to agree on the bridesmaid dresses. Michele has some ideas. I also value your opinion on the perfect wedding dress. We look forward to seeing you. Have a good evening and give my best to William please."

Penelope jumped up on Michele's lap and purred loudly. Too bad she couldn't be part of the ceremony. Some people have their dogs present, but cats are a different story. She thought about some of her favorite phrases about cats. *Dogs have owners, cats have staff. A cat is an example of sophistication minus civilization. Dogs believe they are human; cats believe they are gods.* Although dogs can be trained, cats are not on-command creatures. They pretty much do what they want, when they want, where they want. If the behavior exhibited happens to be what the cat owner requested, it may appear the cat responded to the human command. The real test comes when the command is repeated and properly executed multiple times. Not normal cat behavior. No, Penelope would not be taking part in the ceremony.

Sara was glad that Joseph liked cats. It would have been a deal-breaker if he didn't. Although it would have broken her heart, she could never choose a man over her dear, sweet Penelope. Fortunately, she didn't have to make such a decision. Joseph knew how much Penelope meant to Sara and, although he was more of a dog person, he had connected to Penelope over the past several months. They were all going to get along just fine.

Wednesday dawned sunny with a nip in the air, but not one that would leave a mark. Sara showered and chose an outfit that would be easy to get in and out of since she'd be trying on wedding dresses. She selected a top with buttons down the front instead of a pullover that would disrupt her hair every time she removed it. She didn't want to wind up looking like the bride of Frankenstein. She picked a loose-fitting pair of slacks and some pull-on boots for comfort and warmth. She bid Penelope goodbye as she left the apartment and headed to the dining room for breakfast.

Pam's seat was still empty. There was no annoying ring from her walker bell. She was a sweet person with simple needs, an abundance of positive attitude, and a smile for everyone. Hopefully her health would improve and she would be seated at the table again soon. Joseph sat next to Sara. "This is your big dress shopping day with Allison. Please try to select a dress that doesn't show off your ample cleavage and youthful figure to all the young men. You know how those younger gents can get." He winked and the table erupted into laughter. "We know how former pole dancers can flaunt their stuff." Again, more laughter.

Sara told those at the table, "After we go dress shopping

today, Allison has offered to take Michele and I to the hospital to visit Pam. We'll have an update for everyone at dinner. Pam doesn't have family to visit and care for her, so we have to be her family. If we find out she's going to be there for more than a day or two I think we should send her flowers from her table mates. Do you all agree?"

It was unanimous that flowers would be a good idea. Jim suggested that maybe he should take the transportation van to visit her and share some of his humor. She always liked his jokes. Everyone remembered the blue stain on the tablecloth from Pam's uncontrolled laughter while consuming blueberry pancakes. He was sure some of his humor would be the best medicine for Pam right now.

Sara and Michele waited in the lobby and Allison arrived right on time. Michele took a seat in the back while Sara opened the passenger door and sat next to Allison in the front. They exchanged pleasantries and were on their way in search of the wedding dress Sara pictured in her mind. She only hoped such a dress existed.

Traffic was light and the streets were clear of ice and snow. The sun shone brightly outside and warmly in Sara's heart. Was this really happening or was it all a dream? She was shopping for a wedding dress. She was getting married. She was going to be Mrs. Joseph Zimmerman.

The first stop was an upscale shop that specialized in wedding gowns and had a large number of attendant dresses. The saleswoman reminded Sara of someone but she couldn't remember who. The older she got, the more people's faces seemed to look familiar. Was that a senior trait? She wondered.

"Good Morning, Ladies" the salesperson said. "Please call me Cassandra. Which one of you lovely girls will be the beautiful bride?"

Sara spoke up. "I'm the lucky one. My name is Sara and this is my soon-to-be daughter-in-law, Allison, and my very good friend, Michele. They'll be my attendants. The wedding will be on Saturday, April 14th, so we have less than two months to prepare. The dress I'm looking for should have a nice cream color with the length falling slightly below the knee. It should present a tailored, sophisticated look. I'm hoping for a dress that accentuates my remaining good body parts and camouflages the numerous gravity-damaged ones. I might be your most challenging customer today or, for that matter, this month. Please show me what you have. I'm guessing that I'll need something in the ten-to-twelve size range."

Cassandra thought for a moment. "My, that is a quandary, but I'll put my thinking cap on. I have several dresses that could possibly work for you. Let me go see what I can find. While I'm looking, please feel free to help yourselves to juice, coffee, and muffins. Also, Michele and Allison, please browse the attendant dress selection. We have numerous spring pastels available. I'll be with you shortly."

Although they had all eaten breakfast, the coffee smelled enticing, and who wants to drink coffee without having a muffin? Maybe a light late lunch? After the coffee and muffins were consumed, they browsed around in search of attendant dresses. They wanted street length with maybe a short jacket over a sleeveless tailored dress. It could be cool in April, and the reception might be on the patio, weather permitting. They could select a dress that both Michele and Allison could wear again to a social event in the future—nothing bridesmaid-frilly or lacey or with ruffles. Dresses like that are worn once and hung in the back of the closet to be donated to a clothing drive twenty years later.

"I'm looking for something in a pastel, maybe light blue or pale peach," Michele said.

Allison said, "I know this sounds strange, but black is popular now for attendant dresses, maybe with accents in a light gray or white. It breaks with tradition, but I've looked through several Brides magazines recently and it appears to be a very popular trend. I see they have numerous darker dresses on the racks."

Cassandra returned with three dresses which she felt met Sara's criteria. She held each one up for review. Sara didn't rule any of them out. She took them all into the dressing room to model for Michele and Allison who continued to explore the selection of attendant dresses while Sara disappeared into the dressing room with Cassandra. This process might take longer than they expected. There were other stores, but this was the one Allison liked best and the one she felt had the best selection. It could be a bit more expensive, but who could put a price tag on this special wedding event?

Sara emerged from the dressing room wearing dress number one. It was light beige with a square neck and cap sleeves. There was a lace insert that hid any cleavage (like that was a problem). It was a bit fitted, but not spandex tight. The length was perfect with a bit of lace trim around the hemline. Cassandra commented, "This is a size ten. We also have it in size twelve if this one's too tight. I don't think it is, but that's your call. You can choose a patterned scarf wrap to compliment the dress and provide warmth for the reception if needed. I think the dress looks marvelous. What do you ladies think?"

Michele and Allison both gave a thumbs-up. "You look lovely," Michele said. "I know there are two other dresses for you to model but I think my vote is going to be for this one. Adding a muted beige print scarf will be the icing on the cake. Gorgeous!"

Allison agreed. "I love you in this dress. I know they say not to choose the first dress you try on, but this may be an exception. Try on the other two dresses, but I think my vote has already been cast."

Sara returned to the dressing room and tried on the same dress in a twelve just to be certain that she didn't need to go up a size. It swam on her, so ten was definitely correct, but light lunches and minimal snacking before the wedding date might be a good idea. She tried on the other two dresses. The second one was beige, but on the darker side. The third was mid-calf length and the skirt was a bit too flowy to suit her. It was unanimous. Dress number one in size ten was a definite winner.

They browsed through all the scarves and found one that matched the beige of the dress perfectly with a muted print that didn't distract from the dress's form or fit. Sara gave a sigh of relief as she had found just the look she had hoped to find. "Thank you for helping me," she said to Cassandra. "This is the exact dress I pictured in my mind and adding the scarf was a bonus. I am one happy bride-to-be. I say yes to this dress. Now we have to find the perfect dresses for Allison and Michele."

They discussed the new trend of attendants wearing darker colors instead of the traditional pastels. Cassandra selected a black A-line dress which fell slightly below the knee. The sleeveless bodice was on the fitted side with a skirt that widened toward the hem. The matching chiffon bolero shrug jacket cardigan with three-quarter sleeves completed the outfit. A single string of pearls with matching earrings would be nice complements to the ensemble. Sara wondered about what to give to her attendants. Pearls would be perfect.

Michele and Allison tried on the black dress and jacket and loved them. They also sampled several other dresses but none fit or presented themselves like the black A-line dress. They agreed and said it could also be worn to an evening event or (bite-your-tongue) to a funeral. It was simple but elegant.

The dress shopping had been highly successful. The seamstress took measurements to make minor adjustments and said the dresses would be ready for pickup in about a week. It was almost one o'clock when they headed to the restaurant for lunch. Afterward they would stop at the hospital to check on Pam.

# Chapter Four

## *Hello Darkness My Old Friend*

The restaurant that Allison chose specialized in homemade soups and sandwiches. It was small but very busy. The hostess knew Allison and they chatted for a moment before she seated them at a table by the window. It was a lovely day and the winter sunshine seemed warmer than it should in February. Maybe Sara's inner glow provided some of the heat.

A perky young woman introduced herself as Maria and spouted off the daily specials, in addition to the multiple soup choices, all from memory. Young people and their fresh memory cells that cooperate on demand: impressive and depressing at the same time. *Maria will learn later in life not to take memory on demand for granted*, thought Sara. She wasn't very hungry. She blamed the muffin and coffee she had at the dress shop and the excitement of the moment. Had she just selected a wedding dress? *Really?* Yes, a dress to wear to her wedding. It was really happening. She was going to be a bride.

Sara apologized to Maria. "I'm so sorry, could you repeat the soups? My mind was somewhere else." Maria repeated the choices almost robotically. Sara thought the cheeseburger soup sounded interesting and decided to have that with some of the fresh-baked bread from the basket on their table. Allison and Michele ordered and Maria disappeared into the kitchen.

The lunch conversation centered on the items that needed to be completed prior to the nuptials. The restaurant that Joseph had owned for decades would prepare the food and cater the reception. Since it would be a morning wedding, they decided on a brunch menu for the guests following the ceremony at Parliament Square. The wedding cake had yet to be selected, but Allison knew a bakery that she felt had the best product to offer. That would be an outing for another day. The flower arrangements would include pastel tulips and other colorful spring flowers. Maybe they could select the cake and flowers the same day. It shouldn't take that long. Allison suggested that they schedule a day in about a week to go together and make those decisions.

The food arrived and everyone began to eat. Sara raved about the soup. She never imagined that the ingredients used to make a cheeseburger would fit so nicely into a soup bowl. Allison and Michele regretted not ordering the same thing and said they would try it on their next visit. It looked and smelled delicious. "Do you think the kitchen would share the recipe?" Sara asked. "I would love to make this for Joseph." Allison replied, "I'll ask. I do think that Dad would love this soup."

Everyone passed on dessert and they headed for the hospital to visit Pam. The warm sunshine tempted Sara to carry her coat to the parking lot, but when she stepped outside the temperature reminded her it was still winter in New England. She shivered all the way to the car and welcomed the heater's warmth as they drove to the hospital. They stopped to select a small, cheerful bouquet which they hoped would brighten Pam's day and lift her spirits.

Allison pulled in front of the hospital and Sara and Michele exited the car and headed for the entrance. The information desk was right inside the door. Sara asked for Pam's room number. The attendant, who appeared to be eligible for residency at Parliament Square, turned to her computer and typed in some information. "Pam is currently being treated in the intensive care unit and, because of her respiratory issues, is not allowed visitors at this time. The flowers are also not allowed. I could take a message if you like."

Sara heard the words but had trouble comprehending them. Pam was so sick she couldn't have visitors? Just last week she was at the table having dinner. How did this happen? Just then she heard a familiar voice: Jim. He sat nearby waiting for a ride back to Parliament Square. He had also come to visit Pam.

"Jim, who's going to talk to the doctor and find out what's going on with Pam? She has no family locally and I'm not even sure who to contact. Maybe someone at Parliament Square knows how to locate her next of kin. Somebody has to deal with this on Pam's behalf. She can't just be left here all alone and so sick. We have to do something."

"Sara, I totally agree. We should go back and discuss this with the staff. We can't see her or to talk to her doctor because we aren't family, but we have to make sure that someone's responsible for her care. What if she has no family?"

The drive back to Parliament Square was solemn and quiet; Sara and Michele were at a loss for words. It could easily be one of them in that hospital bed. With age comes heightened fragility. One day all is well (or the best that can be expected) and the next you're fighting for the ability to awaken another day. Sara thought it put some perspective on what really matters and how the expression *Don't sweat the small stuff* is so very appropriate. Would marrying Joseph make her more vulnerable to pain and suffering if she lost him? Or, worse, what if he developed health issues that required constant care and worry and anguish? Maybe it would be better to remain single and not take on the responsibility of caring for another person, should it come to that. Maybe Sara Jennings should be the end of her own story.

Linda was behind the desk in the office when they returned to Parliament Square. Allison spoke for the group. "We just came from the hospital to visit Pam and got some very upsetting news. Pam is in ICU and isn't allowed visitors except for immediate family. They can't update us on her condition, either. Do you know if Pam has family that could take control of the situation?"

"I don't know but I'll start checking immediately. The hospital may have contacted Lynne, our liaison for resident care. If so, she'll expedite the process based on Pam's condition. I will check with her and let you know. She's on the phone at the moment. I think I remember a niece or nephew attending one of the events here some time ago. I'm not aware of any recent visitors but there could have been some on my days off or when I was busy with something else. I'll let you know as soon as I hear anything."

The three women sat together on one of the large, tufted sofas in the lobby. Sara felt guilty for her newfound happiness after the dress shopping and lunch. It seems like there's no rhyme or reason behind why some are allowed to continue living while others are destined to depart this mortal world. Sure, genetics, lifestyle, and just plain luck seem to be part of the equation. Death takes no prisoners. Why one life is taken while another is spared is a question with no answer. Be grateful for today, but never take tomorrow for granted.

"I worry that when Joseph or I leave the world of the living, the other will self-destruct. We've both suffered the loss of a spouse. Now we're building a life together knowing that our days are numbered but hoping for the best. This sudden health crisis with Pam makes me wonder if I'm doing the right thing. Maybe romance is best left to the young. Maybe I'm being foolish thinking I can start over." Sara dabbed a tear from her cheek.

"Don't be silly" Allison replied. "You and my father were meant to be. Life has no guarantees at any age. You lost your first husband while you were still a teenager. Waking up each morning is a blessing which we too often take for granted. I understand that Pam's current condition is bad, but all we can do now is be here for her and pray for her recovery. You can't let this put doubts in your mind or make you question your future with Joseph."

Linda walked over from the desk, a solemn look in her eyes. "The hospital just called to let me know that Pam has passed. We're trying to contact her nephew to discuss the funeral arrangements. I'm so very sorry. Pam was a special lady."

Sara and Michele hugged and sobbed. Pam's seat at their table would be empty. The annoying ringing of the bell on her walker would be sadly missed by all. Everything had happened so quickly. There was no time to say goodbye or share a final hug.

Allision sat with the ladies awhile and then headed home. She was so glad they had been able to spend the day together even though it ended sadly. "I'll call in a couple of days to set a date and time to visit the bakery and flower shop. You ladies need to mourn your friend and pay your last respects. Give Joseph my best."

The rest of the day was a blur. Sara and Michele talked with the other residents about Pam's passing and shared their memories. She had been a sweet, unassuming lady who always had a kind word for everyone. Her life had been very simple in many ways, and from all outward appearances she seemed to be a happy woman. They couldn't remember a single time that Pam complained or uttered a mean word. Some people find happiness without looking while others search their whole life and are never able to find it. She would be missed

Dinner that night was very difficult. Pam's empty chair was the elephant in the room. The most vivid memory they shared was the blueberry-stained table cloth caused by Pam spitting out a mouthful after hearing one of Jim's jokes. Although the ringing of her bell had been annoying, its silence was deafening. Jim didn't even share any humor. It was a time for reflection and sadness. No mention of the dress shopping or lunch out with Allison was shared. Those activities took a back seat to the loss of their tablemate and friend.

Betsy spoke up as the dessert dishes were being cleared. "I wonder who'll be selected to sit at our table. I hope it's a gentleman. Preferably one who's good looking and has a full head of hair. Women outnumber men at most of the tables. It would be nice to have another man to share meals with us. Maybe a widower who's looking for a woman. Not that I would be interested of course. Who needs a man in her life . . . no offense, Sara. You and Joseph are a match made in heaven. That's not going to happen again."

The group left the dining room and went their separate ways. Joseph and Sara went back to Sara's apartment to feed Penelope. "Joseph, today was a double-edged sword. We had great success dress shopping and sharing time with Allison, but Pam's passing made all that a distant memory. It seems impossible that she'll never walk into the dining room to share another dinner. We'll never hear her annoying bell or experience her childlike innocence. I'm going to miss her."

Joseph hugged Sara and she melted into his embrace. How could she ever doubt this marriage? He was the best thing that had happened to her in many years. Who was she to question fate? This was meant to be.

The mood at Parliament Square was somber. Death wasn't uncommon but it was unsettling. In a community where the median age is eighty, it's expected that the obituaries would frequently list Parliament Square as the last address. It was hard to read Pam's obituary and see the picture, which was a much younger version of her. Everyone had a life story before moving here that would never be known to the others. Existence at Parliament Square was like a second life detached from the first one; a new beginning, but not necessarily a good one. It was somewhere to pass the time while waiting for life's door to close. It was often not a happy place even though friends and family told you it would be.

The funeral was attended by many of the residents. Pam's only living relative, who could be located, resided in California and no longer traveled. Only her friends from Parliament Square were there to say final goodbyes. It isn't the number of people present at a funeral that's important, it's the people in attendance who sincerely grieve for the departed. Pam would be missed. The luncheon following the service was nice. Memories were shared. Tears were shed. Hugs were plentiful.

Life slowly returned to normal, or close to it. Allison called Sara to schedule another outing. The dresses were ready for pick-up, and they needed to visit the bakery and the florist. Michele was under the weather with a cold, so Sara and Allison decided to go without her because time was of the essence. The wedding date was getting closer with each passing day. February was drawing to a close, leaving March and two weeks in April before the big event. They decided to go cake and flower shopping on Monday the 26$^{th}$, weather permitting. Maybe Michele would feel well enough to join them if she rested over the weekend.

Joseph and Sara bundled up on a sunny Saturday afternoon to take a walk outside and get some fresh air. They often walked the grounds in the nicer weather, but the cold winter sentenced them to indoor activities on most days. The brisk wind slapped them in the face as they departed the warm lobby. They held each other's mitten-clad hands as they strolled slowly along the shoveled and salted path around the building.

Conversation was limited as their wool caps and coat hoods muffled the words, making it even more difficult than normal to hear, but they were content to enjoy the New

England winter landscape that reflected the peace and quiet of the season. The snow-covered ground and trees muffled the sounds around them, as if Mother Nature was helping them stop and appreciate this moment in time. They were so lucky to have found each other in their twilight years. Joseph squeezed Sara's hand and smiled. Sara bent down, grabbed a handful of snow, and tossed it into Joseph's face. He laughed and pulled her close for a long, heartfelt hug. They walked back toward the lobby with a spring in their steps and smiles on their faces.

The dinner table wasn't the same without Pam. Her empty seat was unnerving. Although they tried to pretend nothing had happened, they couldn't. Betsy and Jan shared some stories about their recent trip to visit friends in Pennsylvania. They had taken the train and apparently there was a mix-up in their sleeping accommodations. They reserved two lower-level bunks but had been assigned to a sleeping compartment with one lower and one upper bunk.

"Betsy, let me tell them what happened," Jan said. "We realized when we saw the sleeping quarters that there was a lower and an upper bunk. That isn't what we requested, but we decided to make the best of it. I told Betsy that I would take the upper bunk. We prepared for bed in our room"—Jan emphasized the word "room" using air quotes—"which wasn't any bigger than a closet. The ladder to the upper bunk was narrow and Betsy spotted for me as I tried to climb it. Somehow, I wedged the head of my bunny slipper in between the third and fourth rungs and got stuck. I couldn't go up; I couldn't go down. Betsy laughed so hard she thanked the inventor of the discreet woman's undergarment out loud for providing her protection from leakage. The porter heard her laughing and me calling for help and knocked on our door. Betsy yelled 'Come in,' and he did. The door knocked Betsy backwards just as my foot pulled out of the slipper and I fell on top of the porter.

"As we slowly regained our composure, we apologized to the porter and told him about our dilemma with the bunks. He offered to help me climb the ladder, but this time without the slippers. We settled in for the night and laughed about the story he'd tell his coworkers."

Betsy chimed in. "You forgot to tell them what happened when you had to use the bathroom during the night. That ShamWow sure came in handy. Who knew it could hold that much liquid? Maybe they could use that in their infomercial."

"Betsy, I think that is enough sharing for now. There are more stories to tell but let's save them for another time. Let's hear wedding updates from Joseph and Sara."

Sara wiped her mouth with her napkin and tried to regain her composure after listening to Jan's story. "Michele, Allison, and I went dress shopping. We were lucky enough to find not only the perfect wedding dress but also beautiful attendant's dresses. I won't go into too much detail about my dress because I want it to be a surprise for Joseph on our wedding day, but we only had to visit one store to find them. It was a very successful trip. Next, we'll select the wedding cake and flowers. So, preparations are moving along on schedule. It's less than two months away now."

They finished the meal and went their own ways for the evening. The empty seat at the table was still upsetting. They hoped it would be filled soon. The upcoming nuptials brought hope for the future while the recent funeral reminded them how fragile life can be. Any one of them could have departed this world, but this time it was Pam. A life lived in fear of dying is a life not worth living. *Think positive thoughts and appreciate each passing day* should be their mission statement. But some days that was easier said than done.

# Chapter Five

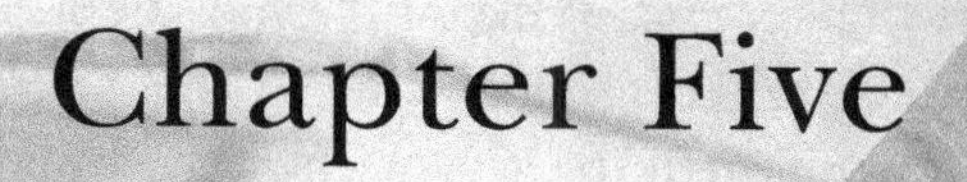

## Buttercream Icing

March came in like a lion. The temperatures were single digits, the snow was drifting, and the winds were brutal. The trip to the bakery and florist had to wait until the second week, and even then, Sara bundled up like she was going dogsled racing in the Yukon. The early afternoon sun did little to warm the day, but Michele felt much better and was able to join Allison and Sara on their outing.

"Allison, I'm so glad that you are able to drive us, but even more grateful that you can help me decide on the wedding cake and floral arrangements. I talked to Joseph last evening about his preferences. He said the flowers were entirely my decision. He would be okay with dandelions and ragweed if that's what I want. The cake, however, is a different story. He doesn't want any little cutesy cupcakes. He wants a three-tier standard-issue wedding cake with an age-appropriate cake topper. He dislikes coconut, so that's out. He said he'd like something in the chocolate family for the cake and definitely a buttercream frosting. Yes, it HAS to be a buttercream frosting."

"Sara," Allison replied, "my father is a gentle and kind man. He'll be more than willing to let you run the show, including the wedding and the marriage. But don't cross him on his cake request. When he owned the restaurant, he had a once-in-a-lifetime baker, Antonio. The desserts this man created were the talk of the town. My father's favorite was the decadent double-chocolate layer cake with a to-die-for buttercream icing. To this day, he raves about that cake. Unfortunately, Antonio retired years ago and took the double-chocolate cake and buttercream recipes with him. There are others who've come close, but none compare to Antonio."

"Maybe we could find him and ask him to come out of retirement long enough to make the wedding cake. Do you know how we could find him?" Sara asked. "That would be a real wedding-day surprise for Joseph. He might be happier about the cake than about his new bride. I've never competed against a cake before."

"He lost track of Antonio after he sold the restaurant. I don't know where he is or even if he's still alive. The bakery we're going to today is relatively new but I've only heard rave reviews about their wedding cakes. My friend's daughter purchased hers from this bakery. She said it was the best buttercream icing she'd ever tasted. She licked it off the groom's face after the cake smashing because she said it was too good to waste. I missed the wedding, so I can't tell you about it first hand, but they should have samples for us to taste today. I'll try to compare it to what I remember of Antonio's version. My father will be the real judge of the cake. Here we are ladies. Let's go taste some buttercream icing."

The sweet smells of baked goods wafted through the air as they entered the bakery. The building was small inside with sparkling glass cases protecting the confectionary delicacies from the potential consumers. There were plates of samples available for tasting. Everything looked delicious. Allison approached the aproned woman behind the counter and asked, "Is Angie here? She's expecting us." The woman (her name tag read *Cookie*—was that her real name or her bakery stage name?) told Allison to follow her to the office where Angie was waiting for us.

Angie was, for lack of a better description, a female version of the Pillsbury Doughboy. She was plump but pretty. Her skin was fairer than Nicole Kidman's, if that is even possible. Her hair was piled high on her head into a chignon with undisciplined strands popping out here and there. Her smile was welcoming, her scent a mixture of cinnamon and vanilla, and her hug would give Jan competition. She greeted us like we were best friends separated for years and reunited at last. She was a textbook extrovert.

Allison spoke for the group. "Angie, it's wonderful to meet you. I've heard so much about your wedding cakes and especially your buttercream frosting. My father will be marrying Sara, the young lady to my left, next month, and he is a buttercream connoisseur. He's never had any that compared to what his friend and baker of years ago, Antonio, made. We're here to sample your best chocolate cake and buttercream frosting."

Angie burst into loud laughter to the point of almost crying. Once she regained composure, she replied, "You're not going to believe this but my Great Uncle Antonio taught me to bake when I was a little girl and he shared his frosting recipe with me when I opened the business. He made me swear on a stack of actual Bibles never to share it with anyone. He was my inspiration to start this business and he still critiques my products. He's almost ninety years old but sharp as a tack, though his mobility is a bit compromised. He lives with his daughter outside of Boston. I'll let him know you were here."

"Small world," Sara responded. "This is going to be so wonderful. Joseph has repeatedly told me he's never had better buttercream icing than Antonio's. Now he'll have to add your name to the list. Let's talk about the cake and the topper. Do they make silver-haired bride and groom figures? I don't want the standard young figures on this cake. No walkers or canes necessary; just a mature-looking bride and groom."

"I'll do some research but I'm certain I can find something appropriate. I'll talk to my supplier today. Now, what type of cake did you have in mind?" Angie asked Sara.

"Joseph requested a three-tier decadent chocolate cake with, of course, buttercream icing. I plan to order floral arrangements with tulips and other spring flowers. Maybe some pastel-colored fluting and flowers on the sides and around the top would be nice. Do you have a sample of your best chocolate cake for us to try, and a book with pictures of decorative floral choices?"

They tasted three chocolate cake samples. One was too dry. One was too sweet. The third was, as Goldilocks put it, just right. It was very dense and moist and made you crave a glass of cold milk to wash it down. Yes, this was the one Joseph would love. If the buttercream icing was made using Antonio's family recipe, this would be the *pièce de résistance*.

Allison assisted Sara with the order paperwork and they spent a short time chatting with Angie. They asked her to tell Antonio that Joseph had wished for Antonio's world-famous buttercream icing on his wedding cake never knowing that Angie was able to provide that. This was indeed a very successful wedding cake shopping day.

The next stop was the florist. Ordering the floral arrangements should be a simple task. How many different options could there be? Tulips and spring flowers. Sounded easy enough.

On the ride to the florist Sara noticed an old, worn leather sofa sitting by the curb. Maybe it was being discarded because the owner had moved and chosen not to take it along. Or maybe it had been replaced by a newer, better one. If only the sofa could talk and share stories about the family gatherings, movies, and intimate moments it had shared over the years. Now it was destined to be compacted and dumped into a landfill or left out in the elements with the other trash to disintegrate over time.

Of course, Sara knew that she wasn't emotionally connected to the sofa, but it served as a reminder that more than just furniture and other material belongings are discarded when no longer useful. People get older and, along the way, the aging process sometimes robs them of their abilities, usefulness, and worth. They have life stories to share and valuable lessons to pass down to future generations, but all too often they get left by the curb. The old sofa can be replaced with a storeroom-fresh model, but the seasoned souls are lonely, lost, and sad when their senior status makes them feel unwanted.

Allison played music on the ride to the florist. Sara closed her eyes for a moment and replayed the bakery visit in her mind. It had all gone so well, just like the dress shopping. Each item checked off the list put her closer to the wedding and closer to being Joseph's wife. This was really happening. She was going to be part of a married couple again. She wasn't going to be alone anymore.

Michele had been quiet for most of the trip. Sara thought maybe she was still feeling a bit under the weather. "Michele, are you feeling okay? This isn't too much activity for you is it? We can return to Parliament Square and visit the florist another day."

"No, Sara, don't be silly. I'm fine. I'm really just along for the ride. I enjoy being invited but the decisions are yours. I loved the cake and frosting sampling. I think the cake is going to be spectacular. I'm anxious to hear what Joseph has to say about the icing. Everything seems to be coming together quite nicely."

The florist shop was off the beaten path in a small building with quaint scalloped green awnings and frosted windows. This was the off-season for the floral industry; Valentine's Day was over and Easter was still months away. The shop was devoid of customers with the exception of a young couple holding hands. Maybe another wedding? Allison greeted the aproned woman arranging daises in a porcelain vase with a friendly hug and hello. "Fern, so good to see you. Please meet my future mother-in-law Sara and her friend Michele. We're here to order the flowers for the wedding and reception on

April 14th."

"I am so glad to meet you both. Allison and I grew up together, so I know Joseph quite well. I spent a lot of time at their house, and I used to waitress at their restaurant during high school and college. I was so excited when Allison called me with the news of your upcoming marriage. Let's get started by going through some of the floral arrangement books. That'll give you an idea of the basics and we can go from there. First question: What are your flower preferences?"

Sara said, "I want the main flower to be tulips, of any color, and mix in some daffodils with a few hyacinths for fragrance. We have to limit those because we don't want the chapel to smell more like a funeral than a wedding. Their scent can be overpowering, but a little bit is nice. I guess mix in some greens and baby's breath too. Does that sound like a good combination? The nosegays for my attendants should be white tulips and yellow daffodils to contrast with their black dresses. My bridal bouquet can be more colorful. Joseph, the best man, and the ushers should have a single white rose lapel flower. I don't think a tulip would look good on a lapel. What do you think?"

"I'm very impressed that you're so specific. Some brides have no idea what they want and we have to start from square one. What you want is certainly possible. Let's decide on the arrangements for the church first. After that, the table centerpieces for the reception, and the attendant's and bride's bouquets. Sounds like a lot but it's really pretty straightforward especially since you know what flowers to include."

Allison and Michele listened while Sara and Fern discussed and then decided on each item. Sara asked their opinion several times along the way. It was evident that this was not Fern's first rodeo. She and Sara clicked almost immediately. In less than an hour, the decisions were made and the women bade Fern goodbye.

"Allison, Joseph told me that he's going to talk with the restaurant about the catering. He knows their menu and feels comfortable doing that. So, we can cross that off our list of things to do. He said you'd take him to the restaurant in the next week or two. We need to lock in the menu with them soon because they may need additional staff that day to keep the business open and running in addition to doing the catering for the reception."

"Yes, Sara, I'm going to call the restaurant today and set up a day and time that my dad and I can visit. I'm glad he offered to do that. I know he wants to stay in the background during the planning stage, but he's comfortable with food service. He wouldn't have enjoyed the dress shopping, florist or bakery. I think it's great that you two already work so well together."

As they drove back to Parliament Square, they passed the discarded leather couch at the curb. There was a group of young people attempting to load it into the back of a pickup truck. Apparently, the couch wasn't destined for the landfill just yet. It's worth had been seen by people who would give it a new home until they could afford a newer, better one. It still had value.

Sara reminded herself that, like the couch, being old, worn, and no longer perfect didn't necessarily mean being unusable. Everyone should be seen for their value and purpose, regardless of age. Sure, some things diminish with time, but there were also a wealth of experience and knowledge there for the taking.

She felt much better after seeing that. She was glad they had driven by just at the moment the couch was rescued. It lifted her spirits a bit. Even though the upcoming wedding had lightened her mood, she still fixated on the fact that she had much less life remaining than there was life already experienced.

Getting older was depressing. No matter how positive your attitude, the inevitable conclusion is always closer than it has ever been. You'll never be younger than you are today. Should you have the good fortune to live into your eighties and nineties, you'll still have to endure the loss of friends and family along the way. It's a double-edged sword. You're fortunate enough to be above the ground, but many of those with whom you shared your life are not. Each time you grieve at a funeral, you wonder if you'll be next.

"Sara, this has been fun," Allison said. "I'm so glad we were able to do this together. The big event gets closer with each item we cross off the to-do list. We need to stop and pick up our dresses, then we can call it a day. I'd suggest we stop for tea and crumpets, but I don't want you ladies to be late for dinner. I know they serve promptly at five and it's already three-thirty."

Cassandra was with a customer, so Allison asked another employee if she could retrieve the dresses for a final fitting. Sara made herself comfortable on the lovely showroom sofa while Allison and Michele took their dresses to the fitting rooms. Sara's dress had fit perfectly and needed no alterations. It had been a long afternoon and Sara rested her head on the back of the sofa. She had almost drifted into twilight mode when Michele appeared and asked how her dress looked. "It's beautiful!" Sara exclaimed. "You're going to make heads turn at the wedding." Allison appeared and she also looked amazing in her dress and shrug jacket. "All you're missing is a single strand of pearls and I think I know just where to find one. Let's get the dresses in their covers and head back to Parliament Square."

Allison parked in the visitor space right outside the main entrance and helped Sara and Michele inside with their dresses. The strong wind almost turned the heavy garment bags into kites. They were glad Allison was there to assist them inside. The heat in the lobby felt almost tropical in comparison to the Arctic air outside. It was good to be back. They had accomplished a lot, but it was tiring. Allison bade them goodbye and headed out to the parking area. She was such a nice young woman. Sara wasn't just getting a wonderful husband; she was also getting a lovely stepdaughter.

Dinner that evening was hearty vegetable beef soup with crusty rolls. It was perfect for a cold New England night. The conversation centered around the day's activities with Allison. Betsy and Jan had been practicing several songs to sing while the guests were being seated in the chapel. They wanted to perform them for Joseph and Sara (and anyone else who was interested) in the activity room after dinner.

It saddened Sara to think that she had suggested they ask Pam to make it a trio when she came back from the hospital. But in the blink of an eye, Pam was gone. Sara tried not to think about her mortality, but at her age it wasn't an easy thing to avoid. *Appreciate the present*, she kept telling herself. *Be glad for what I have and don't fear what is yet to come.* Good advice although hard to remember at times.

"Betsy and Jan, that would be wonderful. Joseph and I are anxious to hear your songs. Everyone should join us and we can vote for our favorite ones. The guests will appreciate your singing and maybe the media people will include some in the broadcast. You could be famous!"

After dinner, the group went to the activity room. It was practically deserted since it wasn't Bingo night and many of the residents normally returned to their rooms after dinner to listen to the evening news followed by *Wheel of Fortune* and *Jeopardy!* Some might venture out after that, but most stayed in for the night.

Jan and Betsy stood in the front of the room and announced the first song. "We'll start out with Stevie Wonder's "Signed, Sealed, Delivered I'm Yours" which Google says is a very popular wedding processional. We did our research. The second one we'll sing is "Over the Rainbow." The final one we chose is "Marry Me" which many of you might not recognize because it isn't a classic like the other songs, but the lyrics brought tears to our eyes. It is sung in a high key so we'll try to keep it within reason. Here Goes!"

Betsy and Jan played instrumental recordings of each song while they sang. At the wedding, the pianist would play the music for them. Everyone applauded loudly after the first two songs. The third one none of them had ever heard before and they wondered if maybe an older, more traditional song might be better. "I had trouble deciphering the lyrics while you sang. I may not know all the words to the first two songs, but I could guess at the ones I didn't know," Jim said. Michele agreed.

"Okay," Jan responded. "We'll practice and fine tune the first two songs and search for a third one that's more age appropriate. We just thought the lyrics were so nice, but I'm sure there are many oldies that would be just as nice and people will recognize the words. Thanks for listening."

The group dispersed and Sara and Joseph returned to Sara's room to check on Penelope and enjoy some alone time. It had been a busy day. Sara told Joseph about their visit to the bakery but made no mention of meeting Antonio's niece Angie or the buttercream recipe. That would be a secret saved for the wedding day. The trip to the florist had been pretty uneventful, but it checked one more item off Sara's to-do list.

"We should talk to a travel agent soon to make our reservations at the Sandals resort. Are you sure you really want to go there for our honeymoon? It'll be expensive and I'm still not sure about flying. I'll definitely need medication if I'm going to get on a plane. It's been a long time since I flew and I must confess, honeymoon or not, I'm very nervous about it. I understand it's a safe way to travel, but that doesn't calm my nerves when the plane takes off or flies through turbulence. Just talking about it makes me anxious."

"Sara, I assure you that flying is the safest mode of transportation based on the numbers. Yes, I do want to go on a honeymoon and I want it to be something special. Unbeknownst to you, I already made our travel reservations. These venues need to be booked well in advance and I was cavalier enough to reserve a honeymoon suite before I even popped the question. How about *that* for confidence? Although I must confess, I opted for the refundable deposit just in case you turned me down. So, no worries. We are going to Sandals Montego Bay. We leave Sunday morning for a week of fun in the sun. You'll love it, I'm sure."

"Joseph, I love a man who takes control. It makes you even more attractive if that's even possible. I guess I have no choice but to say yes and stock up on Xanax. I can't pretend that flying doesn't scare me, but if it means that you and I have a week alone together in a tropical paradise, count me in. I'm sure we'll be the oldest honeymooners there but then again, maybe we won't be. Age is just a number, which I choose to ignore whenever possible. Let's dim the lights and practice for the trip."

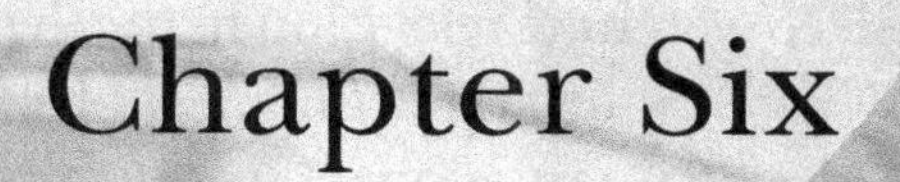

# Chapter Six

## *Guess Who's Coming to Dinner*

On most nights Joseph would bid farewell to Sara and go back to his own apartment to sleep. He felt it was appropriate to do that until after the wedding. One night he fell asleep watching television in the living room with Sara and didn't awaken until morning. Sara had covered him and retired to the bedroom alone. On this morning, Joseph didn't wake up on the couch. He was in bed with Sara when Penelope jumped up to demand her breakfast. "Sara, I was going to leave last night but I must have fallen asleep after our dress rehearsal for the honeymoon. I remember being very tired and trying to leave but I couldn't find the key to the handcuffs."

"I didn't have any handcuffs, but you're giving me ideas for the honeymoon. I woke up several times during the night and basked in the warmth of your body next to mine. It's been a long, long time since I experienced that feeling. It was very nice and I look forward to it being a permanent part of my life. But for now, you better sneak back to your apartment. You don't want to do the walk of shame when people see you leaving. You'll ruin my reputation as a woman of high standards. They won't know that our cuddling and sleeping together was purely innocent and not sexual. Now get dressed and off with you. Thanks for staying, handcuffs or not."

"I'll see you at breakfast. No one will be the wiser. It was nice spending the night with you. We have so much to experience together in the years to come. Younger people are starting with a clean slate. They have their careers, child rearing, house hunting, retirement planning, the list goes on and on. We have already done all that. We simply have each other. Ours is a match made by a higher power. We need to smile and accept our destiny. Love You!"

Just as Joseph opened the door to leave, he heard the elevator doors open. "Sara," he said loudly, "your toilet should be fine now. Next time wait until after breakfast to call me please. You woke me up."

One of the maintenance crew exited the elevator and asked if he could help. "No thank you," Sara responded. "My fiancé came over early this morning and fixed it." Joseph headed for his apartment with a skip in his step and a smile on his face. Maybe this aging process wasn't all a downhill battle. He felt happier than he had in years and he wanted it to last forever.

When Joseph arrived in the dining room Sara was already seated at the table. Joseph winked at her with a cat-ate-the-canary look on his face. The others seemed none the wiser, although Sara felt like she was wearing a large scarlet letter on her sweater. She might even be blushing, but no one seemed to notice.

Midway through breakfast, which was cinnamon French toast served with a side of bacon, a tall man of African descent approached their table. "Hello, my name is Charles, but you can call me Chuck. I've been assigned to fill the empty seat at your table. Sorry I'm a bit late, but we were finishing up the paperwork in the office. I just arrived yesterday. I heard about Pam. I offer you my sincere condolences. I've lost some good friends myself lately, but I look forward to becoming friends and sharing many meals together. The woman in the office referred to yours as 'the fun table' which I must admit sparked my interest."

Each person extended a welcoming hand as they went around the table introducing themselves. They were all glad to have the empty seat filled. Each day it reminded them of Pam's absence. They did miss her innocent presence and that darn bell. Jim and Joseph were glad to welcome another male to the table. They were still outnumbered five to three, but hopefully Chuck would be someone to discuss sports with instead of love stories or daytime TV soap operas.

Michele was happy to have a man of color at the table. She was comfortable with all the white residents but, truth be told, she welcomed another dark-skinned tablemate. He was quite tall and good looking, too.

Linda approached the table to welcome Chuck. "You're very lucky to get assigned to this table." She pointed at Sara and Joseph. "These two are going to tie the knot next month right here at Parliament Square. There's going to be a wedding, and it might even be on television." Then she turned to the happy couple. "I spoke with Nancy today and she'd like to interview you privately first. She needs to know your availability for the next two days. Then she'd like to join your table next week to discuss the plans and talk with each of you. She wants to get some background on Sara and Joseph's relationship from the rest of you. Are you all okay with that? There will be a camera crew and some of the discussion will be aired on *The Local Moment* segment of the evening news. You'll all have to sign a waiver. Is there anyone who does not want to be included?"

"I will pass," Deborah replied. "I am not comfortable doing that. I will make plans to sit at another table that day."

Everyone else was fine with it. Chuck said he couldn't contribute to their story since he had just arrived, but he'd still like to be included. It sounded like a lot of fun. Jan and Betsy were enthused. They started to discuss their wardrobe options for the telecast. Jan had some very colorful outfits with, of course, matching accessories. Some of her ensembles were so loud you could hear her coming before you saw her. Well, fingers crossed, she would select something suitable for the television cameras.

Jim stood and said, "I've been working on a couple of one-liners for the wedding toast. Stop me when you hear something you like.

"—Just think, if it wasn't for marriage, men would go through life thinking they had no faults at all.

"—Getting married is very much like going to the restaurant with friends. You order what you want, and when you see what the other fellow has, you wish you had ordered that.

"—A honeymoon can be defined as a trip a man takes before he starts working for a new boss.

"—Eighty-five percent of married life consists of yelling 'What?' from the other side of the house.

"I have plenty more where those came from. You can cast your votes later. Remember, laughter is the best medicine."

Chuck laughed heartily at Jim's humor and commented, "I think I'm going to like sitting here. I'm recently widowed and my two children felt I needed to move to a community that would engage me in life again. I was alone in a large house with few neighbors. I kept to myself and I was finding life a bit lonely since losing my wife two years ago. I didn't put up much of a fight about moving here because my older son is going to move into my house and he told me that if I'm not happy, I would always be welcome to come back and live with him and his family. That made me feel a little better, even though I never want to live with either of my adult children and interfere in their lives. What do they want with an old man wandering around the house getting in the way? It's better this way and I plan to make sure my transition works. I'm hoping you can help me do just that."

"Chuck," Betsy said, "we'll get you involved. There is bingo night every week, which is a lot of fun. Also, there are many day trips and group events. They post a bulletin each week in the lobby with dates and times. Linda, who stopped by earlier, is the social director. She keeps us hopping. Her energy level, even for a younger person, is off the charts. She gives the Energizer Bunny a run for the money."

Jan practically leaped from her chair and ran to Chuck. He learned first-hand the depth of one of her hugs. "Welcome, Chuck. We're so glad to have someone fill the empty chair. We're sure that everyone else envies us for our camaraderie and fun. Well, they can just make their own merriment. We're glad to meet you and look forward to sharing stories and making new memories."

After breakfast, Joseph and Chuck talked as they headed for the lobby. They discovered they had something in common: They both had owned and operated restaurants for most of their adult lives. Sara excused herself while they looked for somewhere to sit and continue their discussion.

It would be nice, Sara thought, if Joseph and Chuck became friends. Sara had Michele, but Joseph really didn't have anyone. He got along fine with Jim at meals, but they didn't have a friendship as such. Jim was very outgoing and quite the comedian, but he and Joseph didn't seem to have a lot in common.

Sara returned to her apartment and decided to give Michael a call. She hadn't talked with him in quite a while and she wanted to update him on the wedding. After three rings his answering machine picked up. "Hello, Michael. I hope all is going well for you in California. I'm certain that your weather is much better than our New England cold and snow."

"I've selected my wedding dress, the floral arrangements, and the wedding cake. Joseph is working on the catering and he made our honeymoon reservations all on his own. We're headed to the Sandals resort in Montego Bay. I may have to medicate for the flight, but I am certain it will be worth it. Just wanted to update you on our progress and let you know I anticipate your visit and look forward to you walking me down the aisle. You're going to love him! Call me when you can. Have a great day. Love you."

Sara cuddled up with Penelope on the rocking chair. So much had changed since she moved in last July. Had it only been eight months since she sat in the lobby waiting for Michael to complete the paperwork and escort her to new "home"? Sometimes it seemed like she had just arrived at Parliament Square, and other times she felt like she had lived there forever. The memories of her beloved beach house dimmed. The sadness she felt over the loss of her independence lessened as the months passed. She had new friends. She had new purpose. She had a new love in her life. She was going to be okay. In fact, she was going to be better than okay. She was going to be happy again.

Sara decided to take off the month of April from the day care center. Two weeks before the wedding to prepare, and two weeks after the wedding for the honeymoon and time with Joseph. She would continue there on Wednesday and Friday through March and return in May. She'd miss the children. She enjoyed their enthusiasm for life which seemed to rub off a bit on her when she spent time with them.

Art Linkletter sure knew what he was doing when he aired the *Kids Say the Darndest Things* segments on his television show *House Party*. Their spontaneity and unedited reactions to situations were often priceless. When Sara announced to the children one day that she would be absent for a month because she was getting married, one response was "I didn't know Grandmas could even get married."

Most of the loose ends were being tied up. A little over one month remained until the wedding day. The March weather was brutal, but Sara was certain April would bring warmer days, spring flowers, and the return of the robins. She always loved to see her first robin of the season. Since Sara was a young girl she remembered "stamping" the first robin of spring. You licked your thumb, pressed it into the palm of your other hand followed by a "stamp" with the bottom of your fist. The superstition is that doing this will bring you good luck. Maybe she should stamp every robin she saw this spring. She and Joseph could certainly use all the good luck they could get. Marrying in your eighties wasn't for the weak of heart. Lady Luck would definitely be offered the welcome mat at their apartment.

Chuck and Joseph found they had several common threads. They had both been entrepreneurs in the restaurant business. They both were football fanatics, and both wore their New England Patriots-inspired wardrobe to meals. Joseph would have an enthusiastic fan to share this season's games. Sara tried to feign interest but often dozed off or found excuses to be elsewhere on game days. Watching games in the fall this year would be much better for everyone.

Nancy from the TV station scheduled to meet with Joseph and Sara Sunday afternoon in Sara's apartment. "Joseph, I am a little apprehensive about this meeting. I know we agreed to this but now I am rethinking my, I mean our, decision. If this interview is done properly it could inspire others our age to tie the knot, but it could also turn into a circus sideshow. We could be a sweet silver-haired couple targeted by Cupid's arrow in the twilight of our years, or we could be two dementia-ridden octogenarians looking for publicity."

"Sara, as the young folks say, *it is what it is*. We'll share our story with Nancy. You can tell her how my animal magnetism made it impossible for you to refuse my marriage proposal in front of the other residents. Or I can tell her how you begged me to marry you over and over until I weakened and agreed. It's your call."

Sara laughed out loud and gave Joseph a Jan-like hug. "You better not say those things while we're on camera. I may have to call off the wedding. Leave the groom standing at the altar alone. Wouldn't that be the talk of Parliament Square? Our story might even make the national news if that happened."

Sara asked Michele to assist her in selecting an appropriate outfit for the interview. She wanted to look younger, thinner, and more attractive. Nothing that a face lift, a tummy tuck, and a time machine couldn't achieve. But those were not an option. She had to lose ten pounds and twenty years in two days. As she got older, the phrase *what you see is what you get* seemed to be more meaningful.

"Michele, I think we should select something from my wardrobe in the slimming color of black. That shouldn't be difficult since ninety percent of my clothes are either black or dark gray. Or I could check with Jan and possibly borrow one of her colorful, putting it mildly, ensembles. I hate to admit it, but some of them actually look quite attractive on her. I don't think that would be the best choice for television, though. They always say the camera adds ten pounds. That's not a good thing."

"Sara, you'll look great in anything you choose. You don't have a weight problem, nor do you look a day over seventy . . . maybe even sixty-five. Remember, age is only a number. The best accessory you can choose is a big, friendly smile. All the diamonds and pearls can be upstaged by a sincere and genuine smile. The real beauty comes from within, which will shine in Joseph's presence. Relax. You got this, girl."

After reviewing her wardrobe selections, Sara decided on tailored black slacks, her favorite red sweater, and her cherished plaid scarf that Michael had given her for Christmas. She would look very chic, yet sensible. Age-appropriate clothing was both functional and stylish. She would model the outfit for Joseph and discuss his wardrobe options. Then they'd show the television-viewing public that old does not mean frumpy and worn. This was no longer the day of housedresses and velour pantsuits. Age no longer meant dressing like your appearance wasn't worth the effort.

Dinner that Friday was baked haddock, stewed tomatoes, and macaroni and cheese. The better Sara's mood, the tastier the food. Could there be a connection? Sara told the others that Nancy from the television station was coming Sunday afternoon to interview she and Joseph. If that went well, then she'd be back next Wednesday before lunch to meet the others (excluding Deborah, of course) in the dining room. The show was scheduled to air two weeks prior to their April 14th wedding date. They were still discussing the possibility of the network televising the wedding itself.

Jim spoke up. "Sara and Joseph, I know that you really enjoy my sense of humor so I've been practicing some jokes for the event. I'll remember to keep it clean since the program will be aired during family viewing time. You are a very special couple, so I want to be certain whatever I say isn't misinterpreted. I'll leave out the part about Joseph ordering blue pills in bulk and Sara's pole dancing career. Any other requests?"

Before Sara could answer, Linda appeared out of nowhere and gave Sara a big hug. "Nancy told me that she'd be here Sunday afternoon to interview you and Joseph for the segment. This is so exciting. Have you ever been on television before? I was on one time when they interviewed shoppers at a new grocery store. Of course, it was nothing like this. You're going to be celebrities here at Parliament Square."

"Thanks for your encouragement," Sara said. "Joseph and I have been so consumed with planning the wedding that we haven't focused on our TV appearance, which is probably a good thing because I don't want to get anxious about being in front of the camera. We're hoping that Nancy can present our story with a human-interest flavor instead of a curiosity from

*Ripley's Believe it or Not*. We understand that not many people marry in their eighties but maybe that's because they just don't find the right person. Joseph and I are blessed to have connected later in life. We're entering uncharted waters with only our love and respect for each other to serve as our compass. There are no guarantees in life. Each day we have together is a gift we look forward to unwrapping together."

The diners at the table all stood and loudly applauded Sara's message. Betsy and Jan had tears in their eyes. Yes, they were old. Yes, their days were numbered. Yes, life at this age was as fragile as bone china. However, the fear of dying should not keep you from living. Remember, no one gets out alive.

# Chapter Seven

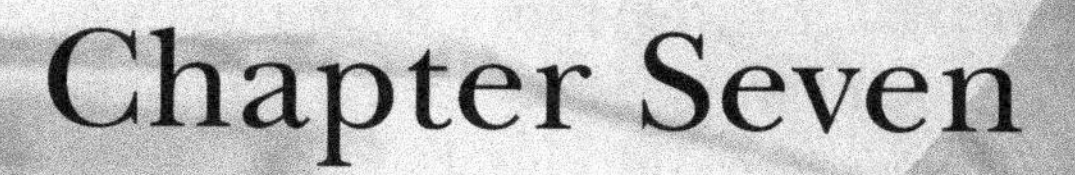

## *Lights-Camera-Action!*

Sara could hear the telephone ringing as she fumbled trying to get the key into the lock on her apartment door. She almost fell over Penelope racing (in a manner of speaking) to answer it. Not sure what makes answering the telephone before hearing a click at the other end when picking up the receiver so important, but it just is. Maybe it dates back to the good old days when everyone in the house tried to answer the phone first, thinking it was for them.

She had a flashback to the days when her family had what was referred to as a party line, which meant several households shared a single telephone number. The caller had to wait until the other family's conversation ended before placing a call. The youth of today would think she was making that up if she ever told them about it. Sharing a telephone number with another family? That was the stone age. Today the landline is pretty much extinct, replaced with the mobile "smart" phone. My how times have changed.

Nowadays, rushing to answer the antiquated landline (if it even exists) is like openly admitting you're over the hill. If you don't use a mobile device for your calls and texts, you're a dinosaur. So much technology, but it's often surprisingly less effective for communication than what we used in days of old when factoring in the learning curve for understanding and using the new devices.

"Good morning, Aunt Sara" the voice at the other end said. "I'm sorry I missed your call. Glad to hear the wedding preparations are going well. I'm looking forward to my trip east to walk you down the aisle. I was wondering if you'd mind if I brought a friend along.

"Marcy and I are officially separated and I think it may be permanent. We haven't been a functioning couple for several years and this move may have been the icing on the cake, so to speak. Maybe it's the best thing. She seems to be happy without me and I feel a new sense of freedom not having to walk on eggshells around her. I know you and my mother never approved of her, but we did try to make it work."

"I'm sorry to hear that, Michael, but like you say, it may be for the best. You're more than welcome to bring a friend along. I'll be moving into Joseph's apartment after the honeymoon, so you and your friend are welcome to stay at my place while you're here. I look forward to seeing you. The wedding may be televised locally; I'll tell you all about it when you arrive. Have a safe trip. Love You."

Sara placed the phone back on the receiver and paused a moment. She really wanted someone better for Michael but she hated to see his marriage end. He and Marcy were together for years and now he had to start over. But that was all right. Not all marriages were destined for wedded bliss. Sometimes it was better to cut your losses and move on. Michael deserved to be happy.

There was a knock on her door. Sara opened it to find Jan and Betsy in sequined dresses that would make a disco ball jealous. They were so excited to show them to Sara. They had ordered them for their musical performance on Sara's wedding day. Oh, my . . . it was a bit much but how could Sara burst their bubble and tell them the dresses were too over the top? She bit her lip and said, "Ladies, you will certainly shine brightly in those dresses. They are very unique, and I'm certain the guests will enjoy your wardrobe as much as your singing, but I wish you hadn't gone to the expense of purchasing new dresses." *Especially these gaudy dresses* she thought.

"We wanted to wear something unique," Jan replied. "I would have selected something more extravagant but Betsy thought we should go with something conservative so she talked me into these. We can return them if you think they're not fancy enough."

"Ladies, Joseph and I are so fortunate to have you singing at our wedding. The dresses will certainly set the stage for the event. I'm certain they'll be the talk of the town." *And hopefully wont blind the television crew.* "We appreciate your enthusiasm. Have you found a third song to sing?"

"Yes, we have," Betsy said. "It is an oldie but a goodie: 'The Way You Look Tonight.' We've been practicing it and would like to sing it for you and Joseph. Maybe after dinner?"

"Great. I'll talk to Joseph about it today. Nancy and the television crew will interview us this afternoon. I'm a bit nervous about being on camera. They say it adds ten pounds and who can afford that?"

As Betsy and Jan walked away, dresses brightly glittering in the sunlight that streamed through the floor-to-ceiling hall windows, Sara couldn't help but smile. So much had changed since last year when she was begrudgingly starting to pack her belongings for the dreaded departure from her beloved cottage by the sea. It all seemed to be a vague memory now as her new life unfolded before her eyes. She was so lucky.

Penelope jumped up on Sara's lap and purred loudly. She seemed to sense the contentment in Sara's heart. Animals are very perceptive of their human's emotions. Some think it's all in the owner's mind, but Sara knew better. If Penelope could talk, she would congratulate Sara on her newfound happiness.

"Penelope, our lives are going to change soon. We'll be moving in with Joseph. It will no longer be just the two of us. But don't worry, you'll still be my favorite. Just don't tell Joseph. We don't want to hurt his feelings. You'll like him, though, and he'll like you. I may have to limit my one-on-one conversations with you when he's around as he may think I'm a bit wacky. Sometimes people think talking to cats is strange, but you and I know better."

The day seemed to evaporate and soon it was time for

Nancy and the camera crew to arrive. Sara dressed in the outfit she and Michele has selected for the occasion. She did a double take when she caught her image in the mirror. The basics were still good. Her posture was straight, no back hump due to years of poor posture and spinal deterioration. Her weight was within the reasonable range for her ever-decreasing height, although a ten-pound loss wouldn't be problematic. Donna had returned her hair to its original brown color with auburn highlights. They say wrinkles are the result of many years of laughter. Better to be wrinkled and happy than smooth and sad.

Joseph knocked on Sara's door. He hugged her tightly when she answered. "My, don't you look lovely young lady? The viewers will think I'm a cradle robber. They'll wonder how this old coot got such a lovely, vibrant beauty to accept his proposal. I'm a little nervous. How are you holding up?"

"Joseph, believe it or not, I am not a bit nervous. Of course, that could be directly related to the several Xanax pills that I washed down with a couple glasses of wine after lunch. I feel quite mellow. I'm thinking this could be my pre-flight cocktail for our trip to Sandals. Hopefully, I won't fall asleep or, worse yet, snore on camera. Wipe that scared look off your face, I'm just kidding. Or am I?"

Sara put Penelope in the bedroom and closed the door. She was a bit skittish with strangers and would be scared of all the activity and unfamiliar people in the apartment. Joseph straightened the stack of magazines on the coffee table and fluffed the throw pillows on the sofa. His OCD was showing. Several minutes of silence passed until Nancy knocked on the door. Sara squeezed Joseph's hand and got up to answer the door.

"Hello, Sara," Nancy said. "Are you and Joseph ready for our crew to set up for the interview? I know it looks like a lot of equipment, but they'll set up quickly and the taping shouldn't take more than sixty minutes. We expect the piece to be between eight to ten minutes long, and we'll review the final cut with you prior to presentation. Any questions?"

Sara mentioned that she hoped they brought the cameras that erased wrinkles and age spots. Maybe they could airbrush the entire video? "Nancy, we're a little nervous, but once the cameras get rolling, I think we'll be okay. We've never done this before and new experiences at our age can be a bit unnerving. We're as ready as we are ever going to be."

The questions started. Joseph and Sara sat close together on the sofa. Sara felt Joseph squeeze her hand several times during the interview. She sensed that he would have passed on this "opportunity" if she hadn't shown interest. Maybe their interview would be too boring and the editors would cut the entire segment?

"Joseph, statistics show that women far outnumber men in senior-living facilities. Sara had something special that attracted you. Can you put that quality into words?"

"If I reply that her outward beauty was her most attractive attribute, I would be skirting the truth. Although I find Sara's appearance very alluring, it was her kindness and gentle ways that made my heart skip a beat when I was near her. She never tried to lasso me into a relationship. On the contrary. Many older women feel they can't survive without male companionship. Sara isn't one of those women. She is confident without being part of a couple. She told me when we started seeing each other that she never felt another man would be a part of her life. I wanted to prove her wrong."

Sara squeezed his hand. "Nancy, I must admit that although Joseph's outgoing personality and gentlemanly manners were a definite draw, his handsome features and senior *GQ* qualities had me from the day I first looked into his icy blue eyes. I am one very lucky lady!"

Nancy asked more questions about their courtship and Joseph's public proposal to Sara at the Parliament Square Valentine's party. Their story was certainly one that the viewing public would find interesting and engaging. Not many seniors find a soulmate in their eighties, and some of those that do are not interested in getting married and living with someone full-time. Often there's a direct negative correlation between age and willingness to change. The higher the age the lower the desire to accommodate another person's lifestyle and make compromises to maintain marital harmony. Sara and Joseph were willing to take on that challenge, and were excited about doing it.

"Sara, can you share your honeymoon plans? I'm sure our viewers are interested in knowing if and where you'll be going."

"Joseph made all the reservations for our honeymoon. We're going to a Sandals resort where we'll stay in the honeymoon suite. We may be the oldest couple there, but we don't plan to behave that way. We're anxious to show those millennials and Generation Xers a thing or two. I may need to get a couple of B12 shots before we leave and pack an industrial size drum of Geritol."

"Sara, that sounds fantastic. We're currently discussing the possibility of taping the wedding to televise for our viewers. I'm sure they'll tune in after seeing this clip and hearing about the Sandals honeymoon. We appreciate you both sharing this private and personal occasion with us and our viewers and wish you both the best in your marriage. Congratulations!"

After Nancy and the camera crew departed, Sara turned to Joseph. "Are you certain that you're okay with them televising the wedding? I think it would be great publicity for Parliament Square. Betsy and Jan have their hearts set on being on TV. But I don't want to do it if you feel it violates our privacy. I understand we're an oddity of sorts, but having all those viewers watch as we pledge our love to each other gives me the chills. I never thought in all my years that I would remarry, let alone do it on TV."

"Sara, as I said before, getting married is the big event. If there is a mariachi band playing, men juggling balls of fire, or monkeys dancing in the aisle, I won't even notice. My focus will be on my beautiful bride and nothing else. You have changed me from a sad, lonely old man to someone who looks forward to each new day. I get up in the morning with a smile on my face and fall asleep with a song in my heart. I don't know how I could be any happier."

Dinner that evening was—wait for it—cheeseburger soup. Sara couldn't believe it. She had talked so much about the soup that she had enjoyed when Allison took her to lunch that when the residents were asked to suggest new meal ideas, cheeseburger soup was the winner. She never expected them to research the recipe and make it. It was delicious.

Her tablemates asked how the interview went that afternoon. "Nancy and the camera crew were very nice. They were patient with us as we sometimes took a minute to gather our thoughts before answering a question. I think it went well. They plan to come back to interview you soon. They want to get your input into how Joseph and I went from tablemates to a betrothed couple. They plan to include excerpts from that interview when they televise our story. I think Nancy said they'll be back before lunchtime Wednesday. I'll verify that and let you know."

Jim suggested a toast to the soon-to-be celebrity couple and they all clinked their water glasses. Jim continued by sharing with them a humorous story he had recently heard. "A friend of mine was sitting in the waiting room for her first appointment with a new dentist. She noticed his DDS diploma on the wall, which bore the dentist's full name. Suddenly, she remembered a tall, handsome, blond-haired boy with the same name from her high school class some forty-odd years ago. Could he be the same guy she had a secret crush on way back then?"

"Upon seeing him, however, she quickly discarded any such thought. This balding, gray-haired man with the wrinkled face was way too old to have been her high school classmate. After he examined her teeth, she asked him if he had attended West End High School. 'Yes, I did. I'm a Crusader through and through,' he said with pride. 'When did you graduate?' she asked. He answered, '1979. Why do you ask?' 'You were in my class!' she exclaimed. He looked at her closely. Then, that ugly, old, balding, wrinkled faced, big butt, gray-haired, decrepit SOB asked, 'What subject did you teach?'

Everyone laughed. Many times, we see ourselves differently than others see us. We know the years have aged us, but our minds play games. We still think like we did when we were younger, but others can't see the wheels turning inside our heads. They see our visibly aging bodies and more limited physical abilities and label us as *old*. We are chronologically old but mindfully young. It's not always a good combination.

# Chapter Eight

*Just a Dream . . .*

*Just a Dream . . .*

Sara, Michele, Joseph, Jim, and Chuck went to the activity room after dinner to listen to Betsy and Jan's singing presentation. Deborah passed. Sometimes it was difficult to understand why Deborah isolated herself from the others. It seemed like such a lonely, sad existence she chose. She had few visits from family and refused to participate in any of the organized activities or events. The more her tablemates encouraged her to get involved the more distant she became. Such a shame to spend what were labeled as your golden years that way.

Sara tried not to visualize Betsy and Jan in their disco-ball dresses but it was all but impossible. If the television station decided to air this event there would certainly be comments about the sequined singing sisters of soul. Maybe those with cataracts should be warned not to look directly at the dresses or, better yet, wear sunglasses?

The music was delightful and everyone applauded at the end of each song. Betsy and Jan bickered a bit about who was off tempo or held a note too long. They apologized and reassured Sara and Joseph that they would practice every day until the wedding. After a bit of conversation, everyone dispersed to their rooms or headed to the lobby. Sara overheard Jan tell Betsy that she couldn't carry a tune in a bucket, to which Betsy replied, "I'd like to put a bucket over your head right now."

Sara turned to Joseph. "Their singing is great but their relationship appears to be a bit stressed. Hopefully it's just pre-wedding jitters. They have four weeks to work out their issues. I'm certain they'll be fine. They're best friends and have been for decades. Speaking of pre-wedding jitters, do you have any concerns? You aren't getting cold feet, are you? Leaving me standing at the altar would certainly be newsworthy but not in a good way."

"Sara, not a chance. There is no way you're getting out of

this now. One month and counting. I think we've located all the ducks and they're forming a line. I hear quacking in the distance. We've completed most of the items on our to-do list. We're in the home stretch. Little to do now but relax and check off each day until the 14th. Let's go back to my place for a little game of touch and giggle, if you know what I mean."

"Joseph, it's not our wedding night yet. What kind of 'girl' do you think I am? I have morals, I have standards, and I have to stop and feed Penelope before I can come to your place. I'll see you there in thirty minutes."

Sara spooned the wet cat food into a dish and called for Penelope. Normally she would run into the kitchen to eat her dinner but tonight she didn't appear. It was certainly out of character. She called again but still no response. Oh please, don't let anything happen to her precious Penelope at this happy time in her life.

Sara went in search of her kitty. She looked under the bed. She looked in the bathroom and everywhere she thought Penelope might hide. Then she heard a faint meow. She moved back to the bedroom and listened. Again, she heard the meow. She opened the closet door and out bounded Penelope. She must have gone into the closet when Sara was getting something out earlier in the afternoon and somehow got locked inside. Poor Penelope. No time to make up, she was off to the kitchen in search of her dinner. Phew, that was a scary moment.

After Penelope finished, she licked her paws and cleaned up a bit. Sara sat on the couch and Penelope jumped on her lap. "My dear, sweet kitty. You had me scared there for a minute. I can't even imagine life without you. You've been my best friend, roommate, and confidante for years and years. You simply have to live forever. I hope you still have all your nine lives. Promise me that you won't scare me like that again!"

Sara started thinking about life. She almost felt like a "What If" moment was about to happen but it didn't materialize. When we let people or animals into our lives, we allow ourselves to be vulnerable. We hurt when they hurt. We're sad when they're sad. We worry about them even when we tell ourselves that our worry won't make anything better. However, without those loved ones our lives wouldn't be worth living. It's certainly a double-edged sword.

Sara was going to marry Joseph and in doing so, his well-being would become her top priority. She would fret when he didn't feel well. She would be defenseless against constant daily worry. Her logical side would tell her that worry was a waste of energy, but her emotional side would argue with that and always come out the winner. She loved Joseph and their upcoming nuptials added him to her list of family members, friends, and pets for whom she invested emotional involvement and concern. Caring opens the door to the heart allowing grief, suffering, and pain to enter as unwelcome visitors. On the flip side, caring also allows love, companionship, and happiness to be ushered inside with open arms.

Sara patted Penelope on her soft, furry head and told her that she'd be back in a couple of hours. She explained that she and Joseph were going to look around his place in order to make a list of what items of his would stay when Sara moved in after the wedding. They needed to consolidate the furniture and personal belongings from two residences into one.

Fortunately, Joseph had never furnished the second bedroom, so Sara had plenty of space for her bedroom furniture. They had to combine the kitchen, living room, and patio items. What they didn't use would be stored until the annual spring garage sale at Parliament Square. If it wasn't sold then it would be donated to a local homeless shelter.

Chuck walked past as Sara locked her door. "Sara, I was

wondering if you could give me some advice? As a man of color, I've always been more comfortable around women of color. I understand that's old school, but I am all about old school. I know that you and Michele are very good friends. I wanted to know if you thought she'd be interested in going to dinner with me sometime. I still have a driver's license and a car. I know she lost her husband some time ago. Although the loss of my wife is more recent, I miss the company of a woman. You and Joseph are so happy, it makes me realize that level of happiness might be possible for me again, too. Michele may not be interested but the only way to know is to ask her. What do you think?"

"Chuck, I can't speak for Michele. Her transition after moving here appeared to be almost seamless but I sense that she feels a bit of loneliness. She's a wonderful woman. We've known each other since college and I think you should definitely ask her to dinner. If you feel more comfortable going with another couple, Joseph and I would be happy to join you. Neither of us still drives, so going to dinner off site would be a welcome change. Currently, we have to ask Joseph's daughter to drive us around and pick us up which is inconvenient for her. Let me know if you would like us to join you."

"Thank you, Sara. I appreciate your offer and I think it's a great idea. Kind of an ice breaker for our first dinner together. I haven't dated anyone since I met my wife when we were in college. I'm sure my dating skills are rusty and having you there as my safety net would be great. I'll work up my courage to ask her and I'll keep you posted."

Sara headed for Joseph's place. He was probably wondering what was taking her so long to feed Penelope. Wouldn't it be nice to have another couple to spend time with? It would be like the old days when she and David played pinochle with Michele and Ted. They used to spend hours together talking, eating, joking, and sometimes even playing cards.

The older we get, the more a network of friends and family seems to make everything more tolerable. Aging alone is scary, but when you can share with others and they share with you, the common denominator of the senior years puts it all in perspective. You're no longer an island of aches, pains, medications, and doctor appointments. Others are right there with you to share their own stories. It gives meaning to the saying *misery loves company*.

Joseph appeared to be half asleep when he answered the door. Of course, that could be expected. It was after eight o'clock for heaven's sake. "Joseph, sorry it took me so long. Chuck paid me a visit. He wanted my opinion on asking Michele out for dinner. And guess what? Chuck still has his driver's license and his car. He can drive us to dinner if he and Michele go and want company. It's like being sixteen again and having your friend drive you around. It's newfound freedom!"

"Sounds good to me. I like the food here, and sharing meals in the dining room, but going out to dinner without having to ask Allison would be great. Although I did hear through the grapevine that we may be allowed to use Uber or Lyft soon. The staff is interviewing several drivers and will allow only those who are approved. It'll be like getting a little slice of our independence back. No longer being able to drive is number one on my list of the disadvantages of aging. That and living with all these older people when I'm still so young."

They both laughed and settled down on the couch together to watch a special on Sandals resorts. They wanted to be well educated on the amenities so they could hold their own with the younger couples. Parasailing and scuba diving were out of the question, but long walks on the white sand beaches and cocktails on the porch while watching the sunset were not. They were going to have a wonderful time together as Mr. and Mrs. Joseph Zimmerman. It would be a week to remember.

Sara insisted on leaving after the eleven o'clock news. She wouldn't leave Penelope alone all night, although she was tempted to crawl into bed with Joseph and feel his body next to hers. The younger generation can have their lovemaking. Not that there is anything wrong with that. As age increases, the closeness and warmth of the other person's body may be all that is necessary to satisfy romantic urges. A hug, a kiss, a soft caress gives us a feeling of intimacy without any sexual encounter. Although the benefits of that little blue pill shouldn't be underestimated.

Sara listened to Penelope's rhythmic purring as she settled in for the night. It would be interesting to see how she adjusted to living with Joseph at his place. She might be jealous of Joseph. It had just been the two of them for so long. She might have to be shut out of the bedroom on those "special" nights. Sara could imagine Penelope loudly meowing on the other side of the door. That would certainly diminish a romantic moment. Maybe some extra kitty toys or treats would be needed.

Sara drifted off to sleep quickly and David came to her in a dream. He was still young and handsome. She wanted to reach out and touch his face, feel his embrace, kiss his lips. David told her that he was happy for her. She shouldn't feel guilty. She shouldn't feel badly for moving on with her life. It was what he wanted for her. To be happy again. To have a man she loved and who loved her. It was meant to be.

Sara and David reminisced over the life they had shared, the good times and the bad. Because David lost his life in an accident there was never any time for goodbyes. One day they were a happily married couple and the next day Sara was a widow, grieving for the love of her life. It was so unfair. David encouraged her to enjoy each day as another one is never guaranteed. Life is a delicate balance of ups and downs. Enjoy the ups as long as possible. She felt his spirit was in the room with her that night. When she reached for him, he was gone.

Sara awoke the next morning with the dream still on her mind. It was so vivid. It was so real. Were our departed loved ones really able to visit us during our slumber? Or was it just a figment of her imagination? Was it something her mind conjured up to put her at ease about remarrying? Was her subconscious secretly dealing with the guilt she felt in marrying Joseph and forsaking David? How would the experts in dream interpretation explain it? Did this dream reflect concerns that she was afraid to address during waking hours?

Sometimes dreams are blurry moments in the night, not to be remembered upon awakening. Sometimes dreams are scary and jolt you awake from a sound sleep. Some are vague memories in the morning that are totally forgotten as the day progresses. This was a dream to remember and believe. David was happy for her. He was glad she had found Joseph and was getting married. She had his blessing.

The breakfast table was abuzz with activity when Sara arrived. Linda had visited the table minutes earlier and announced that the television crew would be taping the tablemate interview today at lunchtime. They were arriving early, around ten thirty, to do the interview before the dining room started serving lunch. It would be too noisy and crowded to actually tape during the meal.

Betsy, Jan, and Michele were discussing their wardrobe for the event. They didn't want to clash colors or look like they were twins or, worse yet, triplets. Linda told them to avoid white and very busy patterns because they play "tricks" with the cameras. Hopefully, the no-pattern request would eliminate the majority of Jan's colorful wardrobe. She might be forced to wear something conservative, if she owned anything that fit into that category. It is said that the camera adds ten pounds, so darker solid colors might be the antidote to that problem.

Jim, Chuck, and Joseph were discussing the weather and the March Madness brackets. They had no concern or interest in what they were going to wear on camera. Men were definitely wired differently than women. Maybe that was all a part of the big plan. Keep the thought process of the sexes different in an attempt to keep life interesting. And that it did.

Michele spoke up. "Sara, do you and Joseph have a preference for what we wear to the interview? This story is all about you two and we want your input. We might not be able to stop Jim from telling questionable jokes, but we can avoid a motley-attired group for the cameras. Maybe we should label our dress code as conservative and hope for the best. We all understand what conservative attire means, right?"

It was decided that the men would all wear dress trousers and collared shirts. The women would wear some combination of navy, black, or red. No whites, no prints, and no reflective fabrics. Keep it simple and basic. The conversation should be the focal point of the interview, not the clothing.

When breakfast was over the women went their separate ways to explore their closets for suitable apparel. It wasn't every day that you were dressing for a television interview. This would be the talk of Parliament Square for some time.

The men went to the lobby to read the paper, talk about the weather, or simply pass the time until they had to get dressed. They didn't have hair to style, or makeup to apply, or six outfits to try on, or nails to polish or . . . the list went on. Life in the testosterone world is simple and to the point. Maybe that's where the *Men Are from Mars, Women Are from Venus* thinking originated. The brain circuity definitely differs between men and women.

The hours passed quickly and soon it was time to face the cameras. Nancy sat with the residents and went over camera protocol and expectations. The crew set up in preparation. They were warned that any part of the interview could end up on the cutting-room floor as the tape was edited before being aired.

Nancy spoke to the group. "We will introduce Sara and Joseph first, give a little background on the upcoming wedding, and then go around the table asking questions. Take your time in responding. Try to speak slowly as sometimes being on camera causes folks to talk quickly, making them hard to understand. If it takes a minute to gather your thoughts, no problem. We can edit any part of the tape. Just be yourselves. Any questions?"

Jim spoke up. "On occasion, I've been known to tell a joke or two. I'll certainly keep it family oriented and use no offensive language. I wanted to give you a heads up as the group could consume some of the interview time laughing at my humor as they often do." "Jim," Betsy replied, "I don't think we have to worry about that. We'll restrain ourselves today. But I can't guarantee the same for our eye rolling or groaning."

Nancy smiled. "Okay, Jim, thanks for the heads up. I think we're about ready to get started. Please relax and enjoy the interview. Just be yourselves and it'll be fun. You'll soon forget the cameras are even rolling."

Nancy introduced Sara and Joseph first and provided a bit of background on their engagement and upcoming nuptials. Then she went around the table asking questions about the betrothed couple. The consensus of the group was it was pretty much love at first sight. Sara and Joseph seemed to form a visible bond from day one. Although they weren't a couple immediately, there was certainly a connection between the two from the start.

Jim, of course, had to sprinkle some humor on the conversation. "These two are going to soon find out the difference between love and marriage. Love is blind. Marriage is a real eye opener. Love is one long, sweet, uninterrupted dream. Marriage is the alarm clock. But all kidding aside, I would like to share a heartwarming story about Sara and Joseph. One evening they were alone cuddling on the sofa while watching television. Joseph lovingly embraced Sara. He then continued what Sara thought was his show of affection by gently rubbing her back and arms. Other areas were involved, but this is a family program. Long story short, Joseph abruptly stopped and moved to the other side of the sofa. Sara, wondering what happened, asked him why he moved. He replied, "I was looking for the remote."

The table erupted in laughter and Sara let everyone know the story wasn't true. Too late. Even if it wasn't, it was funny.

Nancy thanked everyone for their participation. The tape would be edited and a final copy would be presented prior to it being aired, probably next week. She would notify Sara so the group could assemble to watch the edited version together.

# Chapter Nine

## Flu, Snow, and Zumba

March had been kind to the residents of the New England states that winter. Not like it is in California or Florida, with ample sunshine and balmy temperatures, but a kindness revealed by a lack of substantial snow and ice and howling Arctic winds. Even so, the weather had taken a turn for the worse. Sara awoke to find several inches of freshly fallen snow covering the ground with higher amounts predicted. Today was going to be an inside day. The children who loved to sled, build snowmen, and welcome a snow day home from school would be celebrating along with the avid skiers anxious to hit the powdery slopes.

Normally, Sara would have breakfast and walk over to the daycare center to spend the morning with the children, but the daycare center was closed due to the inclement weather. The breakfast conversation centered around the snowstorm and the prediction of more than a foot of snow yet to come. Would the power go out? Could the employees drive though the storm to get to work? What would happen if there was a medical emergency? The room was abuzz with storm related concerns and questions.

Chuck said, "When I was a kid, we had to walk to school in weather like this and it was uphill both ways. The kids of this day and age have it easy. They don't walk to school anymore. They have buses or parents to drive them. They close the schools when the weather is marginally bad. If you ask me, we're raising a generation of softies who won't be able to take care of themselves when they reach adulthood. The hard times are what teach us valuable lessons. Too much is handed to the youth of today. It's not good. But I guess that makes me sound like the grumpy old man that I am."

Everyone agreed that times had changed dramatically from the days of their youth, sometimes for the better with technological advances making life seem like something from

*The Jetsons.* But hand-in-hand with new technology comes the challenge of mastering its use. For the youth of today, that's a piece of cake, but to the technologically challenged senior population, it's intimidating.

Jim chimed in. "The other day I tried to change the channel on the TV using my cordless phone because the TV remote was on the cell phone charger. I wondered why I had such trouble getting it to stay on the charger. In my defense, they do look a lot alike. To say I'm electronically challenged is putting it mildly. I know this makes me sound like an old fogey, but all this new technology is hard to understand and even harder to remember. Give me the good old days, except for the TV remote. That was a godsend."

What to do on this snow day? Kids love having a snow day from school. They get all bundled up and build snowmen or go sledding. Adults enjoy a day off from work, savoring the time inside enjoying a hot cup of coffee until the cold, snowy procession of children coming inside from their playtime begins. Piles of wet clothing, coats, boots, hats, and mittens piled high in the entranceway or the mudroom. But for the folks at Parliament Square, a snow day is pretty much like any other day. There will be indoor activities, conversations in the lobby, and maybe some hot cocoa in the activity room. Retirement brings lots of snow days, many without a trace of snow.

Michele, Chuck, Joseph, and Sara decided to head to the activity room for a friendly game of pinochle. They had played a couple of evenings over the past several weeks and enjoyed each other's company. Sara wanted to hear about Chuck's dinner invitation and was curious to learn if she and Joseph would make it a foursome. She didn't want to ask Michele about it in case Chuck had gotten cold feet. Sara looked forward to leaving the residence in Chuck's car: A bit of independence in this new world of conventionality. The mere thought of sitting in the back seat with Joseph gave her goosebumps, like going on a double date to the prom. My how some things changed so much while others stayed the same.

The card games were fun. There was laughter and sharing and more laughter. The snow continued to fall. Being inside and able to watch the white flakes accumulate, while knowing there was no possible reason to venture out into the winter wonderland, made the snow-covered landscape even more captivating. Also, knowing that it was mid-March, and sunshine and warmer temperatures would melt the frozen precipitation quickly, made this probable last big snow of the season tolerable.

As the game was ending, Chuck said, "Sara and Joseph, Michele and I were wondering if you would join us for dinner one evening, after the snow has melted and the roads are clear. We thought it would be fun to go together, and having you along will ensure that there are no breaks in the conversation. I haven't been on a first date in decades and I may need some backup in case I forget what to do. Since I have my car here, we can hit the open road as long as we're home by curfew."

Sara smiled. "Chuck, we'd be honored to join you for dinner. Having a licensed driver with a car is like being back in high school and going on a double date. Just don't look at us in your rear-view mirror on the way home please. Sometimes Joseph gets a bit frisky and can't keep his hands to himself."

The foursome broke into laughter. It would be nice to spent time socializing with another couple. Before moving to Parliament Square, communication with friends and neighbors was both spontaneous and unlimited. Now, that was not the case .

No longer being able to drive was life-changing. Instead of getting in your vehicle and driving wherever whenever, every trip had to be planned in advance. Although others offered to drive you places, you felt that you were inconveniencing them, so oftentimes you just didn't go. Nothing robbed senior citizens of their independence like revoking their driving privileges and taking away their vehicles.

The blaring ambulance sirens were almost deafening as the group walked through the lobby. A crowd gathered as the paramedics wheeled the gurney into the building and approached the elevators. Although this wasn't an uncommon event, it was certainly an unwelcome one. Sure, the senior population was more susceptible to medical events. Sure, this was a senior community. Sure, this was expected. However, that didn't make it any easier to experience.

Sara squeezed Joseph's hand so hard he winced. "Joseph, this is so scary. They could be coming for you or me. I can't even imaging losing you. We just have to live forever."

"Sara, we both know that's impossible, but we can live each day to the fullest. We've been offered the chance to spend our remaining years together, and we're going to do that no matter how many weeks, months, or years remain in our hourglass of life. I hope our book has many, many unwritten chapters waiting for us to author. Positivity and optimism will be our ink, while love and compromise will supply the paper. We'll show the world how it's done."

"Joseph, you always know just what to say. I realize there are never any guarantees in life. We should appreciate the fact that we've made it this far. Too many people don't. Even worse, some believe they're no longer part of life's equation. They say they're ready to leave this world. I feel badly for them. I vow to you that I will never join their ranks. I will live to the fullest with you until my expiration date arrives."

Just then, the elevator doors opened and the paramedics exited with a patient on the gurney. Everyone tried not to look even though they all wanted to know who it was. Many of the residents were quarantined to their rooms as there was a surge in the annual flu. Although flu shots were mandatory, unless religious beliefs or allergic reaction prohibited it, many had fallen victim anyway. The infection rate had increased so much there was talk of requiring all residents to take their meals privately instead of eating together in the dining room. So far, that hadn't happened.

With spring just around the corner, according to the calendar but disputed by the new-fallen snow outside the window, everyone was anxious for the winter to end. Sara and Joseph had attended a couple of Cynthia's exercise classes but hadn't found one that they both enjoyed. Sara thought the stretching class was something she would rather do in the privacy of her own apartment. Joseph felt the balance class was boring. So, they decided to try something new: chair Zumba.

They were told there would be motivating music and that each participant could work at his or her own comfort level. Some may be more agile or energetic than others, but everyone was welcome.

Cynthia welcomed Sara and Joseph to the class, identifying them to the others as first-timers. That struck Sara as funny and she chuckled to herself. At her age, doing something for the first time seemed like an oxymoron. But yes, she was a virgin in the world of Zumba.

Cynthia explained, "A chair is available for each person if you need it for support and balance. Your movements on the floor will, of course, be more limited using the chair, but feel free to use your body and arms to dance while you're seated. Each of you should work inside your comfort zone. Don't overdo it. This class is all about having fun while getting some exercise. It's certainly not a marathon, but rather an hour to spend together listening to music and socializing. Any questions?"

No one had any questions, so the class started. The music was quite loud. Those with hearing aids quickly adjusted the volume. It was like being in the movie theater and covering your ears when the movie starts because the volume was so intense. Sara was good with it because her hearing was a bit compromised, but Joseph made faces and held his hands over his ears. This was going to be fun.

Cynthia gyrated in front of the class encouraging them to follow her lead. It was obvious that no one in the room was able to dance at her level. Jan and Betsy were in the class, standing right next to each other. They declined the use of the chairs and instead used each other for support. Jan's outfit was a sight for sore eyes. The colors were intense, one shade away from neon, the fit left little to the imagination, and the light-up sneakers were the *pièce de résistance*.

After each song, Cynthia encouraged them to hydrate. Each break lasted longer than the last. Betsy and Jan stopped to chat for a minute. "Isn't this fun?" Betsy asked. "Jan and I have been coming to this class for a month now. We feel so energized by the music and the movements. After last week's class I even skipped my afternoon siesta. You and Joseph should come with us each week until you get married. It'll get you into shape. It might even make your honeymoon more eventful."

"Betsy, behave yourself," Jan replied. "Sorry for her behavior. These classes energize her body and her mind. She made me binge watch two seasons of *Grace and Frankie* after last week's class. She said the actors and stories remind her so much of us. I just wish that we looked more like them and had their money and lifestyle. Oops, time to get back to dancing. See you at dinner."

The hour class did pass quickly. It was fun. It was exercise. well, it was kind-of exercise. Best of all, it was social time with Joseph and other residents. Although Parliament Square offered numerous activities and social events, many residents didn't participate and instead isolated themselves in their apartments watching television and napping.

Sara and Joseph weren't going to hibernate in their apartments before or after the wedding. They were going to participate, socialize, and get involved as a couple, although Joseph might take a raincheck on Zumba next week. He felt it was more targeted toward the women. He said his body just didn't move that way normally.

Cynthia said goodbye and headed off to lunch. Sara decided to have lunch at her apartment instead of the dining room. She wanted to check on Penelope and she was a bit tired from the class. "Joseph, please join the others for lunch. I'm going to make myself some soup, feed Penelope, and take a nap. I have a bit of a headache, which will hopefully go away with some medication and sleep. Tell the others hello for me. I'll give you a call when I wake up. Don't worry about me. I'll be fine."

Sara didn't want to share the fact that she had a bit of a sore throat. And she did have a headache. The class was fun, but maybe she should've waited until a later date to participate. With the number of flu cases increasing, she would rather be safe than sorry. With some hot soup, some acetaminophen, and a nap with Penelope, she would be as good as new in time for dinner. With the wedding just around the corner, there was no time to be sick.

Joseph seated himself in the dining room and explained, "Sara decided to have lunch alone and take a nap. She was feeling a bit under the weather after the Zumba class. I must admit that I broke a sweat. The music was a bit loud, but Cynthia has a knack for getting folks involved. She really enjoys her work and it shows. We're lucky to have so many dedicated staff members.

Although, if someone asked me a year ago about living in a senior community, I would have told them no way. That's for old people. That's for people who can no longer take care of themselves. I never thought in my wildest dreams that I'd give up my home and move to a place like this, but it was one of the best decisions of my life. I'm still close to my family and I've made many new friends. I'm well taken care of and have no residential maintenance to worry about. And the biggest advantage of moving to Parliament Square is that I met Sara and we're going to get married. It sure beats living alone and eating cold baloney sandwiches for dinner."

The rest of the discussion centered around how life changes as the years pass. We understand the normal progression of physical capabilities. Starting at birth, each passing year brings new capabilities and strengths. We learn to crawl, we learn to walk, we learn to run. Some retain their bodily flexibility and endurance into their senior years, but most don't. They say that seventy is the new sixty, but sometimes our geriatric body parts refute that. Only the very naïve expect physical stamina in their golden years to mirror that of their youth.

Our brains, however, age differently. Along life's journey, our knowledge base grows like a sponge absorbing a bucket of water. We learn academically through our school years and beyond. We learn specific skill sets based on our chosen vocations. We learn life lessons through our personal experiences and relationships.

Age may diminish some of the details of that acquired intelligence, but it doesn't change our thinking process. While our values of right, wrong, and in between do not waiver, our brains can't help but question the stranger in the mirror. We don't mentally feel or think like that wrinkle-laden, gray-haired older version of our younger selves.

"I'm going to check on Sara. I think the Zumba class may

have activated some dormant muscle groups. I was rather sedentary, but Sara was determined to keep up with the other seasoned participants. Betsy and Jan, you were very agile. How long have you been attending?"

"Jan and I have been going to that class for about a month. I'll admit the first couple of weeks were difficult, but it gets better with time. As they say, *no pain, no gain,* but at our age we can experience the pain by simply bending down to tie our shoes. I no longer think about parachute jumping or rock climbing; stepping into my underwear and pants are dangerous enough. Definitely best to stay seated for those perilous movements. Tell Sara we said hello and we hope she feels better soon. If she wants some help selecting Zumba attire, let her know Jan and I will be glad to serve as her fashion advisors."

"Thanks, Betsy. I'll certainly pass that along. See you all at dinner."

Joseph met Jean on the elevator. She looked concerned and said that Parliament Square may mandate residents to receive their meals in their rooms until the flu infections started to decline. "It'll be so lonely if we have to stay in our rooms. I enjoy sharing with others at mealtime. Hopefully, the new cases will decrease soon and isolation won't be necessary. Your wedding could be impacted if this becomes worse. That would be tragic."

Joseph said goodbye and stepped out of the elevator on Sara's floor. He didn't want to awaken her if she was dozing, but he was concerned about her. He had a key to her place. He quietly unlocked the door. It was silent. He tiptoed to the bedroom. Sara was on the bed covered with her favorite fuzzy coverlet, Penelope by her side. Joseph walked closer to be sure she was breathing.

# Chapter Ten

## *Nothing but Blue Skies*

As Joseph leaned over Sara to check her breathing, he spooked Penelope who jumped straight up and landed on Sara's head causing Sara, in turn, to bolt upright, launching Penelope through the air and into the nightstand lamp which crashed to the floor along with Penelope. "Holy bejesus, Joseph, are you trying to scare me to death? If you want to cancel the wedding just tell me. Don't kill me in my sleep please!"

After attempting to subdue his uncontrollable laughter, Joseph exclaimed, "Sara, I am so sorry. I didn't want to disturb you. I was simply checking your breathing to be sure nothing was amiss. I admit, in hindsight, it was a bad decision. I should have tempted Penelope off the bed with treats before getting so close. I'll remember that in the future. Other than almost being scared to death by my wake-up call, how are you feeling?"

"I think the hot soup, Tylenol, and brief nap helped. However, the cat jumping on my head and the nightstand lamp crashing to the floor may have negated all the benefits. Possibly I overdid it at Zumba class this morning. I want to move like I did when I was younger. My mind says I can, but my body disagrees. I'll take it slower next time. How was lunch?"

"Betsy and Jan offered to help you select some tasteful clothing for Zumba class. I just ask that you buy the opposite of whatever they suggest. Definitely no sneakers that light up when you move, please."

"Joseph, I'm concerned that the spread of this flu bug is going to put a crimp in our wedding plans. If the management decides to isolate us in our apartments we could be locked down into April. I realize I should be more concerned about everyone's well-being, but right now I'm focused on our big day. I understand our health is priority one. I'm trying to think positive thoughts and pray this epidemic will be over soon with no impact on you, me, or any of our friends."

"Don't worry about the flu. I think the worst is over, with spring and warmer weather just around the corner. The flu is more of a winter illness. I heard the number of new cases is decreasing and no one has been deathly ill with it. Just more of an annoyance if you ask me."

Sara nodded. "Changing the subject, let's talk to Chuck and set a dinner date. I'm really looking forward to him driving us to dinner. He and I are becoming good friends. I hope he hits it off with Michele. It would be so nice to have another couple to spend time with." Just then the phone rang and Sara jumped off the bed to answer it.

"Hello? Oh Nancy, it's good to hear from you. Yes, tomorrow afternoon should work for everyone. Around one in the activity room. Okay. Great. See you then." She hung up and turned to Joseph. "That was Nancy from the TV station. They've edited the interviews and they plan to air them in the coming week. Nancy wants to bring the edited version over for us to watch tomorrow afternoon. I'm anxious to see it. We can tell everyone about it at dinner this evening. I hope it turned out well. She also mentioned that she'd like to talk with us tomorrow about televising the wedding. This is so exciting."

"Sara, I think it's great that the station wants to tape and broadcast the wedding, but before we commit to doing that, I want to be sure that it's really what you want. It will mean TV personnel and cameras in the chapel with our guests. It will definitely heighten the stress level on an already demanding day. I say demanding in a *good* way. We both want our day to be special, and having strangers there to share it may be uncomfortable. If you don't want to pursue this, just say the word and we'll tell Nancy that we've changed our minds. It's your call."

Sara considered for a moment. "You make a good point about the extra people and gear in the already crowded chapel. There are pros and cons to consider. Let me think about it and ask our tablemates for their input before we give Nancy our final decision. I appreciate your concern. I also value the fact that you'll be content with my decision. You're a good man and I'm lucky to have you in my life."

She took Joseph's hand and squeezed it. "I recently heard a song that I remember from years ago. It's always been a favorite of mine and I used to sing it to Michael when he was younger. I think instead of the traditional *Here Comes the Bride* I'd like to have that song play as Michael walks me down the aisle. However, I can't promise there won't be any tears. By the time I get to the altar, my dripping mascara may have me looking like the Bride of Frankenstein. The song is called 'Blue Skies.'" She smiled at the thought of it. "I'm sure you're familiar with the melody. That song has always made me feel that good times are just around the corner. It triggers sad and happy feelings for me, but the happy definitely outweighs the sad. Would that be okay with you?"

"Sure. That would be fine. Maybe we could make that our song? Remember how couples used to do that back in the day? That was when the lyrics were short and recognizable. Not like today's music. There I go, showing my dinosaur-era age. I do know that song. I'm looking forward to many days ahead with blue skies."

That afternoon, Sara and Joseph shared more life stories and cuddled together on the sofa enjoying each other's company. Sara brought out a photo album and shared some of her photos and the memories they evoked. They had both experienced the biggest parts of their lives before meeting. Their life's memories were separate and, although they held special places in each of their hearts, they were memories of times that they could never share together. Those events were over, but the memories remained. Now they would make new memories together.

"Oh, Joseph, look at this picture of Michael and me at Disney World. We were both wearing our mouse ears. I can remember that trip like it was yesterday. We had such a wonderful time. It was, as they say in the commercials, truly magical. I always thought that we'd return there together but it never happened. Little did I know when we left the Magic Kingdom that day that we'd never visit there together again."

"Maybe the three of us could go there sometime. What do you think? I know we wouldn't be able to ride some of the more adventurous attractions, but there would be plenty that we could enjoy together. Pirates of the Caribbean and the Haunted Mansion are two of my favorites. And of course, flying high in Dumbo and spinning in the teacups. Oh, we could have so much fun. We are young at heart, which is all we need."

"Joseph, did you ever see the movie *The Way We Were*? David and I loved that movie. It made me cry every time I watched it, so I watched it whenever I felt I needed a good cry. Something only another woman would understand, needing a good cry. It's a love story, but one with a sad ending. We especially enjoyed the theme song. I'm sure you've heard it. It explains memories. How some are too painful to remember so we simply just forget. It's like that for me when I pick up old photo albums. So many good times and so much laughter. I love the pictures, but not the mixed emotions. So many people in those pictures are no longer alive. So many places in the photos, gone forever. You can turn back the hands of time, but you can never turn back the clock."

The pictures brought smiles and tears. Memories are like that. Seeing photos of family and friends brings back warm, comforting feelings but at the same time makes you miss family and friends who you'll never see again, and times that you can no longer share. Remembering good times that will never come again is a double-edged sword.

As we get older, we come to realize that every experience might be the last. When we visit special places, or spend time with family and friends who live far away, as we wave goodbye we wonder if this could be the last time that we will see them or the last time we will visit that place.

Our younger selves don't think this way because we believe in unlimited tomorrows. The thought that any experience might be the last never crosses our minds. We can try to suppress those depressing last-time thoughts as we age, but it's more easily said than done.

At dinner that evening, Sara mentioned that Nancy would bring the edited version of the television segment the following day at one. "Joseph and I agreed that taping the wedding would be nice, but we're a bit concerned that the camera crew could crowd the chapel. We wanted to ask you what you think about it. You're an important part of our day, so help us decide if the pros outnumber the cons. Let's go around the table and get a yea or nay from each of you. We will let you make this difficult decision for us."

Jan was first. "I understand your concern. For me, the pros are that people at home will be able to see good news for a change. There is so much turmoil and bad news, your love story gives hope to all the lonely, older folks out there. If anyone had asked you a year ago if you were going to find love and remarry, I doubt you would have answered yes. Also, I'm anxious for my friends and family to see me on their fifty-inch high-def big-screen TVs, but that's an item from my selfish pro list. The only con is, like you mentioned, the small amount of space in the chapel. So, my vote is yes."

Betsy replied next. "We have seen your relationship blossom into love and, soon, marriage. We're so excited for you both. This is your day and, speaking for the group, we all hope that it's wonderful. My pros and cons pretty much mirror those of Jan's. I think Nancy and the camera crew will afford you every courtesy when it comes to space and interference. This isn't their first taping and they understand the importance of this very special day. I too vote yes for taping your wedding."

Michele had tears when she spoke. "Sara, you are one of my oldest and dearest friends. And by oldest I'm referring to the number of years we've known each other." Everyone laughed. "In all the time we've been friends, I've never seen you happier than you are today. You and Joseph deserve nothing but the best. I feel that by sharing your story with the media you are allowing a morsel of your happiness to be consumed by those who need it most. Older people will believe for a moment that anything is possible. A seed of hope will be planted. A ray of sunshine will gleam. A smile will be seen on faces otherwise lacking emotion. So, I too vote yes for media coverage."

"Well, I guess it's my turn," said Jim. "One more yes vote and we have a majority, and with Deborah not attending, we may already have reached a decision. I am certainly not a romantic. In fact, I'm pretty much the opposite of one. I was never lucky enough to find the right person for me, so I have no marital experience on which to base my vote. Maybe a bit of humor first?" The groans were audible, but Jim continued. "A man was out walking one day and went by a retirement home. As he passed the front lawn, he saw nine senior ladies basking in the sun in lounge chairs. When he looked closer, he realized they were all stark naked. He went to the door and rang the bell. When the director answered the door, the man asked if he realized there were nine naked senior ladies lying in the sun on the front lawn. The director said, 'Yes' and went on to explain that the ladies were all retired prostitutes and they were having a yard sale."

The table erupted in laughter. Jim certainly had an unlimited number of anecdotes. At times his ability to present a joke on any subject caused some to wonder how his memory worked. Especially since, for most, brain cells seem to jump ship as the years progress.

"Well, I'm glad you enjoyed my dinner-theater humor. There are more where that came from. I'm saving the best for my toast to the newlyweds. I know you're all looking forward to that." More groans. "My vote is a definite yes for the taping. I look forward to seeing myself on camera. I'll be sure to record the program so I can watch it over and over and over. Maybe I can post it on my online dating profile. If Chuck votes yes, then it's unanimous. And should he vote no, the majority rules. Chuck, you're next."

Chuck stood and addressed Sara and Joseph. "I am so honored to be seated at this table with all of you. In the short amount of time we've spent together, I feel like I'm already one of the group. I know that my vote really doesn't impact the decision because the majority has voted yes; however, I also feel there are many more pros than cons. We are all looking forward to your wedding and being there to share the day with you both. Let's raise our glasses and toast to the happy couple and their upcoming wedding."

Glasses clinked and hugs were exchanged. The big day was fast approaching. Sara made a mental note to call Michael after dinner. She hadn't talked with him for several weeks and she wanted to make sure he was still coming.

When Michael first moved away, she missed him terribly. He had been her closest family member for so long and had always been there for her. She thought of him as the son she never had. Then she met Joseph and her whole world changed. She was remiss in calling Michael since she began spending time with Joseph, but she knew that Michael's new job and his new friend kept him very busy. Yes, a much-needed telephone conversation would happen that evening.

After dinner, Sara told Joseph that she was going to return to her place to make the call. Joseph said that he and Chuck were going to the activity room to see if they could find any of the women from Jim's joke. They hugged and went their separate ways.

As she rode the elevator, Sara thought about how life had changed for her since she arrived at Parliament Square less than a year ago. Never in her wildest dreams could she have imagined falling in love and getting married. It was like a *what if* moment, but she wasn't dreaming. She was wide awake.

Penelope greeted her at the door, demanding her dinner. Sara dutifully filled her dish with wet cat food and petted her softly as she began to eat. She really loved this little kitty.

After retreating to the bedroom and selecting a warm sweater, Sara sat on the rocking chair and dialed Michael's number. She knew the time difference would make it about three p.m. California time. She didn't want to disturb him at work, but he often worked from home. He picked up after five rings. "Hello, Aunt Sara. How is the bride to be?"

"Michael, it's so good to hear your voice. It's been too long. I apologize for not calling sooner. I wanted to hear you tell me that you've purchased your plane ticket and will be here with bells on to walk your old Aunt Sara down the aisle in three weeks. The big day is almost here."

Michael laughed. "I've missed our weekly chats. Yes, I have my ticket and will be arriving early on Friday the 13$^{th}$ so I can attend the rehearsal. Good thing I'm not superstitious. Do you think for a minute that I would miss this red-letter day?

However, I saw the winter weather you're having and I insist that you make that go away before I show up. I'm a California resident now and winter weather is a vague memory."

"This should be the last of the winter. I'm certain that sunny, spring weather is just around the corner. Don't even pack any warm clothing. I am that optimistic. How is work going? How's your new relationship? What have you and Marcy decided about your marriage?"

"Well, my job is going very well. I work from home pretty much every day unless there's a meeting or presentation in the office. I recently got a promotion which means more money but also more work. My new friend and I are thinking about moving in together soon. I can't wait for you to meet. Marcy and I have decided to call it quits. She's moved on and I think I have too. We're going through the divorce process and she is actually being very civil, which surprises me. It appears that we weren't a match made in heaven, but it took us years to figure that out. Fortunately, we're in agreement, so no ugly divorce or difficult property settlement."

"How is your husband to be doing? You never told me about your honeymoon plans. I hope they don't include Niagara Falls or Dollywood. Maybe a tropical cruise or a trip to Europe?"

Sara and Michael talked and talked and talked. They shared stories and updated each other on personal current events. It had been too long since they talked and laughed together like this. They were still very close in spirit, although they were far apart in miles. Their relationship was strong. Their bond was unbreakable. They were family.

When Sara said good night, she felt so fortunate to have a nephew like Michael. She may not have been lucky enough to have a child of her own, but she had Michael. She rested her head against the back of the rocking chair and closed her eyes. She rocked and rocked while Penelope purred loudly on her lap.

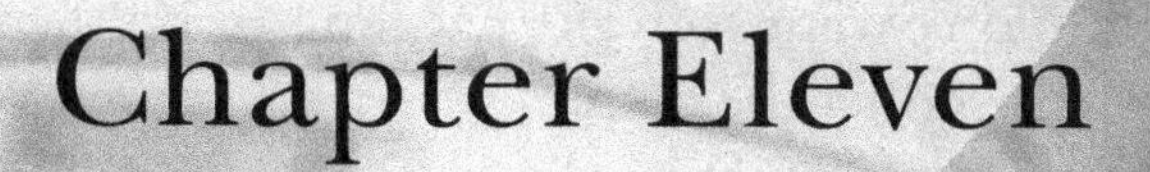

# Chapter Eleven

## *The Local Moment – Autographs, Please*

The piles of snow left by the recent storm melted in the March sun. Sara's favorite season was definitely on the way. Many brides favor June, hence the phrase *June bride*. Sara didn't want to wait that long to tie the knot. At their ages, the sooner the better.

Joseph knocked on Sara's door on his way to lunch. This afternoon at one Nancy was going to preview the taped interview prior to it being televised on *The Local Moment* segment of the evening news next week. Sara opened the door and greeted Joseph with a warm embrace and a gentle peck on the cheek. "I know you can't keep your hands off me, young lady. Want to skip lunch and grab a quickie? I think they refer to them as *nooners*. No one will miss us."

Sara blushed. "I am much too prim and proper for that sort of behavior. And besides, I'm really hungry. Let's have lunch and then watch the tape. I feel sorry that Deborah isn't interested in being part of the group. I've tried numerous times to get her involved with activities. She even RSVP'd that she wouldn't be attending the wedding and reception. Such a shame that she distances herself from everyone. She must be very lonely."

"Personally, I wish she would move to another table. She puts a damper on things. Everyone else is fun and social except for her. If she left, maybe we could get another Chuck or Jim. I know that sounds harsh, but I do feel that way. Deborah just seems to think we're all below her. She feels that Parliament Square isn't up to her standards and quality of life. With any luck, she'll find another residence and move away."

"Joseph, that is not nice. I feel that way too, but I would never verbalize it because maybe there's more than meets the eye. Maybe she has family problems or health issues that we aren't aware of and she doesn't want to share. You're correct that she isn't a good match for our table, but who are we to say she should go? She was seated at that table before you or I lived here. She has seniority. Let's simply hope that she comes around at some point. Until then, no more discussions about Deborah, please."

When they arrived at the dining room, their six table-mates were all seated. It was unusual for everyone to be there for lunch. Breakfast and dinner, yes, but lunch was hit or miss depending on daily schedules and planned activities.

"Hello everyone. Glad to see you all. Remember, we're meeting Nancy in the activity room at one to see the edited tape. I'm excited and also a little nervous. I hope we all like what we see. We're going to be sharing dinner with thousands of viewers. We are going to put Parliament Square on the map."

Everyone talked at once. Apparently, Sara wasn't the only one anxious about the tape. Jan clicked her knife against her water glass to quiet down the noise. "I'm worried I may have exposed some cleavage when I bent over the table for a Kleenex. I knew better than to wear that blouse. It's happened before."

Betsy added, "Don't be silly. If that happened, which it probably didn't, they would cut it out because this is going to be aired during family viewing time. Let's finish our lunch."

Of course, the situation sparked Jim's need to lessen the tension with some humor. "I was talking to a good friend last week who seemed to be upset. I asked him what was wrong. He mentioned that he had rear-ended a car the other day. When the driver got out of the car, turns out he was a dwarf. My friend was surprised. The dwarf looked up at my friend and said, 'I am not Happy!' My friend replied, 'Well, which one are you then?' It didn't go well from there."

Even Deborah smiled a little, although she tried to hide it by wiping her mouth with her napkin. Jim certainly knew how to turn a frown upside down. Lunch was served and the conversation quieted.

Afterward the group headed for the activity room. Much to everyone's surprise, Deborah joined them. This was certainly a surprise and totally out of character. Maybe she was rethinking her behavior, or possibly she was just nosy and wanted to see the tape. Either way, she was more than welcome.

Nancy was setting up the television. She had some kind of device that fit into the 'smart' TV which would allow the program to be broadcast on the screen. New technology. Embraced by youth and younger adults, feared by non-technical and the geriatric population.

Chuck and Jim walked around the room and closed the blinds to make it darker. Everyone took a seat and waited for the show to begin. Linda bounded into the room in her normal kangaroo-like mode, greeted the group, and congratulated Sara and Joseph. The room grew quiet and the show started.

Unfortunately, it was true what they say about the camera adding extra pounds. Several people asked if that was how they really sounded. The voices they heard weren't what they expected. Overall, there were no bloopers or exposed cleavage. It was like a senior version of *Friends*. The connections were there, as were an ample supply of wrinkles and age spots. Maybe the editors could airbrush the entire tape?

As the program concluded, the group applauded and thanked Nancy for bringing the tape over for them to preview. Jim said he was upset that a couple of his humorous moments didn't make the cut. The others pretended to empathize, and several eye rolls were exchanged in the process. No doubt more jokes would surface at the reception. Although they had searched for an *OFF* button to squelch Jim's endless supply of jokes, to date none had been located.

Nancy asked the group what they thought. It was a unanimous thumbs up. They were anxious for their friends and family to see them on television. Sara and Joseph expressed their gratitude for doing such a great job. Their story was tastefully told without the sensationalism that is so typical nowadays. It captured the personal side of the event, a human-interest piece to which many older folks could relate. It was a ray of sunshine in a sometimes dark and dreary world. It was inspirational.

Nancy packed up her things and said farewell. She expected the segment to air on the following Tuesday. She gave Joseph something called a *flash drive* which contained the edited recording, telling him he could view it on his smart TV or on his laptop. Joseph chuckled because he had neither, but he would give it to Allison who had both. Maybe he and Sara should look into purchasing a laptop so they could talk remotely with Michael or Joseph's daughters who lived on the West Coast. Yes, they would look into doing that.

Sara and Joseph remained seated as the others said their goodbyes. The daytime soap operas or an after-lunch siesta were popular activities for many residents. "Sara, I wanted to update you about the menu for the reception. I chatted with the restaurant and ordered several items for the late morning gathering after the wedding. I thought finger foods would be better than a heavy sit-down meal based on the time of day and the guest list. The buffet will allow our family and friends to pick and choose their selections while sharing conversation. No assigned seats except at the head table. I think I'll keep the menu a secret. My guess is that you'll approve. You have enough to deal with already. At my request, I have remained in the background, but I will take responsibility for the reception menu and the honeymoon. I received the plane tickets in the mail today. They said I could have them sent to a cell phone application, but I declined. We old-timers like to have a piece of paper, don't we? Let all that technology to the young folks."

"Thank you, Joseph, for taking care of the food decisions and for making all the honeymoon plans. There is more planning and work involved than I remember. Probably because I was much younger last time. I think I'm going to elope next time. Yes, I am definitely going to run off without telling anyone when I marry again!"

They both shared a bit of laughter. Although sometimes difficult, maintaining a good sense of humor is one of life's best anti-aging secrets. Taking life too seriously at any age has a negative effect on the quality of life. Worry and anxiety cannot always be avoided, but more often than not they are unnecessary, unproductive, and exhausting. They rob you of true happiness without you even realizing it.

Chuck stopped to talk with them just as they were getting up to leave. He suggested that maybe they could make reservations for an evening next week to have dinner with he and Michele. Of course, it would be weather permitting since he promised his son that he wouldn't venture out if conditions were bad. It was a bit of role reversal. Chuck remembered giving his son that same advice when he started driving. Funny how the parent-child relationship seems to go full circle when the parents reach a certain age.

"Chuck, we would love to do that. Sara and I haven't been out to dinner in some time. I know we eat together every evening in the dining room, but leaving the premises and being on our own seems so inviting. The food here is good but sometimes I'm just not hungry for what's on the menu. What night were you thinking?"

"Let me discuss it with Michele and I'll get back to you.

We don't have to eat at five either. We can be wild and crazy. We can make reservations for five-thirty or six! We'll show the world what rebels we are. Maybe we'll even order an appetizer and dessert."

As Chuck left Sara mentioned to Joseph that she was so happy Chuck had been assigned to their table. Maybe that was decided based on Michele being seated there. There were few people of color at Parliament Square. This area of Massachusetts was predominately white, and the majority of residents were Caucasian. "Joseph, I've been meaning to ask you whether Allison's sisters and their families will be attending the wedding. I realize it's a long trip for them, living on the West Coast. I was hoping to meet your other two daughters. If they are anything like Allison, I'm certain that I won't be disappointed. Tell me more about them. You don't talk about them much except to tell me that they called or sent you a card."

"Yes, they both accepted the invitation and will be traveling together. They're leaving their families behind since it will be a short visit and the airfare is quite expensive. I offered to pay but they refused, saying it would be a bit of vacation for them traveling together without their families. They're seldom able to spend sister time together and this will give them an opportunity to do just that."

"I must warn you that Sofie, the youngest, was a bit of a free spirit when she was younger. She lived in a commune for years before getting married. We worried about her, but she welcomed a traditional lifestyle as she got older. She could easily have lived in the Haight-Ashbury neighborhood of San Francisco back in the 60s. She was a true flower child and experimented with potions and pot for years. Fortunately, she met and fell madly in love with a young medical student who treated her when she was hospitalized for a ruptured appendix. Brett settled her down. They moved to an affluent neighborhood, raised three children, and Sophia became the perfect housewife, mother, and doctor's wife. She's the daughter who reminds me most of my late wife, Laura. Although their behavior isn't similar, their appearance is. Sometimes when I look at Sophie it's if I am seeing young Laura again. Almost to the point where it scares me."

"Annette, the middle daughter, is more like me. She is a hard worker who tends to stay in the background and not want the spotlight. She's content with life but never questions the boundaries. She always did very well in school but unfortunately had very limited self-confidence. She never pushed herself to excel, but she did so without even trying. She and her husband chose not to have children, which I feel was more of her husband's decision than Annette's. She is content being an aunt to Sophie and Allison's children".

"So that, in a nutshell, is the story of my daughters. I must admit that I really wanted a son. In fact, I was so sure that Sophie would be a boy that I painted the nursery blue and picked out only boy names. I hid my disappointment from Laura when Sophie arrived. We celebrated having a third healthy, happy baby. Somehow, I think she could sense my discontent even though I never verbalized it."

"Thank you, Joseph, for sharing with me. I hope the girls like me and don't feel that I'm marrying you for your money. We did sign the prenup agreements, as I requested. I don't want any hard feelings now or later about that. I am financially comfortable. You're much more valuable to me alive. I don't want to even think about either of us being taken away from each other for many, many years."

The rest of the afternoon passed quickly as they chatted and shared stories, some of which they may have shared before and forgotten. Older people do not like being told when they repeat themselves. Sure, they sometimes do, but please don't remind them. Be polite, smile, and listen. Maybe this time the story will be a bit different, or some new details may surface. Growing old is hard enough; being reminded makes it worse.

Only two weeks to go until the wedding. Time was passing so quickly. Most of the larger items were crossed off the to-do list. The weather was beginning to cooperate. The temperatures were warmer. The spring flowers were replacing the dirty piles of winter snow. The trees were beginning to bud. It was another reawakening after the long, cold, dark winter. Those who live in warmer climates miss the four seasons in all their splendor. It's a wonderful experience, but maybe we could shorten winter just a bit?

Everyone was seated and had been served dinner when Deborah asked for her tablemates' attention. This was very out of character, as was her attendance at the tape screening earlier in the day. Something was different about her presence. Everyone at the table stopped eating and listened.

"I understand that I have not been the best of company recently. Well, really, ever. I have been very unhappy living here as I totally expected to live with my daughter and her family when the time came for me to leave my home. I was disappointed to say the least when I was told that I would be living here permanently. I refused to accept my daughter's decision to move me here instead of in with her. I did not realize the reason was that her marriage was in shambles and about to self-destruct."

"Her husband announced that he is leaving her for another woman and she is devastated. She called me several times over the past weeks to discuss the situation. She said it was her husband who did not want me living with them and now, with him out of the picture, she wants me to leave Parliament Square and move in with her. I have accepted her offer and will be leaving in the coming weeks. I wanted you all to be the first to know. I also want to ask your forgiveness for my difficult behavior. It was never about you; it was always about me."

The group was quiet for a moment. Deborah had tears in her eyes. No one knew the right words to say. She really wasn't friends with anyone at the table, or with anyone else at Parliament Square. She had isolated herself from everyone, hiding the real reason for her callous, unfriendly behavior.

Jim cleared his throat and said, "It's quite obvious that we have an elephant in the room. If we all remain quiet, it won't leave. So, to break the silence and make the elephant disappear, I have some pachyderm humor. A man took his son to the zoo one spring day and they visited the elephants. The son said in a loud voice, 'Dad, look, there's a frickin' elephant.' His dad was slightly upset as everyone around stopped to stare at them. 'What did you just call it?' his father asked. 'It's a frickin' elephant, it says so on the picture,' he said. And so it did: A F R I C A N Elephant."

The tension eased and everyone chuckled over Jim's evening joke. Again, proving the point that Jim had a humorous story or joke stored in his seemingly endless supply of memory cells, just like the elephant who never forgets.

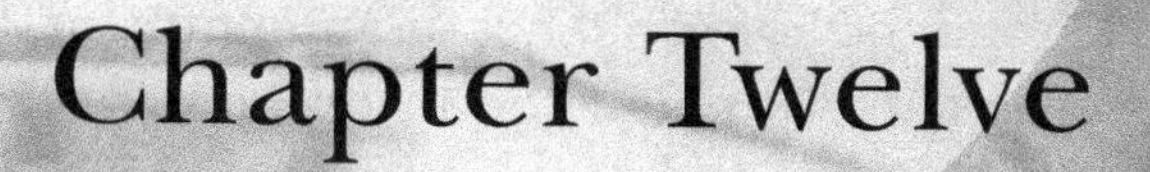

# Chapter Twelve

## *Buon Italiano Appetit*

The news that Deborah was leaving came as a surprise to her tablemates. Many felt she was abrasive and unsocial, but behind the scenes was a sad and unhappy woman. Deborah never shared her disappointment, but then no one ever asked. Although she made herself very scarce, except at meals, anyone at the table could have visited her and possibly discovered the cause of her unhappiness. No one did.

Often, we deliberately or sometimes unintentionally choose not to get involved and perhaps miss an opportunity to make a difference in someone's life. Maybe we're too busy. Maybe we're uncomfortable. Maybe we don't know the right words. Maybe we feel no connection to the individual. Whatever the reason, we miss a chance to listen, possibly a chance to lend advice, and offer a solution. This may have been the case with Deborah.

The change in her demeanor since getting the news that she would be living with her daughter was a true Jekyll and Hyde transformation. She got involved in the dinner conversation. She apologized to Sara and Joseph for declining their wedding invitation and wished them all the best in their married life. Since her daughter lived in Florida, she would be too far away to attend the wedding. She told her tablemates that she was sorry for her unsocial behavior over the past months. She would be leaving before the end of the week. She couldn't be happier.

She promised to stay in touch, but most at the table knew that she probably wouldn't. No one had heard from Mary since she left. However, had anyone attempted to contact Mary since she moved away? Maintaining connection was a two-way street.

We often say to friends, or they say to us, "Let's get together soon." It's done with good intentions, but more often than not it doesn't come to fruition. Weeks, months, and even years pass as we're busy with school, work, family, and simply life in general. Sometimes we think about getting together but we never take the initiative to make it happen. Friendships that could develop and grow are never given a chance. Relationships that could flourish and mature are uncultivated. So many opportunities are lost.

Friendships become more important as the years advance. When the hustle and bustle wind down and life moves at a slower pace, the need for a strong social network becomes clear. However, by then your co-workers are retired, your neighbors have moved away (to a new address or to the hereafter), and your options for friendship and interaction are few.

New friendships are possible at any age, but they don't hold a candle to relationships built and maintained over a lifetime. Instead of saying "Let's get together," say "Does next Friday work for you?" One of life's truisms is that you can never have too many friends.

Sara and Michele decided that Monday or Tuesday would be good for their first double dinner date. There would be fewer people out those nights. For the younger crowd, Wednesday was over-the-hump night. Thursday was celebrate-that-the-weekend-is-coming night. Friday started the weekend and was the night to unwind after a long week of work. Saturday was the romantic date night. Sunday was the night some of the restaurants weren't open. So, Monday or Tuesday appeared to be the best over-the-hill dining-out nights of the week.

Michele was glad that Sara and Joseph were coming along for their first date. Sometimes there can be awkward pauses in the conversation when you're getting to know someone. Michele and Chuck hadn't spent time together alone and they weren't sure a relationship was even a possibility, but there was only one way to find out. No one expected Sara and Joseph's love story to repeat itself. Just having someone of the opposite sex to share time and a meal with was an event. Geriatric baby steps.

"Michele, I'm looking forward to seeing Parliament Square in the rear-view mirror and ordering off a menu. They don't serve many good Italian dishes here, so how does an Italian restaurant sound? Luigi's got a good writeup in the paper and it's only about eight miles away. I checked the prices. They seem reasonable. They even have Monday-night specials. I can make a reservation for six on Monday if that works for you and Chuck."

"That sounds wonderful," Michele replied. "I'll check with Chuck but I can't imagine he won't be on board. Maybe next time we could try Chinese or Thai. I love that style of cooking, but Parliament Square keeps everything simple and healthy. Sometimes it's nice to have something different. When they ask for suggestions for new menu items, I always request chicken chow mein and chicken pineapple fried rice, but neither has been served."

"I tell my daughter that I'm sometimes food challenged here because everyone eats the same thing with no choices. I understand why it is that way, I just don't like it. We get too used to eating what we want when we want it, then we come here and lose our options. I can live with it, but getting out and ordering off a menu will be a welcome change."

"I totally agree, Michele. I said the same thing to Joseph about the dinner menu. They seem to serve ten to twelve different entrees and repeat them over and over. Like you said, they have to keep it simple, but even having two dinner selections each day would be nice."

Chuck and Joseph walked into the lobby and joined the ladies. Chuck said, "We just asked Linda for some restaurant ideas. She suggested Luigi's on Market Street. She told us they have homemade pasta and marinara sauce that is the best around. How does Italian sound?"

Sara and Michele burst into laughter. Sara said, "Your timing couldn't be better. Michele and I were just discussing dinner and thought Italian might be a good choice. Let's get a reservation for Monday or Tuesday. We thought those evenings might be less crowded. It should be easier to talk without a bunch of people around. We might not even have to turn up our hearing aids."

So many activities are taken for granted until they're no longer accessible. With the aging process, the list of once spontaneous, mundane events becomes abbreviated. When driving privileges are revoked because of impaired vision, cognitive concerns, and slow response time; independence is stripped away. The senior citizen without a driver's license must rely on others for transportation. Dependence on others can sometimes be the hardest pill to swallow.

At dinner on Saturday, everyone said their goodbyes to Deborah. The table even ordered a going-away cake to share for dessert. It was a shame that no one had befriended her during the many months that they broke bread together. She kept to herself and appeared unapproachable. Now it was too late. She would be leaving Parliament Square tomorrow afternoon.

Jim spoke up. The group expected his normal funnyman approach. "Deborah, speaking for the group, we wish you well. Please let us know how you're doing once you're settled in, and we'll keep you posted on life here at Parliament Square. We're sorry that you'll miss the wedding and honeymoon stories. You're the third member of our dining room family to leave us. Mary left to help her daughter while she receives cancer treatments. and Pam was taken to the great hereafter."

"I know you won't believe me when I tell you this, but

I can't think of one appropriate joke about you leaving us. Maybe there's just no humor to be found in the situation. All I can say is—please take me with you! Don't leave me here with these crazy old people!"

The group chuckled. "I can't believe that you are at a loss for a joke. I am so disappointed," Sara said sarcastically, accompanied by an almost audible eye-roll.

Jim replied, "Well, I don't want to disappoint my funny story groupies. I certainly have plenty of humor to share, just not any that relates to Deborah leaving Parliament Square. Did you hear the one about the three sisters, ages ninety-two, ninety-four, and ninety-six, who lived in a house together? One night, the ninety-six-year-old drew a bath. She put one foot in and paused. She yelled down the stairs, "Was I getting in or out of the bath?" The ninety-four-year-old yelled back, "I don't know. I'll come up and see." She started up the stairs and paused. Then she yelled out, "Was I going up the stairs or down?" The ninety-two-year-old was sitting at the kitchen table having tea and listening to her sisters. She shook her head and said, "I sure hope I never get that forgetful." She knocked on wood for good measure. Then she said, "I'll come up and help as soon as I see who's at the door."

Oh my, that was an old joke but certainly an age-appropriate one. Living life in the slow lane takes courage, tenacity, and, most of all, the ability to laugh at yourself. Your mind seems to have a life of its own. Your body marches to a different drummer when it marches at all. So much changes yet so much stays the same.

As dinner ended and Deborah said her goodbyes, Sara regretted that she never took the time or made the effort to befriend her. Deborah led an isolated and lonely existence at Parliament Square. Although it was her choice, it could have been different. Sara told herself that she would not allow that to happen again. She would vow to try her best, no matter what the circumstances, to make a difference. She was so lucky to have good friends, family, and soon a new husband. Everyone should be so lucky.

Date night arrived. Michele and Sara were very excited. With Deborah gone, there would only be Betsy, Jan, and Jim at dinner. Surely Jim could keep the conversation going. Betsy and Jan commented at breakfast how jealous they were that the fabulous four, as they had been nicknamed, were able to drive to dinner. They thought a date night was exciting and very romantic.

Chuck pulled his car up to the front door. Joseph stepped out with Sara on one arm and Michele on the other. "I feel like a rose between two thorns," he said.

"I think you have that wrong," replied Sara. "It's a thorn between two roses." Thorn or roses, it didn't matter. They were ready to depart for the long eight-mile ride to the restaurant. The freedom and independence were invigorating.

Joseph opened the back door for Sara and helped her into the car. "I'm sure glad this is a sedan and not a coupe. We'd probably need help getting in the back seat without the rear door. People over sixty should never purchase coupes. We aren't flexible enough."

No sooner had they left the parking lot then there was a commotion in the back seat. Sara's foot shot up between the front seats and her shoe flew off, hitting the dashboard. There was thrashing and screaming and a couple of words that Chuck didn't know were in Sara's vocabulary.

"Heavens to Murgatroyd, Joseph. What in tarnation is going on back there? Please refrain from any crazy behavior. Save it for the ride home. I know you warned me not to look in my rear-view mirror, but really?"

"When is the last time you cleaned out this car?" asked

Joseph. "There's a spider back here big enough to walk on a leash. I hope he's on the bottom of my left shoe, and I hope his family isn't in here with him. Maybe we should spend a warm, spring afternoon at the car wash? I thought the back seat would be exciting, but not because we'd almost be eaten alive by an *Araneae*. I learned that term from a National Geographic special. Now I've had a chance to use it."

"Sara," Michele said as she handed back her shoe, "Are you all right? I must commend you on your quick response and excellent mobility. I know how much you dislike spiders. That must've been really frightening. I'm afraid to look around up here in the front seat. There could be more. I agree with Joseph, Chuck, please take your car to the car wash and clean it inside and out. This isn't the way to impress me on our first date. I may have to lower my scores on the evaluation. Anyhow, I'm sure Betsy, Jan, and Jim will enjoy hearing about it tomorrow. If there's going to be this much excitement, maybe next time we'll set up a video camera. Actually, with spiders, I hope there isn't a next time. My heart is racing and I'm afraid to touch anything in this car."

Chuck pulled up to the restaurant door and the ladies exited quickly, brushing off any possible residual spiders. Joseph hopped into the passenger seat. "I'll walk from the parking lot with you. We can check the car for more insects and I can clean off the bottom of my shoe. That ride sure was a lot more action-packed than I expected. I thought maybe driving ten miles over the speed limit, rolling through a stop sign, or running a yellow light would make the trip eventful. Little did I know there would be heart-pounding, shoe flying, mind-blowing stimulation."

With that comment, Chuck squealed his tires as he raced around the building to the parking lot on the other side, sliding on the gravel as the car came to a stop. "This is only the beginning. Wait until I get the snake out of the trunk for the ride home. Its non-venomous, but no one has to know that."

The ladies were already seated when Joseph and Chuck arrived. As expected, the crowd was light. The specials were posted on a board inside the door and on a menu insert. The smell of Italian sauces and fresh-baked garlic bread wafted in the air. The décor included red-and-white checkered tablecloths, wine bottle centerpieces which held burning, dripping candles and waitstaff dressed in white tops, green trousers or skirts, and red aprons. A little slice of Italy in this New England hamlet.

A perky young woman introduced herself as Maria and said she'd be their server for the evening. She took their drink orders. After reciting the specials for the day, she left promising to return in a couple of minutes with warm garlic bread and to take their dinner orders.

"This is so exciting," said Sara. "Look at all the choices. I'm going to have trouble deciding what to order. I love Italian food. It won't be spaghetti and meatballs. We get that at Parliament Square, although I doubt it can hold a candle to what they serve here. I saw a waitress with a plate of spaghetti topped with a meatball the size of a baseball. My mouth is watering. I think I will have the chicken parmigiana with a tossed salad. That was something I'd make for Michael and I when he visited my cottage by the sea. It's been a long time since I had that. I'm certain their version is much more Italian than mine."

The basket of warm garlic bread arrived along with four glasses of ice water with lemon. Everyone took a piece of bread as Maria went around the table taking orders. The bread dripped with garlic butter. It was delicious, but the company was even better. Hopefully, this was the start of many evenings together ordering from a menu and sharing conversation and friendship.

A party of twelve was seated nearby. They seemed to be celebrating a special occasion. Judging from their ages, it looked like three generations of family. The younger members were focused on their electronics while the adults talked and sipped cocktails.

The two older couples were probably the grandparents or possibly older aunts and uncles. The middle-aged couple, based on their interaction with the two teenagers seated at the table, were likely the parental unit. They all quieted down as their food was served, and they bowed their heads before eating. The older gentleman at the head of the table quietly said grace and everyone joined in the *amen*. Very impressive and very unusual to see in this day and age.

For a moment it reminded Sara of an old Norman Rockwell painting, *Saying Grace*, that used to hang in her grandmother's kitchen. It was of an older woman and a young boy saying grace at a table in a restaurant while the others around them watched with curiosity and amazement. She hadn't thought of that painting for years, but it vividly popped back into her mind as if she had just seen it yesterday.

"Earth to Sara," Joseph said, bringing her back from her memories. "Are you still with us? Chuck asked how you liked the garlic bread."

"Sorry, everyone. I just had a bit of a flashback to another time and place. Nothing like my *what if* moments. This was a real memory. Curious how some things matter little to us when they happen and then surface later and take us back in time, whether we want to go there or not. This was a good memory. I'm back now and here comes our dinner. I'm starved."

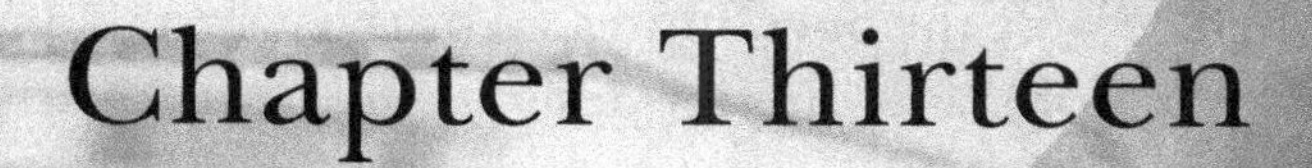

# Chapter Thirteen

## *Not That There's Anything Wrong With That*

The food was delicious and plentiful. The Fabulous Four savored every morsel, raving about the sauce, the garlic bread, and the ambiance. Okay, maybe Sara and Michele were the ones impressed by the waitstaff, lighting (or lack thereof), and interior design. The "boys" were more interested in the food.

No one could finish their dinner, so doggie bags were requested. They all passed on dessert even though the dessert tray looked decadent with several authentic Italian selections, probably baked in-house. This restaurant was definitely on the A-list.

"Ladies please wait by the door while Joseph and I bring the car around. We'll demand that any remaining spiders exit prior to starting the engine. I promise to get the car cleaned inside and out next week. See you gals in a minute."

"Michele, I am hesitant to get back in that car. That was the biggest spider I've ever seen. Maybe I can ride back with my eyes closed?"

"I understand, Sara. I'm terrified of spiders, bees and snakes. They all make my skin crawl, so I avoid them at all costs. Chuck can't get that car cleaned out soon enough. I guess the car sitting in the parking lot for weeks was an open invitation to critters. Hopefully, the ride back will be quick and uneventful. I did really enjoy dinner together with you, Joseph and Chuck. He seems like a very nice man."

Chuck pulled up to the door and Joseph got out to open the car doors for the ladies. He was such a gentleman. Sara visually inspected the back seat before entering. She was sure where there was one man-eating spider, there would be more. Fortunately, they appeared to be gone but they could still be hiding somewhere. Seat belts buckled, doggie bags secure, off they went back to Parliament Square after sharing one of hopefully many dinners and evenings together.

Thankfully, the ride back was uneventful. Joseph held Sara's hand in his. They exchanged smiles and played footsie. This was young love reincarnated. Soon they would be Mr. and Mrs. Joseph Zimmerman. Life was good.

Sara and Michele entered the lobby as the gentlemen parked the car in the resident lot. Linda ran to greet them. "I have great news. I just got off the phone with Nancy. The viewers loved *The Local Moment* segment. The station was flooded with calls asking whether the actual wedding would be televised. Nancy wanted your final approval for them to tape your wedding ceremony and reception. Do I have your permission to tell her yes?"

"Joseph will be here in a minute. I think we're both comfortable with it but I need the final okay from him. It's not like the old days where I could say yes or no without checking with anyone first. Now we make joint decisions. It may take me awhile to adjust to the new process. It has been many, many years since I was part of a couple."

Joseph and Chuck came in from the parking lot with the four doggy bags. They were chuckling about something. Sara asked, "What's so funny, Chuck?"

"We parked the car and were heading for the lobby when we ran into Jim out for his evening walk. You may not believe this, but he told us a joke. It's a bit off-color, though, so maybe we shouldn't repeat it to you innocent, young ladies."

"I think Sara and I can take it. Unless there are numerous swear words involved. I'm not a big fan of cursing for effect. Let's hear it."

"Seems there was an elderly woman named Ethel who loves to charge around the nursing home in her wheelchair, taking corners on one wheel and getting up to a maximum speed on the long corridors. Ethel was speeding up a corridor when a door opened and Mad Mitch stepped out of his room with his arm outstretched. 'STOP!' he said in a firm voice. 'Have you got a license for that thing?' Ethel fished around in her handbag and pulled out a Hershey bar wrapper and held it up to him. 'Okay,' he said, and Ethel sped away down the hall. As she took the corner near the TV lounge on one wheel, Weird Wayne popped out in front of her and shouted, 'STOP! Have you got proof of insurance?' Ethel dug into her handbag, pulled out a pack of Dentyne gum, and held it up to him. Wayne nodded and said, 'Carry on, ma'am.' As Ethel neared the final corridor before the front door, Bonkers Brett stepped out in front of her, stark naked, holding a very sizeable erection. 'Oh, no!' said Ethel, 'Not the breathalyzer again!'

Sara blushed when she heard the punchline, and she tried not to laugh. She didn't want to encourage him. Michele thought the humor was geared more toward the testosterone crowd.

"I'm very glad Jim withholds jokes of that caliber at the dinner table. It was funny but lewd and a bit sad all at the same time. At our age we're often the butt of jokes as a group based only on our age and expected behavior. Kind of like blond jokes. Not all blonds are ditzy, but they are often categorized as such. Not all older people are senile and forgetful, but we're branded that way. Sorry for the lecture. Just not my kind of joke," Michele said.

Linda bounded over before Chuck could point out that it was Jim's joke and he was only the messenger. "Joseph, did Sara ask you about recording the wedding? My friend at the station contacted me about it. I said I would talk to you and Sara. They need to know by tomorrow. Sara told me that she wanted to discuss it with you before giving me a yea or nay. I'm on pins and needles waiting to hear."

"Well, I'm going to discuss this with Sara. We'll give Nancy our decision tomorrow when she calls us. Until then, you're going to have to be patient. This is a big decision for us. It will be one of our first decisions as a couple. We appreciate your support and enthusiasm."

The group dispersed to their rooms. It had been an exciting and enjoyable evening, hopefully one that would be repeated often. Chuck escorted Michele back to her apartment. Sara and Joseph headed for Sara's place to check on Penelope. They ran into Jean in the elevator. She was humming quietly. They exchanged hellos. Jean said, "I saw you on *The Local Moment*. It was very nice and I wish you unlimited happiness in your marriage. I was so upset when Ray left because of his medical issues. He now lives with his daughter and her family in Boston. We stay in touch, but he won't be returning here. However, I did recently chat with Chuck at bingo night. I have a feeling that he's going to ask me to dinner with him, since he has a vehicle here and still drives. I'm keeping my fingers crossed."

When Jean exited the elevator, Sara turned to Joseph and said, "I don't trust that woman. She wanted to get her claws into you and now she has her sights set on Chuck. I understand that I can't change anything, but I want to let you know how I feel. If Chuck invites her out, that's his business. I try very hard not to express my opinion of Jean to anyone but you."

"Jean is not the type of woman I would have any interest in spending time with. She is very lonely and desperately wants a man in her life. That may or may not ever happen. It's often those who aren't looking for love who find it. Or should I say, love finds them? Don't fret about Chuck getting romantically involved with her. I don't think that's going to happen."

As she opened her apartment door, Sara caught her heel on the welcome mat. She tried to catch herself but it was too late and she fell headfirst into the apartment. Joseph ran to her side. "Please don't try to get up. Let's check you out first. Can you move your arms and legs? One at a time. You aren't getting out of the wedding by pretending to be injured. Now, let's try to get you on your feet and over to the couch."

"I think I'm okay. I've tripped on that rug before, but I've always caught myself. Maybe we should attend the balance class more often? Or maybe I should throw out that welcome mat. Let me sit here a minute. I'm guessing that I may feel the effects of this tomorrow."

As we age, we often refuse to accept the fact that our bodily functions and capabilities aren't what they used to be. That's a hard pill to swallow. Mobility is an important ingredient to living a normal life. No one wants to depend on a cane, a walker or, worst of all, a wheelchair. Sometimes it's unavoidable. The goal is to stay as flexible as possible, but that goal isn't always attainable. Another disadvantage of aging added to the growing list.

"Sara, I insist on spending the night here to be sure that you're okay. Nothing appears to be broken but we don't want to take any chances. The wedding is right around the corner and I'm looking forward to seeing my beautiful bride walk, not hobble, down the aisle. Let the others talk. I'm not leaving you tonight."

"Thanks. I appreciate that. Can you please put the doggie bags in the refrigerator and feed Penelope? I'm going to take a couple of extra-strength Tylenol and use the heating pad. My back is a bit sore, but that's not unusual. Maybe a foot rub? I might as well take advantage of all the pampering I can get."

Penelope jumped on Sara's lap. Normally the sound of her dish being filled caused her to skedaddle to the kitchen. Not tonight. She wasn't leaving Sara's lap. Joseph came over with the heating pad and the Tylenol and began the requested foot massage. Penelope didn't budge.

After the 10:00 news, Joseph told Sara that he was tired and ready for bed. "Joseph, I'm feeling much better. I'll have to be more careful. That mat is going in the trash tomorrow. Please go get a good night's sleep at your place. I'll be fine. Penelope will keep me company. But before you go, we need to vote on the television cameras in the chapel. Nancy is going to call me tomorrow and I need to give her our decision. I'm comfortable saying yes but I won't do that if you have any misgivings. This is our day and it just has to be perfect. There are no do-overs."

"My vote is also yes. We trust Nancy's judgement and I feel comfortable that it'll be done tastefully and as unobtrusively as humanly possible. We can share our happiness and love story with others. Looks like we're going to be television celebrities for a second time. Also, I just couldn't break the news to Betsy and Jan that they won't be on TV. Although, depending on airtime, they could cut any or all of their music. Their dresses should reflect well on camera."

"Okay, I'll leave Penelope in charge for the night. Promise me you'll call if you need anything. I'll leave my hearing aids turned on when I go to bed. Sweet dreams."

After Joseph left, Sara remained on the couch stroking Penelope as she kneaded Sara's arm non-stop. Her dinner sat uneaten. She was not leaving Sara. Such a sweet kitty. They were so lucky to have each other's company.

Living with Joseph wouldn't change anything. They would still have their bond. Sara was so comfortable after the foot massage, Tylenol, and heating pad, that she drifted in and out of consciousness. Her thoughts centered around life and death and the fine line that separates them.

Getting older causes a person to wonder when and how they'll meet their demise. As we scan the obituaries for friends, siblings, and acquaintances, many younger than we are now, we wonder how the grim reaper will come for us when our expiration dates arrive.

Will it be sudden and painless? Will it be lengthy and painful? Will it be an accident? Will it be cancer? So many questions with no answers. Younger people may have a passing thought about their mortality, but since it won't likely happen in the near future, the thought is soon forgotten. Older folks see the writing on the wall and understand, but at the same time, fear that their number could be called any time.

David came to Sara in a dream. He was so handsome. Sara would always have a very special place for him in her heart. Joseph wasn't replacing David. There was no competition. One was not better than the other. Life's journey allows us to love many, but not all in the same way or at the same level.

David wanted to comfort Sara. He wanted her to know that he was happy for her. She should have no regrets, nor should she feel she was abandoning him. Finding love more than once is like winning the relationship lottery. Not many hold winning tickets. Accepting a new partner doesn't negate the prior partner's memories or importance. Relationships are individual events; they are not cumulative experiences. Comparisons shouldn't be made. Guilt shouldn't be felt.

It was after midnight when Penelope finally jumped off Sara and went in search of her dinner. Her movement brought Sara back to reality. David's presence was almost real. This was the second time he had visited her since she lost him. Both visits had encouraged her to go on with her life and be happy.

Getting off the couch was a bit sketchy, but after becoming vertical, Sara checked for any damage caused by the fall. She was very lucky. Nothing appeared to be broken. Her back and her right wrist were achy, but not much worse than her routine senior assortment of aches and pains. Maybe two more Tylenol before bed and a nice hot cup of green tea? As the teapot announced that it was ready, the phone rang. It startled her, causing her to jump and aggravating her sore back. Who could be calling this late? It usually meant bad news. She hesitated answering, but her curiosity got the best of her. "Hello," she said into the handset.

"Hello, Aunt Sara. So sorry to call this late but I have been very busy with work. Some days I don't get home until after nine. With the time difference, that's midnight your time. I needed to talk with you before my visit for the wedding. There's no problem. I'll be there to walk you down the aisle. But there's something I must tell you before seeing you and Joseph. I mentioned that I was bringing a friend along. I know that your assumption is that I'll be bringing a woman with me. My new friend's name is Alan. He and I work together. I thought my relationship with Marcy was strained but I was never exactly sure why. I thought we had conflicting personality traits. Turns out, that wasn't it at all. I guess I knew all along, I just didn't want to believe it."

Sara was speechless. She was not offended by same-sex relationships; she felt it was a personal choice. Who was she to judge? She was caught off guard. After getting her wits about her, she replied, "Michael, I am not one to judge. You deserve to be happy. You never seemed truly content with Marcy. Your mother and I always felt that you weren't right for each other. I guess we were right but for the wrong reasons. Finding happiness with Alan was certainly an unintended consequence of your journey. I'm glad that you called to discuss this with me, however. It would have been quite a shock otherwise. If you're happy, then I am happy for you."

The conversation continued for a while. Michael sounded really happy for the first time in a long time. When they said goodbye, Sara went to the kitchen to make her cup of tea and take two more Tylenol. The wheels in her mind were spinning. She was certainly blindsided by Michael's news. She would never have guessed that he was gay. *Not that there's anything wrong with that*, she thought. That reminded her of a Seinfeld episode where Jerry says that exact line in reference to being gay. She still enjoyed reruns of that program. They made her laugh, which many of the current weekly sitcoms did not.

As she sipped her hot tea and lightly buttered a graham cracker, she wondered what her sister, Michael's mother, would have thought about this. She was very strait-laced. It didn't matter, because Barbara was no longer able to judge. Her unfortunate death still haunted Sara at times. If only she had insisted on Barbara seeing a doctor when her cancer was in the early stages. Maybe she would still be here to see Sara get married and find happiness with Joseph. Too many what-ifs.

As Sara prepared for bed, she noticed a bruise forming on her wrist. That carpet was headed for the trash tomorrow. She was lucky this time. She didn't want to take any more chances. Off to bed and maybe more visits from David. She welcomed them as warm reminders of what had been. Good times . . . warm memories . . . great expectations.

# Chapter Fourteen

## *Is That Seat Taken?*

The bright morning sunshine burst into the room, welcomed by an awakening Sara. Any day with sunshine was a good day. The night had been restless. Her thoughts wouldn't quiet down, nor would the throbbing in her wrist. She savored the virtual visit from David. He would always have a very special place in her heart. She questioned Michael's announcement. Although it didn't upset her, she was very surprised. He was such a handsome young man. She was blindsided by the news.

Her wrist was definitely bruised, but she could move it without extensive pain, so hopefully nothing was broken. An arm cast wouldn't be an attractive wedding day accessory. All her fingers worked. She was able to shower and wash her hair without assistance. The heating pad, in combination with pain medication, should provide ample relief.

Sara was the last to be seated at the table for breakfast. Deborah's empty seat wasn't as unnerving as Pam's had been when she was called to her eternal rest. It meant another new tablemate would join the group. Since Sara arrived, Michele had taken Mary's place, and Chuck has taken Pam's. Now someone new would take Deborah's place.

"Sara, how do you feel after your unfortunate fall last evening?" Joseph asked.

"My wrist is a bit sore, and my body aches are a bit more noticeable than normal, but I don't think anything's broken. I'm very lucky," she replied. "That doormat is going out to the trash today."

Betsy asked in a concerned tone, "Sara, what happened? Do you think a doctor should examine you? You can't risk having any medical issues this close to the ceremony. Maybe you should have an X-ray. Better safe than sorry."

"Thanks for your concern, but I'm fine. I can move all my fingers and there are no bones sticking out. I just have to be more careful, as we all do. One second, we can be on our feet and the next we can be on the floor. Those balance classes need to be a permanent item on our weekly agenda. Joseph and I will be attending them as soon as we return from the honeymoon."

The blueberry pancakes and crisp bacon were a welcome sight. The oatmeal mornings, which seemed to occur frequently, were not to be celebrated. Maybe the Fabulous Four could drive somewhere for breakfast one morning. Greasy home fries, scrambled eggs, and scrapple were not on the menu at Parliament Square.

Jan spoke up. "The wedding is a week from Saturday. We are under the two-week threshold. Since Sara refused our offer to plan a wedding shower, are the fellows planning a bachelor party for Joseph? Maybe one final night of freedom and male bonding. Sounds like a recipe for over-the-hill party time. Jim, since you're the best man, are there any plans we should know about?"

"We offered a night out to Joseph. Chuck even offered to drive, but he refused. He said his wild party days were behind him. He doesn't want to risk possible bodily harm and the embarrassment of being asked if he's the groom's father or, worse yet, the groom's grandfather. No, Joseph thinks those celebrations are best left to the younger generation. He appreciated our offer but graciously declined. But I have been working on the material for my reception toast. Here are some contenders:

"—Sara is a bright, charming, wonderful woman who deserves a good husband. It's such a shame Joseph swooped in before she could find one.

"—Someone once said that marriage is a fifty-fifty partnership, but anyone who believes that clearly knows nothing about women or fractions.

"—Hello! I'm Joseph's best man. He told me if I do a good job, he'll make me the best man at his next wedding, too.

"Trust me, there are many, many more where those came from. Since there may be children in attendance, I'll keep it family oriented. So, replace your hearing-aid batteries before the reception, because you won't want to miss any of my punchlines."

Linda stopped by as they finished breakfast. "Sara, have you and Joseph talked to Nancy yet? She mentioned that she called you last evening but you didn't answer and since you don't have voice mail, she couldn't leave you a message. Have you made a decision about taping the wedding? I told her that I'd check and get back to her. Since the wedding is a week from Saturday, the station has to know soon so they can assign a camera crew."

"Joseph and I discussed the taping and we decided to give it a thumbs-up. Of course, Nancy understands that we want the least amount of distraction during the ceremony. They're also welcome at the reception if that's of any interest. The guests are excited and honored to be included. It'll also put a good spin on life here at Parliament Square. Free publicity never hurts."

"Great. I'll call her right now and give her the good news. This is all so exciting. It's not every day that a television studio wants to be part of an event here. The flip side is that it isn't every day an event like this happens. You two are local celebrities. Maybe one of the major networks will get wind of this and want to join the Sara-and-Joseph love bandwagon."

After Linda left, Sara confessed that she was a bit apprehensive about doing this but felt it was the right thing to do. Parliament Square would get free publicity. The residents would have the opportunity to be on television allowing their family and friends to see them. It was exciting but at the same time it added further stress to the wedding day jitters. Maybe they should have simply gone to the courthouse and had a civil ceremony.

Joseph took Sara's hand. "Everything will be fine. It's our big day and our family and friends will be here to watch us say our vows. Nothing is going to put a damper on that. Just focus on me at the altar as you walk down the aisle. All will be fine. You agreed to this being televised based on the benefits to others. That's an example of your selfless nature. You have every right to be a bit nervous. This doesn't happen every day. Deep breaths and calm thoughts, my dear."

Everyone at the table applauded his words of encouragement. He was indeed a very caring man who loved Sara very much. They made such a lovely couple. There is no shortage of songs written about young love. There should be more about finding love in your twilight years. Maybe fodder for a new country music classic?

After Sara's unfortunate fall, she felt strongly that they should attend the balance class held at ten on Thursday mornings. They had attended once or twice before, but had never added it to their weekly schedule. Once they returned from the honeymoon, Sara would work in the childcare center on Wednesday and Friday mornings, they would attend the balance class on Thursday, and maybe fit in a chair Zumba class now and then. They needed to stay active together. One of the most valuable secrets to staying young is to keep moving.

It was a beautiful spring morning, and Sara and Joseph decided to take a stroll around the building after breakfast. There was still a nip in the air, but spring was chasing winter away. The birds were chirping, the sun was shining, and love was in the air. They held hands as they walked.

"Michael told me last evening when we chatted that he was bringing Alan with him to the wedding. I was totally blindsided by the news. I told him that would be fine, hoping that I didn't sound judgmental in my response or in the long silence before I spoke. I just never expected that. I knew that he and Marcy were unhappy together but you could have knocked me over with a feather when he told me. I hope this doesn't upset you."

Just then, Jean approached them from the opposite direction. "Good morning. I'm getting my steps in. I need to stay in shape just in case Mr. Right comes along. I mentioned to Chuck that I would love a ride in his car and I think we may go to lunch next week. I also spoke to Linda about the possibility of my filling the vacant seat at your table. Wouldn't that be great?"

Sara was speechless. Jean sitting at their table? *Oh, please,* she prayed, *don't let that happen.* She doesn't fit in with the group. She isn't a nice person. Oh, this just cannot happen. Sara hid her surprise and dislike by changing the subject. "What a lovely morning. Have you attended the balance class? Joseph and I are going to put that on our Thursday morning schedule after we return from the honeymoon. I think good posture and well-controlled balance can help us avoid falls and injuries. Maybe we'll see you there."

Sara squeezed Joseph's hand so hard he winced. She encouraged him to walk quickly away from Jean. She was worried that her true feelings would escape from her mouth.

When enough distance separated them, she said, "Oh, this cannot happen. Do you think I should talk to Linda privately? I can't imagine pretending to be friendly to Jean every day at meals. I'm sure she has ulterior motives. She wants to sit at our table so she can get her hooks into Chuck. This just cannot happen." They walked a moment in silence. "Joseph, say something."

"I told you before that Jean isn't my type of woman. I'm

guessing that she isn't to Chuck's liking either, but that's none of our business. I'm doubtful that her requesting a table reassignment will be approved. Table seating assignments aren't resident driven. From what we've seen, it appears that new residents get assigned to open seats. It isn't done on the request of a current resident. Think of the chaos that would cause. Don't worry your pretty little head about it. Please, nothing but happy thoughts until next Saturday. And, just so you know, I'm perfectly all right with Michael's news. Don't worry your pretty little head over that. Who am I to judge others? To each his own, as the saying goes."

"I guess you're right. I'll try to put Jean's request out of my mind. I wonder who'll join our table? We'll just have to wait and see. In the meantime, I'll be saying prayers that it isn't Jean. Sorry, she just ruffles my feathers. Also, thanks for being okay with Michael's news. I'm still trying to wrap my arms around it."

The remaining days leading up to the wedding week passed quickly. Betsy and Jan performed their songs for the group one evening after dinner. They sounded good. They were in tune. They were getting along. Best of all, there was no mention of buckets all evening.

Joseph's daughters would arrive before noon the day before the wedding. Michael's flight wouldn't touch down until early afternoon. Everyone would be there in time for the rehearsal at the chapel followed by the rehearsal dinner at Luigi's. Sara and Joseph enjoyed their Italian cuisine so much when they ate there with Chuck and Michele, they decided to reserve the banquet room for the rehearsal dinner.

In attendance would be their Parliament Square tablemates; Joseph's three daughters; Allison's husband William; and Michael and Alan. It would be a small group, allowing everyone to converse and mingle. Joseph hadn't seen Sophie and Annette since he lost his wife two years ago. Sara looked forward to catching up with Michael and getting to know Alan. It should be an enjoyable prelude to the wedding day.

On Sunday afternoon, one week prior to the wedding, Sara decided to try on her wedding dress. She was going to model it for Penelope. Joseph couldn't see her in the dress until she walked down the aisle. She looked at herself in the full-length mirror. Fortunately, she had been able to keep her weight the same as it was the day that she purchased the dress. It fit well in all the right places, if someone her age had any "right places" still intact.

The very low, almost ground-level, heels felt like they were five inches high. Her normal sneakers or arch-reinforced flats were much more comfortable, but certainly not appropriate to wear with a wedding dress. She would just take small, well-calculated steps down the aisle. Tripping wasn't an option. *Positive thoughts*, like Joseph had advised.

As she assessed her reflection, her not quite entirely evaporated female hormones hopped into the driver's seat. She started to cry, without reason. She was so happy about marrying Joseph. Why would her emotional side cause the tears to flow? Was she having second thoughts? Was she having a medical emergency? What was happening?

Carefully, so as not to wrinkle the dress, she sat on the sofa and took some deep breaths. She had to discourage Penelope from jumping up on her lap and possibly making a mark on her wedding dress. She loudly blew her nose and dried the tears from her eyes. Then she realized the tears weren't flowing because she was scared or undecided or hormonally imbalanced. They were tears of happiness. In one week, she would again be half of a married couple. She wouldn't be alone. She was so lucky.

At dinner that evening, the conversation centered around

the empty seat at the table. Sara shared that Jean had stated she was going to ask if she could fill the chair that Deborah had vacated, trying not to express her true feelings as she spoke. She was hoping to get feedback from the others.

"Hell's bells," Jan said in her outside voice. "That is not to my liking. That woman has one goal in her life and that is to snare an unsuspecting male in her net. She is desperate to be part of a couple and will do anything in her power to make that happen. If I remember correctly, she had her sights set on Joseph at one time. I saw her sitting next to Chuck at bingo night last week helping him with his markers. She was practically sitting on his lap. No offense, Chuck."

When Jan finished, Jim spoke up. "I think we are all aware of Jean's tactics. She has approached me several times. She's all sugar and spice on the outside, but if you were able to look below the surface, you would see ulterior motives with selfish undertones. She is all about Jean. I will tell you honestly, I would fight her getting assigned to our table. We have such a compatible group of folks here. Deborah wasn't a good fit, for reasons that we didn't understand. There would be no guesswork when it comes to Jean. She is too obvious."

To Sara's surprise, Chuck spoke up. "I recently met Jean and, although I see the consensus that she isn't a good fit, I beg to differ. I was impressed with her kindness when we sat together at Bingo. She had nothing but good things to say about everyone at this table. I wouldn't sign the petition against her joining us."

The conversation grew very quiet. Looks were exchanged, and there were several eye-rolls. Jean had managed to pull the wool over Chuck's eyes. Maybe if he spent more time with her, he would see her obsession with male companionship. Although Sara had told herself to get more involved with others after learning of Deborah's reason for withdrawal, she didn't feel that Jean was someone she could befriend. Maybe she was being too judgmental. Or maybe she was being realistic. There can be a fine line between the two.

Often people are labeled as being one of three types. *Pessimistic*, the glass is half empty. These people tend to focus on the negative aspects of life. *Optimistic*, the glass is half full. These people tend to focus on the positive aspects of life. *Realistic*, measure the amount of water in the glass relative to the maximum amount of water the glass can hold. These people focus on facts and figures devoid of emotional or perceived involvement.

In this situation, Sara felt she was building her assessment based on actual behavior. Jean had voiced interest in Joseph. She rebounded to Ray when Joseph showed her no attention. Now she was setting her sights on Chuck since Ray was no longer at Parliament Square. Maybe Sara was a realist with a touch of pessimism. Whatever the case, she did NOT want Jean to join their table.

Michele, Betsy, Joseph, and Sara didn't comment. Joseph changed the subject to the weather prediction for the upcoming wedding weekend. It currently looked dry with temperatures in the sixties and seventies. Hopefully that weather would materialize. Predicting the weather is one profession where you can be wrong fifty percent or more of the time and still not lose your job.

As the dessert dishes were collected, Jean passed by the table on her way out of the dining area. She walked slowly with a bit of a sway in her saunter. She said hello to the group as she passed. Did she just wink at Chuck?

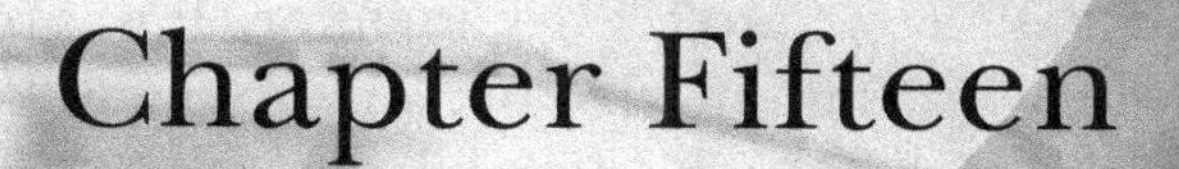

# Chapter Fifteen

## Satin and Lace— Naughty or Nice

Monday was ushered in by clouds, chilly breezes and driving rain. A perfect day to remain cozy under the covers, but Penelope disagreed. She kneaded Sara's arm and meowed to get her attention. It was breakfast time. Although cats do not require a morning walk to take care of business, they can be demanding about feeding time. Their internal alarm clock was not to be ignored.

Sara tried to pet Penelope and encourage her to return to slumber but was unsuccessful. The kneading became more intense and the meowing grew louder. No use fighting it. She would get up, feed Penelope, visit the potty, and return to her warm bed. Maybe she could catch another hour of sleep before showering and beginning her day. How was this going to work when Joseph was still asleep and Penelope insisted on an early breakfast? Would he understand or would he be upset? Maybe Penelope would have to sleep in the guest bedroom. She wouldn't like that at all. Starting Saturday night, their wedding night, changes were coming. Were Sara and Penelope ready?

The dreary weather gave Sara a reason to return to her room after breakfast and begin to pack for the honeymoon. She didn't want to put clothes in the suitcase yet. Having them folded so long would cause them to look crumpled when unpacked. Instead, she'd put all the selected items on hangers ready to be packed Saturday or Sunday prior to departure. They would be away for a week and Sara only had one suitcase, which wouldn't be sufficient, so she borrowed one from Michele. Of course, she could do laundry at the resort, but who wants to be bothered with laundry on your honeymoon?

The weather would be tropical, so nothing but lightweight clothing and a sweater or two in case the evenings were cooler. She had plenty of Bermuda shorts and capris.

Her summer wardrobe was rather extensive because she used to spend plenty of time outdoors at her cottage by the sea. Life there seemed like a distant memory even though she had left it behind less than a year ago. So much had changed in those nine months. What if she had refused to leave? She would never had met and fallen in love with Joseph. Her life would have been so different. A single decision can change everything. She knew that all too well based on the *what if* moments she had experienced when she first arrived.

As she reviewed her sleepwear, she realized that she needed something more alluring for the seven nights they would share at the Sandals resort. She owned nothing that could be categorized as honeymoon eligible. Nothing low cut. Nothing sheer. Nothing frilly. Certainly nothing see-through. Yes, she definitely needed some new sleepwear.

Her first thought was to call Allison and ask if they could go shopping together. She hadn't seen Allison in weeks and it would give them an opportunity to reconnect. However, after giving it some thought, she decided shopping for lingerie did not seem like a good activity to share with her soon-to-be daughter-in-law. Then an idea struck her.

Chuck's telephone rang four times before he answered. "Chuck, this is Sara. I was wondering if you'd be kind enough to drive me to the mall tomorrow to do some shopping. It shouldn't take more than a couple of hours. I can call you when I'm done so you don't have to wait while I shop. Would that work for you?"

"Sure, I'd be happy to do that. Also, I want you to know that I took the car to the local car wash last week and had the interior and exterior cleaned, so no more spiders. Do you think Joseph will allow us to go without him to supervise? I don't want him upset if the two of us go alone. We don't want tongues to wag!"

"No problem. I doubt that he'd be interested in coming, but I'll check. I'd like to invite Michele if that's okay. I'd like her opinion, and it'll give the two of you a chance to spend some time together. I'll call her when we hang up. Does ten tomorrow morning sound good? Hopefully the weather will improve by then so we don't have to go out in the rain."

Sara called Michele who said that she'd love to go along. Michele said she needed a couple things and hadn't been to the mall on the Parliament Square transportation van in weeks. They often went in the afternoon and she wasn't willing to sacrifice her after-lunch siesta to go shopping.

Sara went to Joseph's room to see if he needed help with his honeymoon packing. He didn't answer immediately; in fact, Sara was turning to leave when the door opened. "Sara, sorry to keep you waiting. I was finishing up a call with Allison. Her sisters will be staying there when they're here for the wedding. They have a lot to share and this will give them the perfect opportunity to do just that. In the future, we'll have to schedule an annual West Coast trip to visit the girls and their families. It's been too long. What can I do for you, young lady?"

"I came to see if you need any help packing. I know men don't normally get as involved with packing as women do. Throw in some shorts, underwear, and socks and they're ready to go. Have you decided what you're taking?"

"Actually, I called Allison and asked her to come over and help me select the items I should pack. She's coming Wednesday and will share lunch with us since we have an empty seat. Then, she and I will come back here and decide what I'm bringing. See, I *have* given it some thought. I would have asked you to help but that takes all the surprise out of it. I may pack some speedo suits and muscle shirts. Maybe I'll vacate my comfort zone for this trip."

Sara laughed. "Oh, Joseph, you are too funny. I was just thinking that we haven't seen Allison lately, so it'll be great to have lunch with her on Wednesday. I asked Chuck to drive me to the mall tomorrow to do some last-minute shopping. You're welcome to ride along. Michele has agreed to go with me to assist. I know shopping isn't one of your highest-rated activities, so don't feel pressured into going along. And since Michele is going, Chuck and I won't be seen leaving Parliament Square unchaperoned."

Joseph chuckled out loud. "Yes, we don't want any rumors flying the week before the wedding. I'm glad Michele can go along. I know women like company while shopping and, although I would be company, I wouldn't be *good* company. Waiting outside the women's dressing rooms isn't my cup of tea. Have fun, and maybe a stop at Spencer Gifts would liven up the trip, if you know what I mean."

Sara blushed. "You just never know what you might find in my luggage. Never underestimate the mature woman. They are the ones who will surprise you. If I weren't so paranoid about flying, I'd be even more excited about our honeymoon trip. I am so looking forward to a week alone with you. We can be alone here, but it's not the same. A tropical paradise, and I get you all to myself. How lucky am I?"

They walked to lunch together, holding hands and smiling. Love can be grand at any age. Others may exchange glances, speak in hushed tones, or try to avoid eye contact with those who outwardly display their affection for each other. Maybe it's because they're secretly jealous. Whatever the case, they weren't going to hide their feelings for each other. It was something to celebrate and share, not something to be ashamed of and hide.

The rain slowed, but it continued to fall. Hopefully, it would be better for their trip to the mall tomorrow. The weekend forecast was sunny and cool. The temperatures didn't impact the wedding since everything was indoors, but the sun would certainly brighten the day and allow guests to arrive without umbrellas. Sara hoped the weatherman's predication was correct.

The seats at their table filled for lunch. The smell of egg salad permeated the room. Not a pleasant odor by any means, but the sandwiches were delicious, made with fresh Italian bread, crisp lettuce, and lots of mayonnaise, served with pickles and fruit salad. No crispy, salty potato chips, but that was part of the plan to provide healthy meals to the residents. The dietitian held sessions each month to explain the importance of eating healthy at any age, but especially at an advanced age. It was interesting and informative but not always what seniors wanted to hear.

Jim was in his normal, upbeat mood. It was hard to remember a day when he wasn't outgoing, friendly and of course, funny. He had few relatives, none of whom lived close by or visited him regularly. He had never been married or had children. He was pretty much alone in the world with the exception of his friends at Parliament Square. Some would find his life depressing. Not Jim. If you asked him on any given day how he was doing, his response was always *tremendous*.

Why do some people handle adversity or solitude so much better than others? Is it something in their genes? Is it mind over matter? Is there a secret they could share with others? One person may have a meltdown over a broken fingernail while another appreciates the fact that they only broke one nail instead of two. How do our brains get programmed to react one way or the other? And once programmed, can they be changed? It isn't always about what's happening but rather about how one reacts to it.

Lunch was good. Betsy and Jan said they had butterflies

about their upcoming singing at the ceremony. They said the karaoke night was one thing, but singing in the chapel with the cameras rolling and all eyes on them was another. Fortunately, they were both in good health and their voices were clear and strong. The flu season seemed to be quieting down and hopefully would soon disappear until the fall.

"Betsy and I are ready for the big event. We tried our dresses on and they still fit. We've been attending the chair Zumba classes to avoid weight fluctuations and possible wardrobe issues. So far, so good. We're nervous but excited."

They discussed the open seat at their table. No one had heard any rumors about who would join them. Sara said a silent prayer that it would not be Jean. Doing so made her feel like a bad person, but she just couldn't help herself when it came to Jean.

Tuesday dawned cloudy and breezy but dry. Sara and Michele were meeting Chuck in the lobby at ten to head to the mall. They hadn't spent much girl time together since Sara's engagement.

Soon they heard Chuck's car out front. As they approached, they saw Jean in the front seat. What was she doing here? This wasn't good.

"Good Morning, ladies. Look who I ran into last evening after bingo. I mentioned we were going to the mall and Jean asked if she could tag along. I said of course. I knew you two wouldn't mind. The more the merrier as they say. Although I'm glad Joseph declined because it would've been a bit crowded in the car."

"I love going to the mall," Jean said. "The transportation van doesn't go often enough for me. I enjoy strolling through the stores. Sometimes I don't buy anything. It's just good to get out in the real world now and again. What are you ladies shopping for today?"

Sara replied, "Nothing special. Just some last-minute items for the honeymoon. I need to stock up on the sunscreen. A week in the sunshine is a long time. Although we may not be outside all the time."

The rest of the trip was conversation-free. Chuck turned on the radio to fill the silence. Sara wasn't happy with Jean's presence, but Jean was very happy to be there. Michele was just along for the ride.

When they arrived, Chuck opened the doors for the ladies. Michele and Sara got out, but Jean made a lame excuse that she wanted to shop at a store on the other side of the mall, so she asked Chuck to drop her off there. Very suspicious but not unexpected. Jean was on the prowl and Chuck was her target.

When Chuck pulled away, Sara turned to Michele. "I am so sorry. I know that you enjoy his company. Jean wants to put herself on Chuck's radar. When she sets her sights on a man, she doesn't appear to care how her actions impact others. I'm not saying she knew you and Chuck had gone to dinner together or she knew you had an interest in him. But I feel even if she did know, her strategy wouldn't change. I would never have asked Chuck to drive us if I thought for a minute this could happen. No coincidence that he ran into her at bingo last evening. She's drawn to him like a moth to a flame. She was just waiting for a moment like this. Needed to go to a store on the other side of the mall, my foot. She wanted to spend time alone with Chuck."

"Let's not allow this to ruin our day," Michelle said. "We came to shop for nighties, so let's do that. Whatever Jean and Chuck do together is none of our business. I have no hold on Chuck or he on me. We had one double date with you and Joseph. Hopefully there will be more but that's up to Chuck. You heard him stand up for Jean the other evening when we were discussing her request to be seated at our table. Let's focus on you today."

"Okay. I'll try to do that. I don't like being negative, but Jean brings out the worst in me. Let's head to Victoria's Secret and find something provocative. I want lacey. I want black. I want to have the body that they show in their advertisements. Two out of three won't be bad."

The mall was quiet. "Looks like Tuesday morning is a good time to shop. Maybe the store will be empty and no one will question why a woman my age is shopping there. I can say I'm buying them for my granddaughter. No, I won't. I won't say anything. If asked, I'll say they're for my honeymoon. I don't have to be embarrassed about wanting to look sexy for my new husband, no matter how darn old I am."

Fortunately, the store was very quiet, and there were plenty of options. She didn't want anything see-through. That might be more scary than enticing. She didn't want to give Joseph nightmares. She wanted something opaque with a little structure to support the parts that no longer supported themselves.

She wanted something that was senior sexy if there was such a category. Michele pointed out a couple of possible choices and Sara found two more. She went to the dressing room to try them on. No one but Michele and Joseph would ever see her in them. No one! If there was a fire at the resort, she would either burn in the room or put a sheet over herself before exiting.

The white lacy model was a bit too skimpy and almost transparent. It wasn't form-flattering. At least not for Sara's form. The black satin peignoir set was very sheer but left something to the imagination. At her age, everything was better left to the imagination. This one was a contender.

The next selection was a lacy fire-engine-red two-piece with sufficient coverage. Not something she would wear on a regular basis but definitely suitable for a honeymoon. It was also a contender. The final selection was mainly black with a cream-colored lace bodice. It had matching slippers with a small heel. That could be a fall risk.

Michele critiqued each selection. The clerk must have wondered what was taking them so long. It wasn't easy getting in and out of these garments. As people age, it gets harder to step into undergarments than it used to be. It's also more dangerous. If hospitals kept records of falls for seniors, a large number would be related to simply getting dressed or putting on shoes.

Sara decided on the black satin peignoir set and the lacy fire-engine-red two-piece. They would certainly get Joseph's attention. Where it went from there was up to him. He mentioned he was packing some "special" lovemaking medication. Not sure how that worked or if it was necessary. Sara enjoyed simply being held and cuddling. It should be a very interesting week.

After Sara checked out, they decided to walk around a bit before calling Chuck for a ride home. Sara did need some sunscreen and several other drugstore items. They passed Spencer Gifts and decided to go inside and have a look-see as Joseph had kiddingly suggested. Oh my, there were a lot of X-rated items in that store. Sara felt many of them crossed the line from funny to raunchy. She wasn't a fan of vulgar. She liked a good laugh, but some things were over the top. She did find a pair of feather-covered handcuffs that she decided would be a fun item to take along. Michele purchased some humorous but not-quite-gross greeting cards. Who comes up with this stuff?

It was around eleven-thirty when they passed the food court. Maybe it was time for a not-healthy snack before they called Chuck. He'd probably be at lunch at Parliament Square at noon, so no hurry. To their surprise, Chuck and Jean were at a table sharing a pretzel and an animated conversation. They didn't notice Sara and Michele.

"Hi, Chuck. Michele and I were going to call you for a ride back but thought you'd be having lunch at Parliament Square soon. I guess we were wrong. Hopefully Jean found the store she was looking for on the other side of the mall. It was nice of you to keep her company. We're going to get something to eat. Let us know when you're ready to head back. We're done shopping."

Sara and Michele perused the food court weighing their options. The pretzels with cinnamon and sugar looked tempting. The cinnamon rolls smelled wonderful. Sara was a bit steamed about Jean and Chuck sharing a pretzel, but that was out of her control. Chuck was a grown man, capable of making decisions without her input. It was none of her business.

They decided to get the cinnamon-sugar pretzel bites and a big, hot, gooey cinnamon bun. Parliament Square would never serve these for lunch. They enjoyed every sugary, buttery, calorie-riddled bite.

When they finished, they went back over to Chuck and Jean. "Chuck, Sara and I are ready to leave when you are. We've shopped and we've shared a very unhealthy lunch. It was fun to get out and mingle with the outside world for a while, but it's time to return."

"Okay, ladies. I'll bring the car around and we'll head back."

# Chapter Sixteen

*Jean, Jean, Roses are Red*
*And all the leaves have gone green . . .*

The ride back to Parliament Square was made in total silence. No one had anything to say or, if they did, they were polite enough to keep quiet. Chuck turned the radio to a jazz station and music filled the void. Shopping for lingerie could be checked off the to-do list. Sara and Michele's quality time together had been enjoyable and the food-court food had been decadent and delicious. All would have been positive about the morning's activities if only Jean wasn't sitting in the front seat.

Chuck pulled up to the entrance and the three ladies said their goodbyes and thank yous. Jean said, "Chuck is such a nice man. We had a wonderful time today. Fingers crossed that he'll be calling me soon to schedule a date. See you ladies at dinner."

Jean headed for the elevator while Sara and Michele gathered their purchases and sat on the sofa in the corner of the lobby. "Sara, I know that you'd like Chuck and I to be a couple. It would be fun for the four of us to spend time together. You have to realize you're one of the very few people who is fortunate enough to find love at our age. You're the exception, not the rule. I like Chuck. If he invites me out again, I'll say yes. Whether there's possibly a long-term relationship remains to be seen. Chuck may prefer Jean's company. Or one of the many other people here. The women outnumber the men four to one."

"I understand. I have to accept the fact that wishing won't make it so. I wanted to play matchmaker. Most of all, I didn't want Chuck showing any interest in Jean. I can't seem to get the song 'Jean' out of my head since I saw her in the car this morning. It's an earworm, playing over and over in my head. I hate when that happens. They say chewing gum can help drive a jingle out of your brain. It may take a couple packs to stop this one. Maybe Chuck will tell us at dinner that he had an awful time, fingers crossed.

"Well, I'm off to remove the tags from my purchases and put them with the other things I'm packing for the honeymoon. I really appreciated you going along and being my fashion consultant. It's been forever or longer since I went shopping for lingerie. Flannel and high-necked jammies are my comfort zone. These new pieces are honeymoon appropriate but far from normal. I may pack one mature-woman nightgown as my safety net. Possibly slip into it after Joseph falls asleep?"

Joseph appeared as the ladies walked to the elevator. "I was wondering when I'd see you two. We missed you at lunch. It was just Jim, Betsy, Jan and I. The conversation was sparse so we decided that you two must be the talkers. Jim did share a couple one-liners. What did you lovely ladies have for lunch? A nice green salad? A fruit smoothie? Some other healthy thing?"

Michele and Sara exchanged glances and chuckled in unison. "No, my dear," Sara replied. "We threw caution to the wind and made unhealthy choices. We shared a buttery sugar-and-cinnamon pretzel and a famous cinnamon roll dripping with warm icing. It was liberating. Hopefully, I'll still fit into my wedding dress. Too late for alterations now. On a more serious note, guess who just happened to go along with us today? None other than I-need-a-man-in-my-life Jean. It was unexpected and unpleasant to say the least. Not only did she get herself invited to tag along, but she also corralled Chuck into spending the morning with her at the mall."

"Now, now, Chuck can make his own decisions about women. Maybe he likes Jean. She and I were like oil and water, but to each his own. Maybe he was just being polite today. But remember, Cupid wannabe, this is out of your control."

Michele said, "That's just what I told her. I know she'd like

Chuck and I to be a couple so we could share time with you. That would be great. However, Chuck will decide that, not us. Let the chips fall where they will. If he asks me out again, I'll accept, no questions asked. The ball is in his court."

Their conversation shushed as Chuck entered the lobby. "My ears are burning. Are you three talking about me? I can only guess what the topic was." He stepped closer and spoke more quietly. "I admit Jean coming along was a bit awkward and certainly not planned. I'm not good at saying no, so when she asked if she could come along, I said that would be fine. I have to tell you she's a bit suffocating. I expected her to go her own way in the mall after I dropped her off. My plan was to come back here for lunch and then pick you up when you told me you were ready, but one thing led to another. Before I knew it, we ended up at the food court sharing a pretzel. Michele, I meant no disrespect. Jean seems very nice. She's lonely and desperate for male companionship. Unfortunately, she's going to have to keep looking. I don't want to hurt her feelings, but I also don't want to encourage her. I'll be her friend but only her friend. I hope she finds someone, but it won't be me."

Sara's sigh of relief was audible. "I guess Jean upset me when she said she was interested in Joseph months ago. She did it so matter-of-factly. This was before Joseph and I were an item. Then she stole him away from me at the Halloween party, dressed in the same costume as me. She seemed to lurk around every corner waiting to catch his attention. Fortunately for me, Joseph wasn't interested. Otherwise, the ending to this story would be very different."

Jim strolled by. "Hi, everyone. Is this a private conversation or can anyone join? I just passed Jean. She was whistling and told me she just spent the best morning ever with you, Chuck. It was out of character for her to be so happy and upbeat. So, fill me in. What's going on?"

Sara responded, "Chuck and Jean spent the morning together at the mall. That must be what turned her frown upside down. Unfortunately for Jean, Chuck says it was a one-time thing. He was trying to be sympathetic and a good listener, but it appears Jean interpreted it differently."

The five continued to chat. They agreed that Jean was a woman with a strong desire for male companionship. She wanted desperately to be part of a couple. That, in itself, was nothing to be ashamed of. However, her approach to finding that special someone needed to improve.

She upset other women by targeting men instead of waiting for them to show interest in her. Every day was Sadie Hawkins day for her. She didn't do her homework to determine if her targets were already seeing or interested in someone. Maybe they could play matchmaker and find someone for Jean. But who would it be?

Emily, the resident RN, ran by, headed for the elevator. They didn't like the concern on her face. Hopefully, it wasn't a medical emergency. Soon they heard the sirens and knew her hurried pace and worried expression meant someone was in distress. Sara had a flashback of Pam being wheeled out to the ambulance and never seeing her again. Who was fighting for their life this time? And the more important question, when would Sara or Joseph be on that gurney? Her stomach rolled and she started to perspire. She was feeling a bit faint. She was glad she was sitting down.

Although no one wanted to see who was on the passing gurney, no one could look away. It was like driving past a car accident. You didn't want to see it, but your curiosity wouldn't allow you to look in the other direction. And then they saw: It was Jean.

As the EMTs passed through the lobby where Sara, Joseph, Chuck, Jim and Michele were, Jean told the paramedics to stop. "Chuck, can you please ride with me in the ambulance? I'm so frightened. I missed a step exiting the elevator and I think I may have broken my hip or my leg or my ankle. I'm in so much pain right now. I don't want to do this alone."

Chuck hesitated. His expression and body language said *no*, but he slowly stood and agreed to go. He glanced back at his friends, distress in his eyes. It was apparent that he was going only because he felt it was the right thing to do.

They loaded the gurney into the waiting ambulance. Chuck climbed cautiously into the rear door where he would sit with Jean for the trip to the hospital. The sirens blared as they departed. They sent chills up Sara's spine.

It was unnerving to see one of the residents have a medical emergency. Sara tripping on her welcome mat the other evening could have caused her to fall and break something. She didn't, but it was only a matter of time. It was like walking a tightrope and waiting for a slip to cause a fall.

"I think it is nice Chuck agreed to ride along, Sara said. "I don't think he really wanted to go but he is a nice, caring gentleman. He took the high road. He was just telling us about his experience with her at the mall and then this happens? She managed to play on his sympathies twice in one day."

They all agreed that Chuck going along when Jean asked him to wasn't unexpected. They chatted a bit more and then went their separate ways. It was early afternoon, the perfect time for a little siesta. The shopping had been fun, but it was also a bit tiring. Joseph was curious about what was in Sara's bags. "Let me carry them for you. Maybe I can take a peek inside?"

"Thanks, Joseph, but they're not heavy and you don't want to spoil the surprise, do you? I certainly couldn't wear a high-neck old-lady nightgown on our honeymoon. Sure, it may look better on a younger woman but you'll just have to use your imagination. Just remember that love is blind, so put on your love blinders and see what you want to see. Maybe the wine will help."

Joseph told Sara to enjoy her nap, then he went back to his room to call Allison. He hadn't talked with her for a while and he wanted to check on the plans for the weekend when her sisters would be here for the wedding. The girls always got along well, but Sofie and Annette had grown closer since they moved out west. The three girls hadn't been together since their mother's funeral two years ago. They corresponded and Face Timed each other frequently, but that wasn't the same as seeing each other in person. He was looking forward to having them all together in one place again.

Sara put her purchases in the bedroom, slipped off her age-appropriate walking shoes, and relaxed on the bed. Penelope joined her immediately. She loved cuddle time with Sara. The rhythmic purring of her sweet kitty was soothing and, before long, Sara drifted off. She fell into a deep sleep.

She was awakened by the telephone, but by the time she got her bearings and staggered to the table the ringing had stopped. Probably a telemarketer. She normally turned her ringer off when she napped but today, she had forgotten. When she glanced at the clock, she realized that her catnap with Penelope had lasted almost two hours. Wow, she must have really been tired.

After shaking off the remnants of her slumber, she removed her purchases from the bags. Maybe she had selected sleepwear that was too risqué for a woman her age. It was beautiful but her aging, sagging body couldn't do justice to the satin and lacey garments. Oh well, keep the lighting low, the blinds drawn, and maybe, just maybe, she could pull it off. Joseph knew he wasn't getting a new model. Beauty is in the eye of the beholder. Another saying seniors hoped was true.

The dinner conversation was lively. Jan wore a florescent orange top with lime-green clamdiggers. How she found jewelry to match those vibrant colors was certainly a secret. It was almost as though her clothing shouted *Look at me.* A vision of the reflective dresses Jan and Betsy would wear to the wedding flashed into Sara's mind's eye. She felt another chill run up her spine.

Betsy commented, "Jan, I must tell you that your choice of colorful clothes is off the charts tonight. Soon we'll have to wear dark glasses so you don't blind us. Do tell, is this ensemble new? Please tell us where you bought it. Maybe Sara would like to pick one up to take on her honeymoon."

"Betsy, I know you are pulling my leg. You don't always approve of my taste in clothing. To each his own. I like clothing and jewelry that make a statement. Nothing drab and dreary for me. When I was younger, I worried about what others would think. At my age, as Rhett Butler put it so well in *Gone with the Wind*, frankly, my dear, I don't give a damn. Let others judge and stare and point. It doesn't bother me a bit. Show me a book that describes proper etiquette for the aged and I'll show you a book covered in dust. We've earned the right to act our age. I purchased this online, but I'm not giving away my secret retailer information. I don't want everyone to dress like this. I want to be one of a kind!"

"Well, one of a kind you certainly are. I must say your taste in clothing and jewelry certainly has evolved through the decades. When you were married and raising your family, you could have passed for June Cleaver or Harriet Nelson. As the sand in your hourglass flowed from top to bottom, you changed. I commend your ability to allow judgement to simply roll off your back. I wish I could be more like that. I still dress and behave conservatively, like I always have. We're best friends with different views of life. I guess it's true that opposites attract."

Everyone at the table laughed. It was always fun listening to Betsy and Jan banter back and forth. They were best of friends and they didn't hold their tongues when either had something to say. They certainly livened up the conversation.

Chuck hadn't returned from the hospital. He had texted Joseph around four o'clock letting him know they were taking X-rays of Jean's hip, which appeared to be where the injury was centered. If it was broken, she'd be admitted to the hospital and a hip replacement would be scheduled. She was in a lot of pain and thanked Chuck repeatedly for staying with her. He planned to call the Parliament Square van to pick him up as soon as a diagnosis was made.

Falls can be life-changing at any age, but when they happen during the senior years, they sometimes delineate the beginning of the end. Loss or limited mobility, living with constant pain and risks associated with non-optional surgery, are all game changers. One day strolling around the grounds, attending balance classes, and responsible for your own mobility; the next you're dependent on others for your daily care and physical activity. A tightrope to be respected and carefully, ever so carefully, crossed.

As dessert was served, Betsy said she wanted to share a story with the group. "Last week, Jan and I decided to attend the annual zoo trip. It was over an hour bus ride and, fortunately, the weather cooperated. We went last year and it was wet and cold. Not a good day to walk around outside. This year was different. Sunshine, warm, and no clouds. Since it's almost spring, many of the male animals were feeling their oats. Parents covered children's eyes and pulled them away from the mating animals. Jan was different. She pointed it out to me just in case I missed it, laughing and making adult comments. We got a lot of glares and eye-rolls. But the animal sexual encounters weren't the highlight of the trip, although they were certainly entertaining. We were in the aviary when a rather large bright yellow bird knocked Jan's hat off her head and took one of the artificial flowers that she had stuck in it. Once the bird realized the flower wasn't real, it dropped it and made some loud, cackling sound as it flew away. I guess it wasn't happy about the situation. Everyone in the aviary had a good laugh, with the possible exception of Jan."

"Betsy, you know that's one of my favorite hats. That darn bird snatched one of the most colorful flowers and now there's an empty spot where that flower used to be. I'm going to have to find a new one to replace it. Maybe I'll skip the aviary next year or wear a non-floral hat."

Everyone at the table enjoyed the story, except maybe Jan. Her unusual and often colorful choices of apparel and accessories caught the eye of not only the humans but also our feathered friends. Jim piped up. "Maybe next year we can all go on the zoo trip to witness all the activity for ourselves. Sounds like you gals had a great trip. Oh, that reminds me of a funny zoo story." Jim was oblivious to the synchronized eye-roll. "A man took his eight-year-old son to the zoo. They found the monkey cage very entertaining until the father noticed two monkeys in a compromising position which embarrassed him because his young son was watching. The man walked up to the zookeeper and asked if he could stop them. The keeper told him the monkeys were in their natural habitat and he couldn't do anything about it. The father asked the keeper, 'If I throw peanuts at them, do you think they would stop?' The keeper looked the father in the eye and answered, 'Would you?'"

Linda approached the table just as Jim presented the punchline. "Good evening, ladies and gentlemen. Sounds like your table is once again enjoying dinner together. I think people at other tables are sometimes jealous of your camaraderie. In fact, we've had several people ask to be reassigned to your empty seat. That's why I stopped by." Sara felt her stomach churn as she waited for the announcement. Who would become the eighth diner at their table?

# Chapter Seventeen

## *Ray of Sunshine*

Linda sat in the vacant chair that would have been occupied by Chuck if he weren't still at the hospital with Jean. "As you are all aware, the women at Parliament Square far outnumber the men. This table already has three gentlemen assigned to it, which is more than most of the other tables. So, we're going to seat another female here. I wasn't kidding when I said several women have asked to sit here. We don't process such requests. The management would have an uprising on our hands if we did. How the seating assignments are determined is a deep, dark secret, and I'm not involved. I'm just the messenger. Anyhow, a new female resident is arriving in two weeks and the powers that be have decided to assign her to your table. It'll happen soon after Joseph and Sara return from their honeymoon. All I'm at liberty to tell you is that you'll be getting a new female tablemate in about two weeks."

Chuck arrived just as Linda was finishing. He looked tired. He greeted the group with a forced smile. One of the waitstaff said she'd check to see if there were any leftovers she could bring him since he missed dinner. "Jean has a broken hip and she was admitted to the hospital. They hope to fit her surgery into the schedule tomorrow or the next day. She asked me to tell you that all visitors are welcome. When I was leaving, I heard her on the phone with one of her children. Hopefully, a family member will be able to come."

Linda shared that Lynne would be notified. Lynne would, as the resident liaison, contact Jean's family members, send flowers, and be sure that a member of the staff visited. Parliament Square was very dedicated to their residents. This was their home now and they were treated like family.

Just hours ago, they had been at the mall. Now Jean was in the hospital waiting for surgery and the rehabilitation that would follow. How life can change in the blink of an eye.

Never take tomorrow for granted.

Before David's accident and untimely death, Sara was a real worry wart. She fretted about everything. David used to tell her that worry wouldn't change things. He said it was okay to be concerned about situations but it was not okay to worry about the unknown. The worry wouldn't stop bad things from happening, but the concern would allow her to assess the current state of affairs and hopefully change them for the better. The worry would simply kill the joy of today, while having no ability to better tomorrow.

She had been wise enough, for the most part, to follow David's advice and live by it. She did not throw caution to the wind but she also didn't allow fear and anxiety to control her life, like it once had. She remembered David telling her that you lose the joy of the present when you're consumed with worry for the future.

It had been a long day. Sara was tired and a bit depressed. Although she didn't really like Jean, she also didn't like to see anyone suffer. Only a couple days until the wedding. Maybe Chuck could drive them to visit on Thursday. The surgery should be over by then and Jean would be ready for visitors. Yes, she would suggest that at breakfast. She bid Joseph good night, telling him that she needed a good night's rest and Penelope needed some company since she had been alone most of the day. He squeezed her hand, kissed her cheek, and wished her sweet dreams. "Looking forward to seeing you at breakfast. We can discuss Chuck possibly driving us to the hospital on Thursday."

Once inside her apartment, Sara broke down in tears, unexpected and plentiful. Penelope followed her into the bathroom where Sara loudly blew her nose.

"Penelope, the future is so unpredictable. One day the world looks wonderful through rose-colored glasses and the next the color has faded to black and sadness lurks around every corner. The secret is to not let anyone rob you of your special optimistic outlook. Hold on to that as tightly as possible for as long as you can. It won't be easy but it will be worth it."

A good cry always made Sara hungry. David used to say, "Your tears aren't even dry yet and you're spooning out the ice cream." Dear, sweet David. Although she truly loved Joseph, her heart still ached for her David. They had a wonderful life together that was cut short. Things would be so different if she hadn't lost him. Okay, enough of that. Get yourself together, girl. You're going to be a bride on Saturday. Let's see what flavor ice cream is in the freezer. Not too much, though. You have to fit into your wedding dress.

The morning dawned clear and sunny, the temperatures rising as spring approached. The weather forecast for Saturday looked good, with little chance of rain and a good chance of sunshine and seasonal temperatures, although the weatherman wasn't always accurate. Hopefully, this week he would be.

Breakfast was scrambled eggs, Canadian bacon, toast, and a fruit cup, plus lots of freshly made coffee. Sara liked lots of milk in her morning cup of Joe, and she favored the caffeinated version to get her engine running. Never more than two cups, though, or it would interfere with her afternoon nap.

Sara spoke up while the others ate. "Chuck, have you had any updates from Jean? I think it would be nice if we visited her. Try to boost her spirits. Being in the hospital alone and frightened must be awful. If I'm ever there, please come visit me. It scares me just saying that out loud."

"I talked to Lynne before breakfast," said Chuck. "She was able to contact Jean's two sons. One lives only an hour away. He'll be there on the day of her surgery and visit during her hospital stay. She'll probably need to stay at a rehab facility for a couple of weeks before returning to Parliament Square. With the wedding on Saturday, maybe we could stop by for a visit tomorrow afternoon. Friday will be very busy, with everyone preparing for the big event. Jean will understand that. If tomorrow doesn't work, the rest of us can visit while you and Joseph are on your honeymoon."

Everyone at the table thought a visit would be nice, but hospitals often don't allow more than a couple visitors at a time. Chuck volunteered to drive asking Michele if she would go with him. Maybe a couple of visitors a day would be good.

"I think that's a great idea, Chuck. Let's plan to go after lunch today. We can call the hospital to check on visiting hours. If surgery is this afternoon, we can wait until tomorrow or even Friday."

Sara was pleased to know that Chuck and Michele would be spending some alone time together, even if it was under these circumstances. From what Chuck had shared about the morning at the mall with Jean, he didn't appear to be interested.

"So, let's make sure we're all very careful for the next couple of days," Sara said. "Betsy and Jan, we're counting on you for wonderful music. Jim, you're the best man, and Michele, you're my best friend and bridal attendant. What happened to Jean should make us all be a little more careful. Joseph, you and I should wrap ourselves in bubble wrap until Saturday."

Joseph chuckled. "I guess that rules out sky diving and skateboarding. I'll just sit in my rocking chair with my lap blanket until Saturday arrives. No, I think we'll all be fine. Remember your approach to life: Concern is acceptable but unnecessary worry is not. Think positive thoughts. Everything will be all right. What happened to Jean was an accident. Your fall the other evening was also an accident, but Lady Luck was watching over you. Only a couple of bumps and bruises. Jean wasn't so lucky. I read that many falls are caused because your hip breaks, not the other way around. Maybe that's what happened to her."

Sara noticed that Chuck and Michele left the table together after breakfast. Maybe they were going to check with Linda about Jean's surgery. Visiting Jean would give them an opportunity to spend some time together away from the others. Jean would do a slow burn if she knew that what happened to her was indirectly causing Chuck to spend more time with Michele.

Sara admitted to Joseph that, although she was very excited about getting married, she was also getting butterflies. With the wedding only a couple of days away, her anxiety meter was running high. Maybe the simple civil ceremony would have been the better way to go. No turning back now, though. Full steam ahead.

"Sara, I understand your nervousness. Believe it or not, I feel the same way. Men are better at hiding it. I guess that's why we die sooner. We keep too much bottled up inside. We'll have our families together, our friends will be there for support, and let's not forget the cameras will be rolling. Or maybe we *should* forget that part. Whatever, it will be a day to remember. I've been lucky enough to find a second love of my life and she has agreed to marry this wrinkled, older-than-dirt guy. What's not to be happy about?"

"Thanks, Joseph. You always know just the right thing to say to make me feel better. I know my worry is unwarranted. I tell my brain that, but it has a mind of its own and refuses to listen. I need to wake up and smell the roses. Everything's going to be hunky dory. Jumping Jehoshaphat, what was I thinking? Remember all those phrases from our day? No one under the age of fifty would know what I was talking about.

Our day was a long, long time ago now."

Chuck and Michele walked over to talk. Chuck said, "We talked to Linda about Jean. She told us they can't schedule the surgery until Friday. Michele and I decided we'd visit after we go to lunch at a restaurant I've been wanting to try. It'll be fun and I think Jean may catch on when the two of us show up to visit her. If not, I'll have to tell her at some point that I'm not interested. Hopefully she'll figure it out on her own. Our visit will be brief and it'll provide her with some company and moral support. Maybe we'll meet some of her family while we're there."

"That sounds great," said Sara. "It's so nice that you can still drive. We look forward to another dinner on the town with you after the honeymoon. Joseph and I were just talking about the wedding. Today we're going to review our Sandals video, finalize some packing, and relax. Only two days before the family starts arriving and the festivities begin. Please tell Jean that we hope all goes well with her operation and recovery. We'll see her when she returns to Parliament Square."

As Sara and Joseph entered the elevator, they met a familiar face: Ray Adams. "Hi, Ray," Sara said. "What a surprise. Are you visiting someone?"

"No, I'll be living here again. My daughter, who insisted I live with her after my heart attack, was in a car accident two months ago, hit head-on by a drunk driver. I'm devastated. I tried to live there with her husband, but I felt like an intruder. He needs to mourn and move on. He was very nice, but I could tell he didn't really want me there. So, here I am. I just heard that Jean fell and broke her hip. I hope I'll be able to visit her. I think she'll be surprised to see me."

"I'm sorry for your loss. I was never fortunate enough to have any children of my own, but people say losing a child cuts like a knife. Children are supposed to bury their grandparents and parents, not the other way around. Please know that Joseph and I are here for you. And we'll soon be newlyweds. Our wedding is this Saturday."

Ray smiled. "Congratulations to you both. It's wonderful to see young love, but the more mature, seasoned variety is even better. I wish you happiness and a long life together. We'll catch up when you're back from the honeymoon. There is a honeymoon, right?"

"You bettcha there is. Joseph and I are going to a Sandals resort with all the young, beautiful people. We may stick out like sore thumbs, but we don't care. We plan to show those younglings how it's done."

They exchanged a little more conversation before Ray exited the elevator. This certainly was a strange turn or events. Sara never thought she'd see Ray again. When he left to live with his daughter it seemed permanent. Life often presents forks in the road that cause detours, sometimes good, sometime not. You can't prepare for them. How you react defines your destiny.

Once inside her apartment Sara hugged Joseph tightly and started giggling. "What's that all about?" Joseph asked. "Jean will be so excited to see Ray, she'll forget all about trolling for Chuck's attention. Even though Chuck told us he wasn't interested, Jean has a way of making men feel sorry for her. Now she can lasso Ray instead. Perfect timing!"

The telephone rang. Sara answered. It was Chuck. "Sara, we're heading out soon. When we were checking with Linda about Jean, a gentleman named Ray stopped by the desk to also check on her. We started talking. He said he used to reside here and was friends with Jean. He was hoping to get a ride to the hospital with the courtesy van. I invited him to come with Michele and I after explaining that we were going to stop for lunch first. He said if he wasn't intruding, he'd love to join us.

I wanted to let you know of the change in plans and check to be sure you and Joseph didn't want to come along."

"Thanks, Chuck. We appreciate the offer but with the wedding on Saturday, we have some items to check off our to-do list. Ray is very nice and was spending time with Jean before he moved to his daughter's place. Have a great lunch and tell Jean we said hello."

The afternoon flew by as Sara and Joseph cuddled on the sofa watching the Sandals resort video. It was so beautiful there. The golden beaches, the blue sky meeting the crystal-clear green water. This was going to be a trip to remember.

If only that nagging little voice in her head would stop reminding her about the airplane ride. She hadn't traveled by air in a long, long time. When she was younger, it was no big deal. In fact, she looked forward to flying. As the years passed, that changed. Just thinking about it could throw her into an anxiety attack. She might have to rely on her expired anti-anxiety medication. She hadn't taken any for quite some time. Maybe only one or two would be enough to take the edge off.

Allison called Joseph to discuss the plans for the weekend. "My sisters will be staying with William and me until they depart for home on Monday. It'll be fun seeing them and spending some time together. I'll pick them up at the airport on Friday, then at five o'clock we'll meet at the chapel at Parliament Square for the rehearsal. Then off to Luigi's for the rehearsal dinner. Saturday morning, the wedding at ten. Is there anything you need me to get, or do you need transportation anywhere before the weekend?"

"Thanks, but I think Sara and I are good to go. We're reviewing the Sandal video right now. The packing is almost complete. I checked the extended weather report today and it looks like Mother Nature is going to give us blue skies and sunshine on Saturday. It's t-minus two and counting."

"Okay, Dad. We'll see you Friday. If you think of anything or change your mind about needing a ride somewhere, please give me a call. I'm so happy for you both. I know I'm going to cry like a baby. Love you. Bye."

"Well that was nice of Allison to call," Sara said. "She's such a nice woman. I'm sure all three of your daughters make you very proud. We're going to visit them at least once a year after we are married. You need to see them and vice versa. I know they miss their mother but they still have you. Maybe we could take the train to the West Coast instead of flying. Or, who knows, maybe after this trip I'll be ready to fly again without fear.

"I haven't spoken to Michael in a while. I hope all is well. I'm so anxious to see him. We haven't been apart this long since he was born. I do miss him, but spending time with you helps me deal with his absence. Before you, Michael and Penelope were my whole life. Now I have you and Michele, not to mention the others. Life is good and I'm thankful for every new day. I look forward to our journey together. We may have gotten a late start, but that's better than no start at all. Thank you for being the man you are and the husband you will be. I am such a very lucky lady."

# Chapter Eighteen

## *On Top of Spaghetti . . .*

After watching the Sandals video, Sara and Joseph dozed off for an afternoon recharge. Although the younger generation views sleeping during the day as unnecessary and a waste of productive time, they may simply be jealous of the fact that they're unable to participate. When you're younger, a nap is often an impossible luxury because of work, children, and a hectic schedule.

Retirement changes that. An afternoon siesta often happens spontaneously while watching daytime television, reading a book, or simply relaxing. Medical experts say mid-day downtime boosts energy levels and improves memory, but they also advise keeping the dozing time short so as not to interfere with quality sleep at night.

Sara awakened before Joseph and tiptoed to the kitchen to make a cup of afternoon tea. Penelope followed, hoping for a kitty treat. It was two hours until dinner. Maybe a cookie or two with her tea would be good.

Her appetite in the golden years was often diminished, but a sweet snack was a different story. Intense dark chocolate was her downfall. Some feel it is too bitter. Joseph loves milk chocolate and refuses to eat dark chocolate. Not a problem; that meant more for her.

Penelope thanked Sara for her treat by rubbing against her legs and purring loudly. "Penelope," Sara whispered, "Joseph and I are going away for a trip soon but you will be in good hands. Michele is going to take care of you while we're gone. You be a good kitty for her until we get back."

Joseph entered the kitchen, rubbing his eyes and stretching. "I thought I heard you talking. I forget that you and Penelope have conversations. It amuses me when you talk in a high-pitched kitty voice to keep the banter going."

"People talk to their pets all the time. Most pets hear their name, blah, blah, blah, treat, blah, blah, blah, toy; but some pets recognize many words. Wouldn't it be great if they could speak? Of course, that could be a double-edged sword. I'm having a cup of tea and some 'calorie free' cookies. Would you care to join me? I hope my moving around out here didn't wake you. You were in dreamland when I woke up."

"Thanks for the offer but I think I'll go check my mail and answering machine. I have to call the caterers about Saturday to be certain everything will be perfect for the reception. I don't want any snafus. I am anxious to hear how Chuck and Michele enjoyed their lunch together with Ray and their hospital visit to see Jean. I'll see you at dinner, my dear."

Sara added milk to her tea. Although she preferred coffee, if she wanted a warm beverage in the afternoon, tea was her drink of choice. No sugar but lots of milk. It was like a latte but with tea instead of coffee. She dunked one cookie, then another, and before she realized it, she had eaten six. Oh, my, better put those away before the whole box is gone.

She was having her hair and nails done on Friday by Donna, the resident hairdresser. She really needed a color and cut. It was due two weeks ago, but she wanted to wait and have it done right before the wedding. Maybe Donna could fit in a pedicure too? She should have matching polish on her fingers and toes for the honeymoon. She didn't want the younger guests thinking she wasn't a classy lady If she had to be this darn old, the last thing she wanted to do was act like it.

The phone rang causing Penelope to skedaddle. She didn't like loud noises or quick movements. "Hello," Sara said.

"Hi, Sara, this is Michele. Do you have a couple minutes to talk before dinner? I can be at your place in fifteen minutes if I won't be interrupting anything."

"Sure, come over. Joseph left a little while ago and it is just Penelope and me here." She hung up the phone. "Penelope, my curiosity is piqued. I know they say curiosity killed the cat, but we both know that isn't true. I wonder what happened at lunch and with their hospital visit? I'm on pins and needles."

Sara started to straighten up a bit. She had items scattered here and there waiting to be packed for the trip. When was the last time she went somewhere for a week? She hadn't traveled since losing David.

Their trip to Egypt might have been the last time she flew and spent more than a few days away from home. Wow, that was so many years ago. Sometimes, when trying to remember when an event happened, the mind loses perspective. What seems like a couple of years is actually a decade or more. Years passed slowly when she was younger, but their passing picked up speed like a runaway train as she aged.

Michele's tap on the door pushed Penelope into the bedroom. Silly kitty. "Hello, good to see you. Please come in and sit down. I can't wait to hear about your adventures. I feel like I should have a microphone so I can ask you questions like they do on the news."

"I may give an abbreviated version to the others, but I want to give you the full-blown story. Lunch was very nice. I had the best cheesesteak sandwich since I ate my first one in Philadelphia as a teenager. It was quite large, but I managed to clean my plate. I hope my dress still fits for the wedding. Anyway, as Chuck told you, Ray went with us to lunch. He seems like a very nice man. He told us about the accident that took his daughter's life. He kept it brief; I could see tears welling in his eyes. It's such a tragedy. Then we checked at the hospital about visitation for Jean and were told that only two visitors were allowed in the room at a time. Ray told us to go first and he'd surprise her when we were done. Jean was glad to see us. Well, she was really glad to see Chuck. She tolerated my being there, but she doted on Chuck's every word.

"She told us her older son would be coming today and

again on Friday, the day of her surgery. He and his wife are in the midst of an ugly divorce after almost thirty-five years of marriage. From what Jean said, her daughter-in-law decided that she wanted to explore her options, whatever that means. Her son was devastated."

"Jean asked Chuck to sit by her bed and hold her hand for support. Made me want to gag, but I controlled myself. Her demeanor did a three-sixty when Chuck mentioned that she had a surprise visitor waiting to see her and his name was Ray. I thought she was going to jump out of the bed. She asked for her hairbrush, lipstick, toothbrush, etc. We left her to pretty up after we said our goodbyes."

"Ray went in to see Jean while Chuck and I chatted in the visitor's lounge. He said that hospitals make him very uncomfortable after spending so much time there through his wife's illness. He said he still really misses her but he's trying very hard to move on. I felt a bit of a connection with him as we talked. It was really the first time we've spent time together alone, and I think we'll be spending more time with each other. We have to take it slow; he's still grieving for his wife. I understand, and I am in no hurry."

Sara smiled. "I'm so glad to hear that your lunch and visit went well. I'm thinking that Ray's return will lessen Jean's interest in Chuck. Not that it was a problem really, because Chuck told us that he wasn't interested in Jean. I'm so glad Chuck felt comfortable talking with you about his grief. Sometimes sharing feelings after the loss of a loved one helps us heal. So, tell me, how did the visit with Ray go?"

"I was getting to that. We waited in the lounge for over thirty minutes. I decided to go ask if he was ready to head back. When I got to Jean's room the door was closed. I knocked and Ray answered. He said Jean asked to spend more time with him and he would call the Parliament Square van to pick him up later. He thanked me for taking him with us to lunch and bringing him to visit Jean, so I guess they'll be keeping each other company. As we were leaving, a man approached the nurses station asking about Jean. He said he was her son. I could see the resemblance. We told him she had a guest. Although he was friendly, he also seemed cold. Maybe it was because of his current marital situation or maybe it was just me."

"Thanks for filling me in, Michele. My dislike of Jean has lessened a bit. I still think she can be ruthless when it suits her purpose. Maybe Ray will give her someone to focus on and spend time with. She desperately needs a man in her life and I think Ray may just be the right person for the job. Let's head to dinner a little early so I can check my mail. I'll freshen my lipstick and be ready in two shakes."

The lobby was quiet. It was almost the dinner hour and most residents were heading to the dining room. Sara checked her mail. As she turned, Ray came in the front door. He had a smile on his face and a bounce in his step. "Sara, I just got back from the hospital. Jean is nervous about her surgery. I told her I'd be there for moral support. She asked me if I could stop by tomorrow to spend some time with her. We did correspond several times after I went to live with my daughter, and I missed her. We were just getting to know each other before my heart attack. Now it looks like we'll get a second chance."

"That's good news, Ray. I know Jean did miss you after you left. She'll need someone to hold her hand and keep her company during her recovery, and she'll help you reacclimate to living here. You couldn't have returned at a better time."

Joseph snuck up behind Sara and covered her eyes with his hands. "Guess Who," he asked.

"I warned you about sneaking up behind me before. My fiancé will be here any minute. He has a very jealous streak."

They all laughed and walked together to dinner. Chuck and Michele sat next to each other as they often did. Betsy and Jan were already seated. Sara and Joseph settled into two of the empty seats, Joseph holding the chair for Sara and pushing it in when she was seated. Jim was the last to arrive. He wore an untucked Hawaiian-print shirt and cargo shorts. He asked, "Does anyone want to see me do a hula dance? When I wear this shirt, my hips beg me to sway and my hands and arms second the motion. I learned how to hula when I was stationed in Hawaii many, many years ago. Have I mentioned that before?"

Everyone nodded in unison. Jim had often recounted tales of his life in the Navy. The narratives were entertaining but often long-winded and full of details that could be condensed. He loved to talk about those times and share stories. Too bad Jim never took a mate in life. He was a nice man, but cupid's arrow never penetrated his heart. Too bad. A life without marriage is like salt without pepper, peanut butter without jelly, ketchup without mustard, and hugs without kisses. Nonetheless, he seemed very content and happy. Good for him.

Dinner smelled very good. Spaghetti and meatballs. Not as good as Luigi's, but definitely one of the better evening meals in the rotation. They even had warm garlic bread and freshly grated Parmesan cheese. The conversation quieted as everyone focused on eating the hot plates of pasta and sauce. Jim asked, "Does anyone remember the song *On Top of Spaghetti*? I remember singing that at rec hall with my fraternity brothers when I was in college whenever they served spaghetti for dinner."

"Yes," said Jan, "I remember that song very well. When I was teaching third grade, the kids would sing it in the cafeteria at lunch time. It goes on and on and on. That sure brings back some memories for me. I think I remember the lyrics. Why, I could burst into song right now."

Fortunately, Jim spoke up before Jan could get started. He said, "This reminds me of a funny Italian story. Gianna was just married and, being a traditional Italian, she was still a virgin. So, on her wedding night, staying at her mother's house, she was nervous. But her mother reassured her. 'Don't worry, Gianna. Luigi's a good man. Go upstairs and he'll take care of you.' So up she went. When she got upstairs, Luigi took off his shirt and exposed his hairy chest. Gianna ran downstairs to her mother and says, 'Mama, Mama, Luigi has a big hairy chest.' 'Don't worry, Gianna,' says her mother, 'All good men have hairy chests. Go upstairs. He'll take good care of you.' So up she went again. When she got to the bedroom, Luigi took off his pants exposing his hairy legs. Again, Gianna ran downstairs to her mother. 'Mama, Mama, Luigi took off his pants and he's got hairy legs!' 'Don't worry. All good men have hairy legs. Luigi is a good man. Go upstairs and he'll take good care of you.' So up she went again. When she got there, Luigi took off his socks and his left foot was missing three toes. When Gianna saw this, she ran downstairs. 'Mama, Mama, Luigi's got a foot and a half!' 'Stay here and stir the pasta,' said her mother. 'This is a job for Mama!'"

Jim told the joke in a thick Italian accent and the punch line was too funny not to make everyone erupt in laughter. The folks at neighboring tables gave them hairy eyeballs. They were jealous. Yes, this was a good group of seniors. Soon another would join them. Hopefully, she'll have a good sense of humor and won't be afraid to show it in public.

Betsy asked Chuck how Jean was doing when they visited her at the hospital. "Jean's nervous about her surgery but not in much discomfort. Her attitude improved significantly when Michele and I told her Ray was there to see her. She was very excited to hear that he was back. Seems his return couldn't have come at a better time."

Dessert was a sundae bar. This only happened once or twice a month. Everyone loved making their own ice cream delicacy with several flavors of ice cream, chocolate and caramel sauces, wet nuts, whipped cream, and the best selection of sprinkles around. Each table took its turn at the bar. As residents returned, they teased those waiting at the other tables with their creations. It brought back memories of being a kid and running to the ice cream truck with your friends and siblings to make a selection. The sound of that ice cream truck played quietly over the sound system to remind everyone of days gone by.

Most kids of today don't know the sound of the ice cream truck or the exhilaration of hearing that melodic tune, calling out to their parents in a frenzied flurry of excitement for money to purchase frozen treats. Those days are gone, replaced by ice cream chains and local establishments offering dozens and dozens of toppings and soft-serve or scoopable frozen flavors. It's the norm in the twenty-first century, but seniors who knew the excitement of the ice cream truck think the younger generation is missing out on something.

"Remember when we were kids, waiting to hear the ice cream truck music?" asked Betsy. "I remember my favorites were the toasted almond bar and the Orange Creamsicle. We used to call the driver the Good Humor Man because it said *Good Humor* on the side of the truck. I think they carry those items in the grocery stores now. My brother and I used to race to the truck, each of us wanting to be first in line. Those certainly were the good old days."

"Yes," said Jan, "I remember the white truck with the loud music and the treats. Sometimes my parents would ask me to get them something when I purchased mine. I'd run back to the house so their ice cream wouldn't melt in the heat. Great memories!"

After consuming the creamy, sweet dessert, they all headed for the activity room. Jan and Betsy were going to present their songs for the final time before the wedding on Saturday. Only two days remained before the big day. Time passed quickly since Joseph's unexpected proposal at the Valentine's Day party. Life's unpredictability is what makes it exciting. If we knew what was going to happen, we would be bored, there would be no surprises. The events that make us do a double-take, removing us from our comfort zone and the day-to-day mundanity, are the events that etch themselves in our memories. Expect the unexpected and live for the element of surprise.

Betsy and Jan were in rare form. They were excited about the songs and currently on a sugar high from the sundae bar. Maybe less chocolate syrup and fewer sprinkles in the future? The increase in energy levels for children and seasoned adults is directly proportional to their sugar intake. This would be a performance to remember.

They asked Jim to take care of playing the background music on their cassette player for each of the songs. The younger generation doesn't know what a cassette tape is, or its predecessor, the 8-track cartridge. Nowadays, music is downloaded or streamed on smart phones or other devices and enjoyed on small plastic earphones. Times sure have changed. We still love our music but the method of listening to it has transitioned over the years.

Jim inserted the first cassette, turned up the volume, and gave the "girls" a thumbs-up. Jan and Betsy held hairbrushes, pretending they were microphones, and they sang their souls into them. The first two songs were great. This dynamic singing duo had done their homework. Their hours of practice had paid off. The third song, *Over the Rainbow*, was so beautiful. Sara's dreams were indeed coming true. The lyrics to the song tugged at her heartstrings, tears came to her eyes. She squeezed Joseph's hand and smiled.

Applause rang out when they finished. Jan and Betsy waved their hairbrushes and took several deep bows. "Autographs available at the door," Betsy announced with a smile.

# Chapter Nineteen

## *T-Minus One and Counting*

Thursday evaporated into thin air without a trace. Friday, the day before the nuptials, brought clouds and light showers. Saturday's forecast was promising with sunshine, seasonal temperatures, and no rain expected. Family members would be arriving today. The excitement and anxiety levels were equally high.

The seven tablemates shared breakfast and conversation. Everyone at the table was part of the wedding party, even Chuck. Joseph had asked him to be an usher with Jim. Betsy and Jan would harmonize as the guests were being seated. Michele was one of Sara's two attendants. Jim was the best man. So many new friendships had been established over the past six months. Sara and Joseph had fallen in love. Mary and Deborah had left Parliament Square. Pam had been called home by a higher power. Michele and Chuck had joined the table. Soon another resident would become the eighth person to break bread with them.

"I propose a toast," said Jim. "No, not rye, wheat, or pumpernickel, to the soon-to-be wedded couple. Let's all clink our juice glasses to the lucky couple, wishing them a long and happy marriage. Joseph, I have never been fortunate enough to find my perfect mate, but my married friends have provided me with this advice: When you have a discussion with your wife, always remember to get the last two words in and those words are, 'Yes, dear.' They tell me that is the secret to a happy marriage."

Everyone chuckled as they clinked their glasses. Yes, there was some truth in that advice. Just never let the wife know the husband's response may not be completely sincere. What the marriage experience would bring to Sara and Joseph remained to be seen. It was uncharted waters and smooth sailing was not guaranteed. Every marriage brings challenges, disagreements, and compromise. The secret is open communication and fresh batteries in the hearing aids. Marriage at an advanced age does have common ground with young love: that warm-all-over feeling when you're together, and that sad and lonely feeling when you're apart. You count the hours and minutes until you're together again. Just holding hands makes your heart skip a beat. Maybe not so many similarities in the bedroom, however, as intimate relations bring many challenges. Not to say it's impossible, but it's often not spontaneous or frequent. Medications may sometimes be involved, which must be taken well in advance. Then there are the flexibility issues, coupled with the logistics of the activity itself, not unlike a game of Twister. Not impossible but certainly tricky. Without due care and attention, a romantic moment could quickly become a comedy routine.

Jim continued. "I had a friend who, on his wedding night, watched his bride remove her prosthetic leg, her artificial eye, her wig, and several other attachments and put them all in the nightstand drawer. He wasn't sure if he should climb into the bed or into the drawer."

Sara laughed. "That's very funny, but I am not one to kiss and tell. There will be no bedroom stories shared at this table after the honeymoon. Joseph and I are looking forward to an entire week alone together." She raised her eyebrows suggestively. "I hear they have room service there that is so good, you never have to leave your room."

Everyone at the table, with the exception of Jim, had been married. Although they knew very little about one another's marriages or honeymoons, each person at the table had personal memories that bubbled to the surface, sometimes vague and fractured, but fragmented pieces remained.

Betsy spoke up. "When I went on my honeymoon, a long, long time ago, I was as nervous as a long-tailed cat in a room full of rocking chairs. Being a good Catholic girl, I saved myself for my wedding night. Well, it turns out we partied too long and drank too much at the reception. We woke up the next morning and neither of us could remember our wedding night or if we even consummated our marriage. Needless to say, we joked about that night for years."

Everyone shared a chuckle. "I have a story too," said Jan. "My high school sweetheart and I married shortly after graduation. Our wedding was small followed by a very casual reception at the local VFW. We said our goodbyes around midnight and departed for the local Day's Inn. Our budget was very limited. My parents, wanting to surprise us, had a bottle of very expensive Champagne delivered to our room. The knock on the door came at a very inopportune time, if you get my drift. During our marriage, every time we opened a bottle of Champagne, we would pretend we were knocking on a door and say 'Surprise' in unison. Those around us wondered what we were doing. We told them it was an inside joke."

The friends departed the dining room with smiles on their faces and bounces in their steps. This group of seven, soon to be eight, had countless memories to share about their life experiences and relationships. Except for Betsy and Jan and Sara and Michele, who had been long-time friends, they knew very little about each other.

That would change over the coming months and years, while seated together at their table in the dining room. Old friends bring sparkle to our lives, like precious diamonds that have been cut and polished. New friends, made later in life, are like diamonds in the rough, their true value being hidden under layers of lifetime experiences, to be explored, evaluated, and appreciated with each passing day.

Sara and Joseph had consolidated most of their household belongings at Joseph's apartment. Sara would wait until they returned from the honeymoon to move her bedroom furniture into the second bedroom. Michael and Alan would stay at Sara's place for several nights until they returned to California.

Today was moving day for Penelope. Her bed, toys, dishes, and food would be kept at Joseph's place starting today. While Sara was on her honeymoon, Michele would stop by to visit, feed, and clean the litter box. She and Penelope were best of friends.

Suitcases were packed. Family would start arriving soon. Rehearsal in the chapel and the rehearsal dinner were only hours away. It was go time. The first wedding at Parliament Square in many years would be taking place less than twenty-four hours from now. One could almost smell the excitement in the air.

The tablemates ran into Ray in the lobby after breakfast. "Ray, can you update us on Jean? Today is her hip replacement. Are you going to the hospital?"

Ray looked a bit down and replied, "Her family thinks it best if I wait to visit until she's moved to the rehabilitation facility. The number of visitors is limited and they feel only family should be there for her now. I understand, but I feel badly since I told Jean yesterday that I'd be there today. She doesn't have her cell phone turned on. I tried leaving a message at the nurse's station, but they told me she was on the way to the operating room. I really hope everything goes well for her and she gets my message."

Sara took Ray's hand. "Ray, I'm sure her sons will explain. She'll understand why you aren't there. She'll probably be released by Sunday and transferred to the rehab center. She will need your support and company more then because her family will most likely return to their lives at that point. Don't worry, you and Jean will have plenty of time to be together."

"Thanks, Sara. I'm just so glad that my path led me back

here. As you may know, Jean doesn't like being alone. We were just getting to know each other when I had my heart attack and went to live with my daughter. We did correspond several times since then. Hopefully, we can pick up where we left off."

Sara and Joseph headed to Sara's place. It was time to move Penelope, her belongings, and Sara's suitcases to Joseph's apartment. Sara wanted to change the sheets on the bed and put out her best towels for Michael and Alan. Also, a bit of dusting and vacuuming were needed. Not everyone felt that kitty fur was an acceptable fashion accessory. Maybe taking her focus off the wedding would calm her nerves and lighten her mood. She was excited about being married again but apprehensive at the same time. It wasn't simply putting a ring on her finger and reciting her vows. It was pledging herself to Joseph in sickness and health till death do them part. When younger, the *until death do you part* vow seemed a lifetime away. Now in their eighties, that vow took on a whole new meaning.

The phone interrupted her vacuuming. It was Michael. His flight was delayed but they should arrive prior to the rehearsal at five. He apologized and told her that they would come directly to the chapel at Parliament Square as soon as they landed. He assured her that they should be there in plenty of time to walk her down the aisle.

She hung up and felt the warm tears run down her cheeks. "Pull yourself together, woman," she said aloud. "You are marrying a wonderful man who loves you very much. There are no guarantees. Make the most of the time you have together and leave the rest to a higher power. Your worry is a waste of time and energy. Your concern is understandable and acceptable. Put a smile on your face and a song in your heart. Accept today with a smile. Think of tomorrow as your friend. Buckle up, Buttercup!"

Sara blew her nose and wiped her eyes. The pep talk she gave herself worked. She threw the dirty sheets in the washer, made the bed with her best linens, and continued cleaning until the place was spotless. She sat in her beloved rocking chair to rest her weary bones and drifted in and out of consciousness, fighting to stay awake while embracing the peaceful moments of slumber. Joseph's knock on the door brought her back to reality.

"Sara, are you okay in there? I'm getting worried."

Sara opened the door and threw her arms around Joseph. "I'm fine, no I am wonderful, no I am tremendous. I could not be happier or more excited about tomorrow. I am marrying the most handsome man at Parliament Square."

"Sara, did you decide to marry someone else?" Joseph asked. "The most handsome man can't possibly be me." They laughed and shared a long, warm embrace. This was going to be the beginning of a wonderful life together. No matter what their age, each new day held promise and possibilities.

"Michael called and said his flight was delayed but he expects to be here in time for rehearsal. He'll come directly from the airport. Have you heard from your daughters today?"

"Allison called and said her sisters would be arriving around one and she would be picking them up at the airport. They're going to spend the afternoon together and meet us at the chapel at five. I can't wait to see them and give them each a big, long hug. They're going to love you and vice versa. I'm so glad you finally get to meet them."

Sara said, "I called Luigi's and everything is ready for the rehearsal dinner. They have the private dining room reserved for us. They're expecting us between six and six-thirty, but they understand if we run a little later. It'll be a wonderful evening together with family and friends. I'm really looking forward to it. It's almost lunchtime. Do you want to finish moving my things to your place after lunch? We're almost done. How's Penelope doing? I'm sure it will take a little while for her to get adjusted to her new environment. I'm so glad you two have bonded over the past several months. We'll soon be a happy family of three."

"Yes, let's go have lunch and then finish moving your things. Penelope is doing well. She was curled up on the sofa when I left. I think she misses you but that's to be expected. She and I had a nice chat this afternoon . . . *not*. You know I'm not one to have conversations with animals, not that there is anything wrong with that."

They walked hand in hand from the elevator to the dining room. Some may disagree, but having a significant other makes each day a little fuller. For some, being alone can be difficult. Others are content with their own company. Some choose to be single over their lifetime or after losing their spouse, while others find the single lifestyle hard to accept. Having another person with you when waking up in the morning and going to bed at night provides comfort and security, like having a special blanket or stuffed animal to sleep with when younger.

Jan spoke as they seated themselves at the table. "At this time tomorrow, you will be Mr. and Mrs. Joseph Zimmerman. We will have a married couple at our table. You will be newlyweds. We can't wait to hear all your stories about adjusting to married life. Oh, yes, and share the memories you make on your honeymoon. We want all the details."

"Jan," Betsy said in a scolding tone, "we don't want Joseph and Sara to think we expect to hear details of their honeymoon. Maybe some pictures of the resort, the crystal blue-green tropical water, and the white sand beaches. The rest is private and none of our business. Unless, of course, they *insist* on telling us. I'm more interested in hearing about how Sara handles the flight. I think that might be her biggest challenge."

"Friends, Joseph and I will take lots of pictures to share when we return. I plan to take a couple of pills to help me with the flight. Nothing much, just enough to take the edge off. I'll be fine once the plane is in the air. It's the feeling that your stomach is falling down to your knees as the plane takes off that scares me. Joseph will hold my hand, my meds will have kicked in, and I will visualize Joseph in his skimpy speedo bathing suit. That should do the trick.

"Since this is the last meal we'll share before our wedding, Joseph and I want to thank you for all your support over the past months. We appreciate you being a part of our journey and we look forward to sharing meals and life with you for many years.

"Tomorrow I will have a new name but I will still be the same Sara you have known since we met. Marriage doesn't change a person. Many have tried to change their spouse, thinking the sanctity of marriage would make that happen, but their success rate is low. I remember a quote from a Dr. Seuss book: 'You know you're in love when you can't fall asleep because reality is finally better than your dreams.' I think that sums up the definition of love very well. I may have trouble falling asleep for years and years. And for that, Joseph, I thank you."

The table applauded. Sometimes people live their dreams without realizing it. Busy schedules, distractions, disappointments, misunderstandings, and hectic lifestyles interfere with our assessment of success. Happiness and contentment are often achieved but not realized. Sometimes it's necessary to take a step back to allow the big picture of life to clearly come into focus. Allowing the small stuff to skew one's perspective minimizes the value of our accomplishments. Sad, but often true.

As they left the dining room, Linda approached Sara and

Joseph. "All is set for the taping of the ceremony tomorrow. Nancy just called to say the crew will arrive early, around nine, to set up before the guests start arriving. She wanted me to check with you. The music will start at nine-thirty, followed by the wedding vows at ten. Is that correct?"

"Yes, Linda, that is correct. If the crew is set up and in place by nine-thirty, that would be great. Then Betsy and Jan will begin singing, the chapel doors will be opened and the guests will be seated. Joseph and I appreciate Nancy's attention to detail with this. I'm sure the camera crew will be part of the scenery not part of the event. Thanks for working with Nancy on our behalf. We'll see you tomorrow at the ceremony."

Joseph and Sara moved Sara's remaining items to Joseph's place. Sara went to her salon appointment to have Donna work her magic. Her hair, her nails (fingers and toes), and some waxing (facial hair only). How the young people survive waxing their bathing-suit area is hard to understand. That has to hurt. The facial waxing was punishment enough. The aging process seems to put hair in all the wrong places. It gets thinner or disappears on the head but abounds on the ears, nose, upper lip, and chin.

It was three o'clock when Sara left the salon. Her reflection in the mirror wasn't that of a young woman, but it reminded her of her younger self. Sure, there were wrinkles, each well-earned. The curious part was that although the person in the mirror looked older, that same person often didn't feel that way inside. There was a disconnect between what was perceived and what was reality. Others saw the senior version of Sara, while Sara remembered the younger version hidden beneath the wrinkles, age spots, and sagging skin. Physically there is no way to stop the aging process. Mentally is a whole different story.

Only two hours remained until the rehearsal. Sara went

to her place to prepare. She selected a casual outfit for the evening, with a pair of tailored slacks, a white three-quarter-length sleeve lightweight sweater, and her favorite scarf that Michael had given her for Christmas. It was her favorite item of clothing because it was so beautiful but also because Michael had purchased it for his Aunt Sara. She was so excited he was coming for the wedding. She missed him since he left. They had so much to talk about. She couldn't believe he would be here so soon.

Joseph called to tell Sara that he would come to her place around quarter-to-five and they could go to the chapel together. He said he had a nice afternoon nap while she was at the salon. Men required much less preparation than women. They wondered sometimes why it took women so long to get ready. They knew better than to question it aloud, but they still did it.

"Joseph, I'm ready now. Let's go to the lobby until rehearsal time. I'm too antsy to stay here any longer. I have the heebie-jeebies. See you in a couple of minutes." Sara hung up the phone and took a quick glance in the full-length mirror, which wasn't always her friend. Not too bad for someone who had been around for eight decades. My goodness that was a long time. So much has changed. Both husbands, and many friends and family members were gone. She felt a *what if* moments starting to materialize. She grabbed her purse and headed for the elevator. Not today. She turned after closing her door and ran directly into Michael. *He was here.* She hugged him so hard he cried out "Uncle . . . uncle . . . I give up. I can't breathe."

"Michael, I don't want to let go. It's been too long. I missed you so much. I've been counting the days until you were here. Don't tell Joseph, but I may be almost as glad to see you as I am to get married. Put your luggage inside and join us in the lobby. Where is Alan? How did you get here so early?"

"They put me on an earlier flight. A seat came open and here I am. Alan's working on a special high-priority project and won't able to leave until later today. He'll be here tonight in time for the wedding tomorrow. He said to extend his apologies but, unfortunately, business is business. You'll love him, Aunt Sara. He's tall, dark, and handsome, but his best qualities are kindness and caring. Two attributes that Marcy mostly lacked. We finalized the divorce, amicably. From what I hear, she's already met someone to take my place. I say more power to him."

"Well, make yourself comfortable and then join us in the lobby. Joseph and I will be there waiting for you. I can't wait for you to meet him and for him to meet you. The two most important men in my life. I'm so happy I feel like my heart may explode."

Sara met Joseph in the lobby. They sat side by side on a tufted, floral retirement-village sofa. "I am walking on air. Michael is here a bit ahead of schedule. He's at my place freshening up. He will be down soon. You two are going to get along so well. You are both handsome, kind, gentle men. Joseph, this is really happening. Pinch me . . . I think I'm dreaming. No, never mind. If I am, I don't want to wake up."

# Chapter Twenty

## *Memories Light the Corners of My Mind*

Michael greeted Sara and Joseph with a grin that would have made the Cheshire cat jealous. He looked happier than Sara had seen him in years. His move to the West Coast, his recent divorce from Marcy, and his new lifestyle looked good on him. Both of their lives had changed dramatically since they shared their last meal together at her cottage by the sea less than a year ago. Life was good.

"Michael, I want to introduce you to the young man who swept your old Aunt Sara off her orthopedic flats. This is Joseph. Joseph, this is my nephew, Michael. The two favorite men in my life meet at last."

"Joseph, I am so glad to meet you. Aunt Sara has told me so much about you, I feel I already know you. Sometimes I think I've spent more time with Aunt Sara and Uncle David than I did with my own parents. She was always there to support and encourage me after I lost my mother to cancer. I don't know where I would be today if not for her."

"Thank you for the kind words, Michael," Sara replied. "All I can say is ditto. You've been like the son I never had. I wanted children but unfortunately, they never materialized for me. I've been fortunate to have lived a good life, but it would never have been the same without you being a part of it. I'm so proud that you're here to walk me down the aisle. Thank You."

Hugs and kisses were exchanged and some tears of joy were shed. It was a happy time. It was a memory in the making. As people age, they sometimes fear their memories can only be viewed in the rear-view mirror. That is far from the truth. Memories are timeless and the ability to make new ones has no age limit.

Photographs are our messengers for past events. They capture that special moment in time physically, but our intangible memories are often more vivid and meaningful. They live in our hearts and minds, triggering emotions often without warning. They can be our friend. They can be our enemy.

Joseph took Sara's arm. "Let's all head to the chapel. We can sit and talk there with more privacy and less noise. The lobby can get loud and the chapel doors are always open. My daughters should be here soon and I asked them to meet us there. I'm so excited to see them all together for the first time in many years. I think the last time we were together was at their mother's funeral. It's sad, but funerals and weddings are often the only things that bring families together."

The chapel was empty. It was a small room with a seating capacity of somewhere around eighty. The pews were polished mahogany, matching the pulpit. Sara had attended Sunday services here several times, but she missed her old church, pastor, and congregation.

The pastor at Parliament Square was nice enough, but the message wasn't presented as she felt it should be. It was more of a Sunday-school lesson than a life lesson. She wanted a meaningful message that related to life as she lived it. Maybe she expected too much.

The chapel was freshly vacuumed and dusted. It smelled like a floral room freshener had been sprayed to mask the room's somewhat musky aroma. The flower arrangements would be delivered tomorrow morning before nine o'clock. The bouquets for Sara, Michele, and Allison, and the boutonnieres for Joseph, Chuck, and Jim would be left in the pastor's office.

It was four-thirty. Thirty minutes until rehearsal. Sara introduced the pastor to Michael and told him how lucky she was to have her nephew walk her down the aisle. They reviewed the sequence of events, starting with the guests arriving and ending with Sara and Joseph kissing after the ceremony. It was pretty straightforward.

Betsy and Jan entered the chapel using their outside voices. They seemed to only have one volume level, one that could easily be heard by those who either forgot or refused to wear their hearing aids. "Betsy, I told you we were too early. We aren't supposed to be here until five. We're almost thirty minutes early. Sorry for interrupting you, Sara and Joseph. Jan always wants to be early. We can wait outside."

"No worries, ladies," said Joseph. "We're waiting for the others. You haven't interrupted anything. Let me introduce you to Michael, Sara's nephew from California. She's shared stories about him and now you get to meet him in person. My three daughters will be here soon. I am so excited to see them.

"We look forward to hearing your melodic voices tomorrow. For the rehearsal, you'll only sing the song that Sara walks down the aisle to. The others can wait until tomorrow when the guests are being seated. Jan, I must compliment you on your outfit. I don't think I've ever seen a lime more green or a lemon more yellow than those colors. You certainly are the fashion plate at our dining room table."

"Thank you, Joseph. I found this colorful frock at a yard sale last year. Quite the deal! Can you believe someone would want to part with it?" The entire group rolled their eyes. "Betsy thinks it's too bright, but I disagree. As you know, I like the unusual. I like to set myself apart from the others. You won't find *me* dressing like an old lady."

"Well, it certainly is one of a kind, just like you, my dear friend," Betsy replied. "We've been best friends for decades. We met when the dinosaurs roamed the Earth. The good thing about best friends is that you can tell them anything. No subject is off limits. I remember when you told me I looked like a man after I had my hair cut very short, Twiggy-style. That kind of hurt my feelings until the waitress called me 'sir' at the restaurant. Your unique dress code is what defines you. It makes you who you are. I applaud you for being an individual and standing out in a crowd."

"Betsy, you've always spoken from the heart. That's one of the things I like most about you. You embrace a conservative lifestyle while I support more of a liberal, individualistic one. They say opposites attract. In this case they're correct. But enough about us. Let's get this rehearsal started. I'm ready to sing my heart out with my best friend ever."

Joseph's daughters entered the chapel with William. They exchanged hugs and greetings. His three girls were all beautiful, each in her own way. Allison was a sweet woman who Sara had grown quite fond of over the past months. Joseph introduced Sara to Sofie and Annette, both very attractive. Annette inherited many of her father's facial features, especially his crystal-clear blue eyes. Sofie was tall and slender. She hung onto Joseph's arm as if she was fearful that he'd run away if she let go. Annette was the only brunette of the three and had a bit more meat on her bones. Allison and Sofie were very slender and dressed to accentuate their slim figures. Sofie wore a less fitted, colorful one-piece dress with short sleeves.

"Sara, I want you to meet Allison's sisters. I'm so sorry that it took this long for you to meet them. They live far away, as does Michael, but that's really no excuse. In the future, visiting will be on our agenda. Sophie is married to Brett, a very successful financial planner. Annette is a career woman, who her old dad hopes will find love someday. Marriage isn't for everyone. However, it is for me and you, so, let's get this rehearsal started. I'm starving."

The pastor explained the program. "Betsy and Jan will sing while the guests are seated. Chuck and Jim will seat the guests. At ten, the organist will play 'Blue Skies' which will trigger the processional. Jim, Chuck, Joseph, and I will enter through the side door and stand at the left side of the altar. The attendants will slowly, one at a time, walk down the aisle and will stand to the right of the altar. Michael, with Sara on his arm, will then make the slow walk down the aisle to the altar. When they arrive, I'll ask, 'Who gives this woman to be married to this man?' Michael, that's when you say, 'I do.' At that time, Michael will step back and have a seat in the front row on the right side. Sara, you'll turn and hand your flowers to the attendant to your right and then join Joseph at the altar. Then the ceremony begins.

"Joseph and Sara, when we met you requested that I do the standard wedding nuptials, which I will have you each repeat in short segments to each other. I will then ask that you place the rings on each other's fingers. Following the exchange of rings, I will pronounce you husband and wife, adding that the groom may kiss the bride. At that time, the organ music will begin to play at a louder volume. Joseph and Sara, followed by the attendants and groomsmen in paired sets, will proceed back the aisle and exit the chapel.

"It's very simple. The musical processional, vows, and release will probably take less than fifteen minutes. The guests will leave the chapel and walk to the activity room where the reception will be held. Any questions?"

Jim broke the silence. "Pastor, please be sure to include the no-money-back and limited-warranty-guarantee documents with the marriage certificate. Senior weddings require additional paperwork. *Just kidding.* I can hardly wait for the best man's toast tomorrow at the reception. I have so much material but so little time."

"Thank you, Jim," said Joseph. "Jim is our resident comedian extraordinaire. He has a joke for every occasion. I'm a bit concerned about the toast tomorrow. I don't think we have any questions. Let's walk through the ceremony now and then take off for dinner. Our reservations are for six o'clock."

The rehearsal went well. As they finished, a tall, dark, handsome young man walked into the chapel and quietly took a seat in the last pew. Sara didn't recognize him, but she suspected it was Alan. He looked so young and athletic. Physical appearance doesn't announce sexuality. Often those who are what used to be labeled a hunk aren't attracted to the opposite sex. Sometimes those who appeared to be of the Casper Milquetoast variety are very popular with the ladies. It's a mixed-up world. No assumptions should be made nor judgements passed. To each his or her own.

Michael introduced Aunt Sara to Alan as they walked to the cars. Alan said he thought it was amazing she had fallen in love and decided to get married. He confessed that he had never been married but hoped to one day. He winked at Michael as he said so.

The procession of vehicles left the parking lot headed for Luigi's. Joseph took Sara's hand in his. He could sense that she was tense. That was understandable. He rubbed the top of her hand and looked into her eyes. "This is your last chance to change your mind, young lady. Speak now or forever hold your peace. Understand, however, I will tell everyone that I'm the one who broke off the engagement. I don't want people to think I'm the jilted Joe."

"You're stuck with me, Joseph. Maybe I should give you one last chance to take back your proposal? Possibly you have your eye on one of the younger, under-seventy ladies. I'm certain you'd be snatched up quicker than you can say Jack Robinson. If there were a senior edition of *GQ*, you'd be on the cover. It's you and me, lambchop. Too late to turn back now."

Chuck stomped on the brakes without warning. Sara and Joseph would have been in the front seat if not for their seat belts. "What happened?" Sara shrieked. "I don't want to die the day before my wedding."

"A dog ran right in front of my car. I just missed him. There he is running up the hill. A man is chasing him. Boy, that was lucky for him and for us. My guardian angel is working overtime today. I can't even imagine hitting someone's pet. My hands are shaking. I think I may order a drink before dinner."

He drove slowly the rest of the way. Accidents happen all the time, every minute of every day. Sometimes someone is at fault, other times, like this one, no one is at fault. Driving isn't something to take lightly. One mistake can alter the rest of your life, the lives of those in your vehicle, and anyone else involved. Some seniors are outraged when their driving privileges are revoked. It's the single biggest factor contributing to loss of independence later in life, but it's often for the best.

"Chuck, your reaction time was excellent. I don't know if I could have braked as quickly," said Michele. "I'm glad everyone's wearing seat belts. The wedding party in casts and bandages wouldn't be a good look. Goes to show that you just never know what the day holds. A split-second decision can be the difference between life and death. But I don't want to get all philosophical, so let's change the subject."

When they arrived at Luigi's, Chuck pulled up to the entrance and the ladies went inside. Chuck and Joseph drove around to the other side of the building to the parking lot. "Joseph, I want to say congratulations and wish you and Sara all the happiness in the world. You're so fortunate to have found each other and decided to get married. I wish you years of happiness and health. At our age, or at any age for that matter, there are no givens. Be thankful for each day you have together and make each one count. I'm not sure I could ever marry again. I'm too set in my ways, and it's hard for me to make compromises. I'm just a grumpy old man, I guess."

Joseph smiled. "This is between you, me, and the bedpost:

I am scared to death. I love Sara and I'm not afraid of marriage. My fear is losing her. I watched my wife die slowly and it was the most awful experience of my life. There was nothing I could do to save her. Losing a loved one, slowly and painfully, has to be one of the most difficult experiences. You know what the end result is going to be, but you refuse to accept it. You hope against hope that it will get better, knowing all the while that it won't.

"But enough of that for now. I'll hope for the best, think positive thoughts, and enjoy each day we have together to its fullest. Throwing the good away because we fear the bad accomplishes nothing. Let's go have that drink you mentioned."

Most of the guests were seated and deep in conversation when Chuck and Joseph arrived. The private room was very nice, with two tables of six set up quite elegantly for dinner. At one table were Michele, Betsy, Jan, Jim, and the pastor. Michele motioned for Chuck to come join her. At the second table were Allison, William, Sophie, Annette, Michael, and Alan. The head table had only two place settings, one each for the soon-to-be bride and groom.

It was a large room for such a small gathering, but Joseph insisted on reserving it for the rehearsal dinner. He wanted a private place to share the meal with family and friends. He didn't want a big table in the main dining room as that could be noisy and crowded on Friday evenings. This was perfect. It might cost a bit more, but it was only money.

Michael stood and clinked his knife against the side of his water glass. The room grew silent. "I'm Michael, Sara's nephew from California. She may have mentioned me to some of you from time to time. Aunt Sara and I spent countless hours together for as long as I can remember. She's been like a second mother to me and now that my mother has passed on, I think of her as my adopted mother. When she called me after the Valentine's Day party and announced her engagement, I was silent at first when I heard the news. I didn't think anyone was good enough to marry her. But as she continued to talk about Joseph and their wedding plans, I quickly realized that my old only-in-chronological-years aunt was head over heels in love. She was as giddy as a schoolgirl. That was totally out of character for my very in-charge, I-can-do-anything-better-than-you-can aunt. This was the real deal.I could not be happier for the octogenarian love birds.

"Aunt Sara, I know you were very unhappy initially after I strong-armed you to sell your precious cottage by the sea and move to Parliament Square. I told you it was for your safety, but I could see you didn't agree. I think you resented me for some time, and I felt at times that maybe I made a mistake in forcing you to move. Maybe there were other options. Having said that, think how different your life would be if you hadn't moved. You would still be alone, not even aware of the fact that falling in love again was possible. Sometimes the events that we fear or dislike the most become positive moments. This is one of those moments. I wish you both the best on all that lies ahead. You serve as an example to the naysayers that love conquers all."

Glasses clinked as the guests applauded Michael's words. It's funny how our perspective changes as we travel life's path. When we're children and young adults we can't wait for milestones to arrive. Our first love, our first car, our first apartment, our first job, our first child, and the list goes on and on. We wish to be old enough for this or that to happen. Some say it's wishing your life away.

Then as we mature and reach mid-life through the pre-retirement years, we continue to look forward to life-changing events, but at the same time we accept the fact that many of the items on life's wish list have already been accomplished. We no longer wish our lives away.

As the final chapter unfolds, sooner than we expected, we begin to wish that we would still be alive to experience milestones rather than anticipating the milestones themselves. Hoping to see a grandchild's college graduation, or to dance at their wedding, or hold our first great-grandchild in our arms, remembering when we held our own children for the first time, so long ago it seems like only yesterday.

Over the years, the opportunity to take part in new, never-before-experienced activities or events diminishes. When we're young the possibilities are limitless. As we age, the possibilities decrease. We've already logged that event in our journal of life, or maybe the window of opportunity for that activity has closed.

Then, in our senior years, there is a very limited likelihood that new and exciting undertakings are within our grasp. That's not to say there's nothing new to look forward to, it's just that the looking has to be done with a magnifying glass.

The memories of life's moments massage our hearts with gentle fingers of love. Sometimes they remind us of days gone by, days that are missed but will never be forgotten. Our hearts often ache for those times. Memories make us smile. Memories make us cry. Sometimes they make us laugh and cry at the same time. They make us realize life is too precious to waste a single day. There are always new memories to be make right around the corner, while our old memories quietly light the corners of our minds.

ELAINE C. BAUMBACH

# Chapter Twenty-one

## *Daaa Dum Da Dum*
## *Daaa Dum Da Dum*

The evening was magical. The food was delicious and plentiful. The conversation was animated and abundant. The love in the room was almost palpable. It was an event to remember for years and years to come. The many photographs taken on cell phones would capture the evening in pictures. Their hearts recorded that happiness internally.

The rehearsal was certainly a red-letter event in Sara and Joseph's journal of life. Having family and good friends in attendance to celebrate this momentous occasion made all the difference. Good times.

Many toasts were made while drinks were consumed, dinner was enjoyed, and dessert was served. Family members spoke about special times shared over the years. After dessert, they moved from table to table talking, sharing, hugging, and smiling. They shared old memories and made new ones.

Jim, of course, threw in a couple humorous anecdotes. "Being asked to be someone's best man is like being called for jury duty. You don't really want to do it, but you know you have to. You have to get dressed up and pretend to be an upstanding member of the community. The difference between jury duty and being the best man is I don't get to cast a vote as to whether a life sentence is in order. That's already been decided. Stay tuned. Tomorrow I have the honor of toasting the newlyweds at the wedding reception. *Toasting* being the key word."

Joseph stood and clinked his glass to get everyone's attention. "Sara and I want to thank everyone for coming to share our special day. We wish each of you lived closer so we could get together like this more often. Physical distance may separate some of us, but our heartstrings will always keep us connected. We love you all more than words can ever express." Sara saw a tear run down Joseph's face as he talked. He quickly wiped it away. He was truly a wonderful and caring man. She hugged him and kissed him tenderly. Someone in the room chanted, "Get a room . . . Get a room" as everyone applauded their public display of affection.

The evening came to a close, although no one wanted it to end. Tomorrow was another day and they all needed a good night's rest to prepare. Michael, Alan, Sofie, and Annette were probably suffering a bit of jet lag after their long journeys. The senior citizens were up past their normal bedtimes. They said their goodbyes, more hugs were exchanged, and they headed for the parking lot.

Fortunately, the trip back included no screeching tires or runaway dogs. The air was crisp, and the sky was clear allowing a view of countless stars. Sara said, "Star light, star bright, first star I see tonight. I wish I may, I wish I might, have the wish I wish tonight."

Joseph said, "I haven't heard that since I was a boy and my mother would make that wish. It certainly brings back memories. I remember asking my mother what she wished for and she always said, 'Health, happiness, and wealth, in that order.' I can almost see her, tussling my hair every time. So long ago but never forgotten."

Chuck asked, "Sara what did you wish for tonight?"

"I wished that tomorrow will be as perfect as I imagine it will be and that Joseph and I live happily ever after. Then some additional wishes for our wedding night and honeymoon, but those are X-rated. I can't share them in mixed company."

They all laughed. It had been a wonderful evening. Sara wanted to spend more time with Joseph's daughters and get better acquainted with them. Also, she hardly had any time to chat with Alan. Sara believed in first impressions. Her first impression of Alan was indeed a good one. He was well-mannered, well-spoken, very personable, and most of all he seemed to dote on Michael's every word. You could see the chemistry between them although there was no outward show of affection. Sara wondered if the others knew they were more than just good friends.

It was almost ten o'clock when they arrived back at Parliament Square. Most of the residents had probably retired for the night. Even though daytime naps are common, bedtime is routinely early, sometimes unintendedly so as the sandman visits while the TV loudly announces the early version of the late news. Or the book being read lies open, dropped when sleep took control.

"Chuck, thanks so much for driving tonight. We really appreciate the fact that you are still allowed to get behind the wheel. When we get back from our honeymoon, Sara and I would like to take you and Michele out to a movie and dinner. It's nice getting away from our often mundane way of life. Also, it will give me a chance to share the back seat again with Sara."

They exchanged good-nights and took the elevator together to their apartments. Sara had given her key to Michael as he and Alan would be spending the night there. Sara and Joseph went to Joseph's place for the night. Penelope was so glad to see them when they opened the door. She meowed loudly. Sara went to the kitchen and got her a treat. Penelope ran under the bed with it. All was quiet.

Sara was very tired. It had been a long day. A wonderful day, but a long one. She was ready for a good night's sleep. "Joseph, we can share the bed tonight but that's all. I'm saving myself for our wedding night, not to mention the fact that I am fifty shades of tired. Don't get any ideas. Tomorrow night will be here in twenty-four short hours. I'm worth waiting for. Sleep tight and don't let the bedbugs bite. Love you."

"You get no argument from me. I'm content to have you next to me and feel your body against mine. This is the first night we'll share a bed together, with many more to follow. I haven't slept in a bed with another woman since losing Laura, so I can't guarantee that I don't snore or make other annoying noises. It's probably a good thing that you'll have your hearing aids out. Sweet dreams, my love. Tomorrow will arrive very soon. It is going to be wonderful."

Sara drifted off quickly. Joseph watched her sleep for several minutes, her breathing soft and regular. He remembered watching Laura as she slept near the end of her struggle. He didn't want to close his eyes in fear that she'd be gone when he opened them again.

It was a terrible time. Now Sara will be his wife and he'll once again be half of a married couple. He loved the thought of being Sara's husband. He feared being left behind again if she was called home before he was. It was an honest concern, not an imagined anxiety. He reminded himself not to allow unsupported fear to steal his happiness. He smiled, put his arm around Sara, and was soon asleep.

Penelope jumped on the bed just as the first rays of sunshine entered the room. Sara was a bit disoriented. She was in a different bed, in a different apartment, and there was a man in her bed. She rubbed the sleep away and gave Joseph a morning hug. "Handsome, you are going to make a sweet old lady happy today."

Joseph said, "But won't you be jealous?"

Sara lightly punched him in the arm and he winced, holding his arm as if he had been shot with an arrow. "You pack quite a punch, lady. I guess I'll have to mind my P's and Q's when I'm with you. Do you have a permit to carry that weapon?"

They fell laughing into each other's arms. Penelope was not amused. She meowed loudly and jumped off the bed. It might take her awhile to adjust to a family of three. She had

Sara to herself for years. Now there was this other non-furry creature around. She didn't like sharing Sara.

They decided to skip the community breakfast table and have some coffee and toast together in their robes. Joseph had a veranda that faced east, so the morning sunshine arrived there early. The air had a little nip in it, but the warm sunshine and hot coffee made sitting on the veranda in their robes quite comfortable. They welcomed the sunshine. No rain clouds lurking anywhere, just clear blue skies. They sipped their coffee as the birds provided a morning medley of songs.

The phone rang and Joseph walked back inside to answer it. He returned after a couple of minutes. "There was a question about something on the brunch menu. I took care of it. I think you're going to be very happy with my culinary choices. I'm anxious to see and taste the wedding cake. You know how I love buttercream icing."

"I do. I'm going to get dressed and go back to my apartment. I told Michael that I'd be there around eight to get ready for the ceremony. He said that he and Alan would clear out and give me some privacy. They'll go get coffee and be back by nine-thirty. This is really it, Joseph. Don't look now, but we're getting married today!"

Sara bade Joseph and Penelope goodbye and headed for her apartment. It was almost eight. Her hair and nails were done. Maybe some final touches to her hair. She needed to put on blush, a light application of mascara, and lipstick. Michael and Alan were already gone when she arrived. Everything was in order. They had made the bed and neatly folded the towels.

Sara removed the dress from its protective bag and held it in front of her. It was perfect. She carefully pulled it over her head. She hadn't put the lipstick on yet to ensure that none would soil the dress. The lace insert on the bodice, matching the lace around the hem, made this gown special. It wasn't a run-of-the-mill beige dress. It had a style of its own. She'd add the scarf wrap after the ceremony at the reception.

Sara stepped in front of the full-length mirror. She didn't see the wrinkled, sagging skin of an old woman. Today she saw only a blushing bride. She saw a woman ready to begin a new chapter in her book of life. A woman not afraid of change. A woman not sad because she was on the downhill slope of life.

A woman who, no matter how little sand remained in her hourglass, was ready to enjoy each and every grain as it dropped through the neck to the bottom chamber. It may take a day, it may take a year, it may take a decade or more, but each falling grain of sand would be anticipated, appreciated, and enjoyed.

Sara carefully applied her lipstick. She fluffed her hair a bit and sprayed it well. It was only nine o'clock when she finished. Maybe she should go to the chapel to check on the flowers. She asked Joseph to remain in his room until she let him know she was out of view. Didn't want bad luck if he saw her before the ceremony. Yes, she would go to the chapel and check on things. She was too excited to sit quietly in her empty apartment watching the minutes slowly pass, each one slower than the one before.

The elevator was empty. Many of the residents were more than likely still in the dining room finishing breakfast. Maybe as a married couple, she and Joseph would lounge in their jammies eating breakfast together in their apartment some mornings. Dinner was another story.

Sara, who once loved puttering around the kitchen and preparing meals, had become spoiled. She no longer had to shop for the ingredients, prepare the food, and clean up when she was done. She really didn't miss that process at all. Maybe she was getting lazy in her old age.

As she left the elevator, everyone in the lobby looked in

her direction. Or maybe it was just her imagination. Did she have toilet paper stuck to her shoe? No, they were looking right at her and giving her a thumbs-up. She smiled and hurried off to the chapel.

The television crew was setting up when she arrived. The flowers had been delivered and placed around the room as previously discussed. They were beautiful. Nancy greeted Sara. "Good Morning. You look stunning. What a beautiful day for a wedding. We're almost finished with the setup. We arrived early, so we'd be ready and out of the way when the guests begin to arrive. We want to blend into the background."

"Thank you, Nancy. You have been most accommodating with both the taping of the segment you did for *The Local Moment* and for your presence here today. Joseph and I appreciate that. We're so happy for this joyous occasion and your filming it for others is like the icing on the cake. I better go hide so the groom doesn't see me. Thanks again."

Sara gave the room a parting glance, then left to meet Michele and Allison in the office next to the chapel entrance. They would wait there until the cue was given to start the processional. The bouquets were gorgeous. Fern had done a wonderful job.

While she sat in the room alone waiting for Michele and Allison, she wondered if David could see her getting married to another man today. Would he approve? Would he be sad? Would he be happy for her? She heard it said in church that you are reunited with your loved ones after death. She questioned what happened if there were several spouses involved. Were you reunited with the spouse you were married to the most years, or the one you were married to most recently, or was there some other heavenly formula used to make that determination? Wow, that was certainly something to ponder. She had never even thought about that before. Fortunately, at that moment, the door opened and derailed her train of thought.

"Good morning, dear friend," Michele said, giving Sara a welcoming air-hug so as not to rumple their dresses. "What a beautiful day for a wedding. You make a stunning bride. I'm a bit nervous as an attendant. I can't imagine how excited you must be. Seems like we were just together in the activity room addressing the invitations. Time moves at Mach speed the older we get."

"Thank you, Michele. Yes, time does seem to pass more quickly, although some days feel as though they last forty-eight hours. But today will definitely not be one of those days. It will be over in the blink of an eye, but it will live in my heart forever. Don't get me started. My dripping mascara will make me look like the bride of Frankenstein."

"Hello, ladies," Allision said upon entering the room. "Don't you both look stunning. I heard there's going to be a wedding here today. The lobby was buzzing with chatter when I walked through. I don't think Parliament Square has hosted a wedding in a long, long time. This is a red-letter day. I peeked in on dad and the groomsmen a moment ago. Jim was practicing his toast, which I am certain will be entertaining. William and my sisters will be arriving soon. And you couldn't ask for a nicer day.

"I am honored to have you two ladies as my attendants. You both look stunning. I may have to remind you that it's bad etiquette to look prettier than the bride. I have a gift for you both to thank you. I thought it might look good with your dresses today."

They opened the boxes to reveal a single strand of pearls in each. They would certainly compliment the black dresses. Sara assisted them in putting them on. "This is in appreciation of you being here with me today. You are truly what friendship is all about. Pass the tissues please."

They heard Betsy and Jan arrive through the closed door. They would never be described as being as quiet as church mice. Sara imagined their metallic dresses. Oh my, what a sight. Maybe everyone would be too polite to notice. After all, some of them did have compromised vision.

There was a tap on the door. It wasn't ten o'clock yet. Who could it be? Sara cracked open the door. It was Michael. "Aunt Sara, you look so pretty. Like a senior Barbie doll. Joseph is a very lucky man. I'll be across the hall and come to walk you down the aisle when the organist starts playing 'Blue Skies.' I remember you singing that to me at bedtime when I was little. I didn't comprehend the meaning of the lyrics until I was much older. It is a perfect selection. See you soon." He gave Sara a peck on the cheek before leaving.

Sara checked the time again. It was nine-fifty. Ten minutes to go. They heard Betsy and Jan singing in the distance. The guests must be taking their seats. The minutes ticked by slower than molasses in January. The ladies made small talk to help the time pass. After what seemed like an eternity, there was another tap on the door. Michael popped his head in and said, "Aunt Sara, they're playing your song."

Michele and Allison left the room to start their slow walk down the aisle to the altar. Michael winked and smiled. "You know I love you very much. You've always been there for me. I wish you and Joseph unlimited happiness today and for all the days to come. You deserve nothing but the best and I think you've found it with Joseph. All your tomorrows start today. Let's do this."

They left the room and entered the back of the chapel. Everyone stood and turned in their direction. Sara felt like her knees could buckle at any moment. Her legs were like rubber. She was walking, but her feet couldn't feel the floor. She focused on her handsome Joseph waiting for her at the altar. She saw no cameras or guests. All the faces in the room were out of focus except one.

She kept walking, holding Michael's arm tighter and tighter with each step. When they reached the altar, she felt warm tears of joy moisten her cheeks. She heard David's voice. *Be happy, my love.* Michael took a seat and Sara moved next to Joseph at the altar as Michele reached for her bouquet. The preacher cleared his throat and the ceremony began.

The rest was a bit of a blur. Vows were exchanged, rings were given. There was a kiss. Then the music started and she was walking back down the aisle on Joseph's arm. There were smiles on the faces of all in attendance. She walked into the room as Sara Jennings. She walked out of the room as Sara Zimmerman.

Sara entered this new chapter of her life with all the confidence of a four-year-old in a Superman cape. It was indeed the geriatric version of reckless abandon.

# Chapter Twenty-two

## *A Sense of Humor and Selective Hearing*

Sara felt the butterflies escape from her stomach, the Jell-O leave her legs, and the doubts evaporate from her head as she and Joseph left the chapel. She did not faint. She did not trip and fall. She did not lose her voice. She did it . . . she really did it. She was married.

The activity room was decorated beautifully and the food smelled heavenly. The personnel at Parliament Square had done the decor without Sara or Joseph's knowledge. They expected tables and chairs to be set up and the food buffet to be ready, but not the beautiful wedding decorations and flowers. This was over-the-top. What an unexpected surprise, which is often the best type of surprise.

"Joseph, look how wonderful everything looks. I feel like I'm in a dream. Did you know anything about this?"

"I plead the fifth. As long as you're happy, I'm happy. Now I want to introduce you to the buffet line. We must go first. The guests have a lean and hungry look in their eyes, so let's fill our plates and get out of the way."

"There are several breakfast-oriented selections. The first is the perfect breakfast quiche. It's a flaky, made-from-scratch crust filled with fluffy eggs, sharp cheddar cheese, spinach, and perfectly crisp bacon. The crust is blind baked first. Then the egg mixture is added to the already partially baked crust and placed in a hot oven for 40-45 minutes. It's one of my favorite breakfast foods. I'll make it for you some lazy winter morning. While baking, the smell fills the air with the most aromatic fragrance. It makes your mouth water and forces you to check its progress through the window in the oven door."

"The second morning-themed delicacy is stuffed French toast. The ingredients are layered in a large casserole dish a day in advance and spends the night resting together in the refrigerator. A single batch contains a dozen eggs, sixteen slices of French bread, sixteen ounces of cream cheese, two cups of milk, and one-third cup of maple syrup. Cinnamon and nutmeg are sprinkled on top. They made four batches for today's event. In the morning, the mixture is baked for forty-five minutes until the top is a golden brown. It's eaten warm with plenty of butter and syrup."

"The third and final sun-up selection is what I like to call ooey-gooey cinnamon buns. I remember as a young boy, waking up to a sweet aroma wafting in the air after spending the night at my grandparent's house. My grandmother would get up at the crack of dawn to start the process. The dough is yeast-based, which requires time for the mixture to double in size before being rolled out. A sugary, buttery mixture is combined with cinnamon and perfectly chopped pecans. When removed from the oven, we would burn our mouths on the first bite because we just couldn't wait for them to cool. Mouth-burning delicious."

"Joseph, I'm so glad you took responsibility for making the food decisions. I would have ordered eggs, bacon, and muffins. You've provided our guests with culinary delights that they will be talking about for years. I can't wait for you to cook some of them when we get back from the honeymoon."

"Sara, I'll be happy to do that. I do love to cook, but I never seem to take the time to bother anymore. I promise I'll make you breakfast in bed one morning every week. How does that sound?"

"That sounds heavenly. I don't think anyone has ever served me breakfast in bed. I'm going to hold you to that promise. All three choices look and smell delicious. The guests are going to be very impressed. Now, what are the three luncheon selections on the menu today?"

"Well, I didn't go with the often-served shrimp, or roast beef, or even chicken. I wanted to provide items that were off the beaten culinary path. The first is one that I know you love.

It's also a favorite of mine. It might sound mundane, but the taste is out of this world. It's cheeseburger soup. You've raved about it since you had it at lunch with Allison and Michele. I tracked down the recipe and there is a very large tureen of it here today."

"The second mid-day delicacy is an item that used to be a favorite appetizer at my restaurant. The patrons just couldn't get enough of it. First, you carve out a large, round loaf of Hawaiian bread or Italian bread. The mixture inside is basically what you would use to make an Italian hoagie. It includes pepperoni, Genoa salami, deli ham, provolone cheese, diced red onion, mayonnaise, Italian seasoning, and finely chopped romaine lettuce. All ingredients are mixed well, then spooned out and eaten on the bread cubes made when the loaf was carved out. It is to die for."

"The third and final item is mini salmon cakes. They were another favorite on my appetizer menu. They're made by combining wild sockeye salmon with sautéed onions and peppers, eggs, breadcrumbs, Worcestershire sauce, ketchup, and pepper. All ingredients are mixed together, shaped into small patties, and flash fried until golden brown on each side. The bite-sized salmon cakes are then baked until heated through. They're served with tarter and cocktail sauces. Scrumptious."

"Well, I'm very impressed. First because you're so food savvy, and second because I now realize that I can put you in the kitchen to cook for me. Another event I have never experienced. A man slaving over a hot stove to prepare meals for me. We may never eat in the dining room again."

Just then the guests started tapping their water glasses with their silverware. They wanted the newlyweds to kiss. Sara and Joseph accommodated them. "Pucker up, young lady. We are obligated to give the guests what they want."

The guests started going through the buffet line. Each

item had a printed recipe placed in front of it so the guests could decide if any ingredients were off their list of approved foods. Food allergies can cause unwanted reactions, especially among age-challenged guests. Certainly, no one wanted to call 911 during the wedding reception.

Joseph spotted the cake at the end of the buffet line. He anxiously awaited the buttercream frosting. "That cake is gorgeous. I can't wait until we cut it and I can try the frosting."

Sara replied, "You're going to be in for a pleasant surprise."

The guests followed Sara and Joseph, one table at a time, through the buffet line. The room was abuzz with chatter. Joseph had done a great job. He had many hidden talents, some of which were beginning to surface. What other unknown qualities lurked below that handsome, personable façade? Only time would tell.

The guests stopped by Sara and Joseph's table to offer congratulations and best wishes. The television crew moved their gear into the activity room after the ceremony. They were taping the reception. Hopefully, Jim's toast would be family-oriented and television worthy.

Betsy and Jan, in their almost reflective metallic dresses, were all aflutter. "I told Betsy that I plan to catch the bouquet. I caught the flowers at my great niece's wedding but unfortunately no knight in shining armor ever materialized. Maybe this time will be different. I've been practicing my catches with a pillow in my apartment. I think I'm ready. I was going to bring my catcher's mitt but I thought that might be over the top."

"Sorry to disappoint you, Jan, but I'm not throwing my bouquet. We thought it best to skip that. We'll leave the removal of the garter and the tossing of the bouquet to the younger generation. We don't want anyone getting hurt in a bouquet-grabbing frenzy and, believe me, no one wants to see Joseph remove the garter from my vein-covered legs. That ship hasn't just sailed, it's been put in dry dock."

After everyone finished eating and the buffet items were removed from the room, it was time for the long-awaited best-man words of wisdom. Jim stood and cleared his throat. "May I have your attention please? I know that you will all be very disappointed if I stand up here and present a serious from-the-heart speech, so I won't disappoint you. I do have some kind words. I just can't remember what they are right now."

"Where do I start? He is strikingly handsome. You can find his picture in the dictionary next to the word *gentleman*. He is Einstein-smart. He makes the ladies' heads turn when he enters the room. But enough about me. Let's focus on the happy couple.

"I read somewhere the perfect best man speech should last as long as it takes for the groom to make love. So, ladies and gentlemen, please raise a glass to the happy couple, my speech is over!

"All kidding aside . . . no, wait, there's more. I don't want to disappoint my comedy club followers. Someone once said that marriage is a fifty-fifty relationship. Anyone who believes that knows nothing about women or fractions. Now remember this: There are two things that make a marriage last: a sense of humor and selective hearing. Many of us here today already have age-related selective hearing, so we are halfway there. Let's raise a glass to Sara and Joseph. Cheers. The best is yet to come, my friends!"

The guests lifted their champagne glasses and toasted the newlyweds. Jim did a great job mixing family-oriented humor with a short agenda. Those who know him breathed a sigh of relief when he concluded the toast and returned to his seat. It could have been much longer, cornier, and adult-themed. Good job, Jim.

The guests left their assigned tables and mingled. Each waited for a turn to personally deliver best wishes to the bride and groom. It was a time for sharing. Lots of hugs and kisses were exchanged. After all the guests had a chance to spend a couple of private minutes with Sara and Joseph, Jim asked for everyone's attention once again.

"Now is the time to cut the wedding cake. I understand that Joseph is anxiously awaiting this moment. Word has it that he's a connoisseur of buttercream icing. Once he tastes this icing, he may not even want to smear any on Sara's face. Sara has a little surprise for Joseph. No, not that that kind of surprise. Get your minds out of the gutter. This one is related to the icing."

"Joseph, when Allison took me cake shopping, we met Angie at the bakery and her specialty was buttercream frosting. We started talking to her about the cake and mentioned Antonio's name and you won't believe this, but he is Angie's great uncle. He taught her how to bake and inspired her to open up a bakery. This icing was made from Antonio's recipe. Small world, isn't it?"

Joseph stood. "What are we waiting for? Get me a dinner-size plate and a fork. No little dainty cake plate for me. I'm ready to dig in. I may consider sharing it with the guests but then again, I may want to keep it all for myself."

The guests gathered around the cake and prepared for the couple's first shared bite. Sometimes the bride and groom end up with cake up their noses and smeared on their faces. Not the case here. Joseph gently placed a small bit of cake into Sara's mouth. She, in return, being the lady that she was, smeared Joseph's face from eyebrows to chin with cake and icing. The crowd cheered her on.

"Sara, my love, if this icing was not so darn good, I might be upset. But keep it coming. I'll take this icing any way I can get it. You have outdone yourself young lady. I demand a cake with this icing every year on my birthday. Maybe on *your* birthday, too."

Pictures and videos were taken by many on their smartphones. Funny how taking photos has changed over the years. In the days of old (a mere decade or two ago), everyone took pictures with cameras that had rolls of film loaded inside. When you clicked the camera button to record that moment in time, you had no idea if you got a good photo or not. You took the film to the local drugstore or camera shop for processing. A week later you picked up the prints. Sometimes the pictures were good and what you expected; other times not so much. Of course, the event was long over when you discovered that special moment in time that you thought was captured on film was not.

In this day and age, anyone can take a picture on a phone or tablet and instantaneously see the result. If it's not to their liking they can retake the photo again and again until it is, sometimes even relighting the birthday candles to capture the perfect video of them being blown out. The younger generation is unaware of how picture taking has changed. The new technology is all they've ever known.

So many changes in technology and lifestyles have taken place over the decades. Each generation remembers what they grew up with, but many have little if any idea what their parents or grandparents experienced, a perfect reason for sharing life experiences with the younger generation whenever possible. Family history and stories are lost if not shared prior to losing the story teller.

When seasoned adults share with their grandchildren and, if lucky enough, their great grandchildren, the kids often shake their heads in disbelief when told there was no television, no electronics, no portable telephones. They just cannot imagine life at that level. Living your childhood in the 1940s and 1950s compared to living your childhood today might be the difference between living like the Flintstones and living like the Jetsons.

It appeared the television crew was amused by the cake sharing. They had smiles on their faces while the cameras were rolling. Probably not a good example to show younger children as they might think smearing cake in someone's face is okay. Well, their parents can explain it to them.

The cake was shared by the guests, many returning for seconds. It was the highlight of the reception. As the celebration wound down, Joseph asked, "Sara, would you mind if I spent some time with my daughters before heading to the boudoir? I know you're chomping at the bit to get me under the covers but I think we should at least wait until dark. At my age, everything looks better with less light. Seeing my daughters again made me realize how much I've missed them."

"Joseph, that sounds like a great idea. It's much too early to even think about putting on lingerie. I agree with the benefits of low lighting. I wanted to spend some time with Michael and Alan this afternoon anyway. That will give me time to do that. Let's plan on a rendezvous after dark. If you think you can stay awake that late."

"Very funny. Don't worry about me. I've been practicing staying awake later by watching the early version of the late news, which is broadcast at ten o'clock. That reminds me, remember when the television stations would sign off for the night and show the station information or logo on the screen? Those days are long gone. Now you can watch hundreds of shows on the television at any and all hours of the day or night. That memory sure dates me, doesn't it? Oh, well, if the shoe fits. Let's say our goodbyes and thank yous and then spend some family time. I look forward to seeing some of that frilly nightwear up close and personal. In low light, of course."

The guests began to filter out slowly. The wedding and reception couldn't have been more perfect. The weather cooperated. Family members were in attendance. Memories were shared while more were made. It was certainly a day to remember and cherish.

Michael suggested that Sara change into more comfortable clothing for the afternoon. Sara agreed and told Michael that she'd meet him and Alan in the lobby in thirty minutes. She said she had a favor to ask him.

Joseph, his three daughters, and William left for Allison's house to share the afternoon. They had so much catching up to do. It was wonderful having his three girls together, even if it was only for a short time. They should never be separated from each other this long again.

Sara met Michael and Alan in the lobby. "Michael, I was wondering if you could drive me to the cemetery to visit David's grave. I feel a need to tell him in person about today. I know he isn't there, but in my heart, I feel it's the only place where I'm able to communicate with him. I'm at peace with my decision to marry Joseph. This visit will finalize that for me."

"Sure, Aunt Sara. That's no problem. We can chat on the way. We haven't had much time to talk since we arrived. Sit up front with me and Alan can sit in the back. I'd like you and Alan to get better acquainted. The wedding was lovely as was the reception. I'm so happy for you both."

"Thank you. You being here to walk me down the aisle meant so much to me. I promise we'll be out to visit you in California since Joseph said we'll be going there to visit his daughters. I still have to get over my fear of flying, but Joseph will know the right words to say. I'm so lucky to have found him."

The ride took about thirty minutes. They discussed Michael's job, the new apartment that he and Alan shared, the new dog they had rescued. There were so many items to cover in such a short amount of time. When they arrived at the cemetery, Sara asked that they give her a private moment with David.

"David, I must apologize for not visiting more. I think of you often, but since my driving privileges have been revoked it's more difficult to get here. I feel that we've reconnected over the past several months.

"I married Joseph today. You would like him. He reminds me a lot of you. How I was lucky enough to find both of you is a mystery. I truly feel in my heart that you're smiling down on us. I wanted to visit you today because I felt it would provide closure. You'll always live in my heart. I'll never forget you or our wonderful life together. My marriage to Joseph will open a new chapter in my book of life without erasing any of the previous ones. I love you, my sweet, sweet David."

Sara wiped her eyes as she returned to the car. Today was certainly a mixture of bitter and sweet emotions. Life is often like that. Our journey from the crib to the crypt is a series of ups and downs, with hopefully more ups than downs. We mourn the loss of family and friends while celebrating graduations, weddings, and baby showers. While traveling life's journey, if we can remember yesterday without regret and welcome tomorrow without fear, we will truly find contentment in today.

"Aunt Sara, I know that was hard for you. You and Uncle David were like parents to me while I was growing up. Losing him was so unexpected. Life throws us a lot of curve balls. It's how we react that defines us. Instead of wallowing in self-pity, you always took the high road. You taught me valuable life lessons which I execute whenever possible. Thanks for always being there."

The ride back to Parliament Square was filled with memories and talk of future events. Michael and Alan discussed a permanent relationship and possibly adoption. Marcy never wanted children, which Michael didn't agree with but respected, but now he and Alan shared a desire to be parents. Same-sex marriage is now an approved status, so a marriage would precede the request for adoption. One step at a time.

Michael opened the car door to allow Aunt Sara to exit at Parliament Square. He kissed her on the cheek and gave her a bear hug. "We want you and Joseph to visit us after you return from your honeymoon and get settled in. We'll show you the sights of San Francisco and we'll have a wonderful time together. I'll keep badgering you until you make the trip. Alan and I hoped we could give you a lift to the airport in the morning. I know you arranged for the courtesy van to pick you up but we'd really like to take you. It would give us a little more time together and I hardly had any time to get acquainted with Joseph. We don't mind getting up early. What do you say?"

"That's very nice of you. We'd love that. Your flight is later in the day, so you could come back here and catch a couple z's before heading to the airport. It's a deal. We'll meet you in the lobby at 6:45 tomorrow morning. And no questions about the wedding night. You know I'm not one to kiss and tell."

They had an unwritten code stating that they would always be there for each other. No matter how many miles separated them, their heartstrings would always keep them connected. Blood was indeed thicker than water.

Sara entered the building for the first time as Mrs. Sara Zimmerman. It felt good. The lobby was quiet. Joseph was probably still with his daughters at Allison's house. He was welcome to spend as much time as he wanted. They had a lot of ground to cover. She was going to check on Penelope and, with any luck, sneak a short nap. It had been a big day. A wonderful day. A life-changing day. A first-page-in-a-new-chapter day.

Penelope greeted Sara at the door. The apartment was empty. The room smelled of Joseph's after shave. It was a bit musky but not in a bad way. Her years of being a widow and living alone had come to an end. The wedding vows replayed in her head . . . for better, for worse, for richer, for poorer, in sickness and in health, to love and to cherish, till death do us part. This was the real deal. She was again half of a married couple.

After Penelope was fed, Sara made herself comfortable on the sofa. She felt a little nap would help her stay awake past nine o'clock. She didn't want to fall asleep on her wedding night. She reviewed the day's events in her mind. She held her hand out in front of her to examine the ring on her finger. She wasn't dreaming. She was living the dream.

It was dark when she awakened. What time was it? How long had she been asleep? Where was Joseph? She sat up, slowly returning to the world of the living. She really needed that recharge.

"Good morning, Mrs. Zimmerman. Or should I say good evening?" She caught a glimpse of Joseph on the rocking chair across the room. "I've been watching you sleep since I returned an hour ago. I may have drifted off a little myself. It's been a long, wonderful day. I don't want it to end."

"How was your visit with the girls? I wanted to doze off for a few minutes, but apparently my afternoon nap lasted much longer. Maybe I won't be able to sleep tonight. Or maybe I won't want to sleep tonight. What do you think?"

"My visit with the girls went great. We reminisced. We caught up with current events. We hugged. We made memories. We took pictures to capture the visit. I almost didn't want to leave, but I knew my bride anxiously awaited my return. I brought back the remainder of the cake. Want to share some for dinner? Too late to go to the dining room, but cake sounds better than meatloaf anyway."

"You go enjoy some cake and I'll freshen up. I'm not hungry. I had a snack after my visit with Michael and Alan. Now I'm going to attempt to transform this seasoned body into wedding-night status. Keep the lights and your expectations low. Please put the do not disturb sign on the door. Tomorrow we leave for our honeymoon. Tonight, we get to know each other."

The bedroom door closed, intentionally leaving Penelope on the other side. The remainder of the wedding night activities is censored at Sara and Joseph's request.

The wedding may be over, but that's not the end of the journey. Many more adventures remain at Parliament Square.

# Addendum

## CAST OF CHARACTERS

*(PS indicates Parliament Square Retirement Village Character)*

**Alan**
Michael's Boyfriend

**Allison**
Joseph's daughter, wife of William; they have two sons

**Andrew**
Sara's boyfriend after returning from Ireland; impregnates Sara out of wedlock and marries her; killed in the Korean War on July 14, 1953

**Angie**
Owner of the bakery where wedding cake is purchased

**Antonio**
Baker who makes the best butter cream frosting

**Barbara**
Sara's younger sister born in 1942, died in 2010

**Cassandra**
Bridal store customer assistant

**Carol**
Friend from cottage by the sea, husband still alive

**Celeste** (PS)
Resident Bingo addict

**Charles "Chuck"**
PS tablemate after Pam's passing, two children, wife passed away two years prior to his arrival at Parliament Square

**Cindy** (PS)
Staff member who is very tall and wears too much makeup

**Cookie**
Bakery store clerk

**Cynthia** (PS)
Fitness Instructor

**David**
Sara's second husband born in 1935, died in January 2012

**Deborah** (PS)
Tablemate. Perfect, with an accent on affluence

**Diane**
Friend from cottage by the sea, husband still alive

**Donald**
Sarah and David's pet Airedale Terrier

**Donna** (PS)
Hairdresser

**Emily** (PS)
Registered Nurse

**Elizabeth "Betsy"** (PS)
Tablemate. Effervescent and friend to all, best friend to Jan

**Fern**
Florist for the wedding arrangements

**Jan** (PS)
Tablemate. Outgoing, flashy dresser, best friend to Betsy

**Jean** (PS)
Resident. Met on bus to mini golf, interested in Joseph

**Jim** (PS)
Tablemate. Talkative, comedian, opinionated

**Joseph Zimmerman** (PS)
Tablemate. Crystal blue eyes, handsome, recently widowed; Sara's betrothed; three daughters: Allison and husband William live close to Parliament Square, Annette lives on West Coast, Sofie and husband Brett live on West Coast

**Kathryn**
Baby Sara lost at birth

**Laura**
Joseph's first wife

**Linda** (PS)
Perky social director

**Lynne** (PS)
Resident liaison

**Marcy**
Michael's wife

**Mary** (PS)
Tablemate. Sun-damaged skin, private, quiet

**Michael**
Nephew, Barb's son, Sara's caretaker, born in 1972

**Michele**
College roommate, friend from cottage by the sea

**Nancy**
TV personality who records Sara and Joseph's story for *The Local Moment* TV segment

**Pam** (PS)
Tablemate. Childlike and friendly

**Penelope**
Sara's eight-year-old cat

**Ray Adams**
Jean's love interest

**Sara Jennings**
Main Character, last name Jennings.

Born: September 10, 1934

Went to Ireland: June 5, 1950 (age 15)

Returned from Ireland: June 1952 (age 17)

Married Andrew: December 1952 (age 18)

Lost baby: June 1953

Lost Andrew: July 1953

Began nursing schoo: 1954

Married David: December 31, 1964 (age 30)

Moved to cottage by the sea: 1976

Moved to Parliament Square: July 2017

Resides in room 316, Parliament Square Retirement Village

**Tom**
Sara's older brother.

**William**
Allison's husband

# Preview of Coming Attractions

Sara transitioned from a solitary but independent lifestyle at her cottage by the sea to life at Parliament Square; from frightened, unaccepting, and rebellious to tolerant, friendly, and happy. It was a bit of an uphill battle, but meeting and falling in love with Joseph changed her from a lonely senior citizen into a blushing bride.

Life at Parliament Square will continue after the wedding and honeymoon. Residents will come and go as Sara and Joseph's journey of life continues. Growing older is a process. It's not for the faint of heart. There will be good days and there will be bad days. The hope is that the good days outnumber the bad ones.

Chapter One of the third book in the *Parliament Square* series, *The Best Is Yet to Come*, follows. The journey continues . . .

# *The Best Is Yet to Come*

## Chapter One

### *Up, Up and Away*

Morning arrived much too quickly. The wedding night was better than Sara imagined possible. As she walked through the lobby to meet Michael and Alan, her face felt warm. She was a walking poster for the phrase *blushing bride*.

All their tablemates were gathered to wish them bon voyage. Hugs were exchanged and congratulations were offered. It was time to head to the airport and board the plane. Had she taken enough of her calming medication? She felt butterflies in her stomach and a bit light in the head. Had the doctor suggested she take two or three pills? How many had she already taken?

Michael pulled the car around and helped Joseph load the luggage. "Aunt Sara, what's in your suitcases? I hope nothing flannel or matronly."

"Don't you worry, young man. I left all my flannel, turtleneck nightgowns in the drawer. I packed Victoria's Secret flimsy nightwear, perfect for a honeymoon. I hope Joseph agrees."

Sara and Joseph sat together in the back seat holding hands.

Michael and Alan were up front discussing the best route to the airport. They had plenty of time to get there. Betsy and Jan waved from the curb and shouted in unison. "Live each day like your last, and live each night like your first!"

"Wow, that is great advice. I'll have to remember that one," Alan said. "Your friends are almost as excited as you are. They seem genuinely happy for you. Sometimes people get jealous. They don't seem that way at all. I wish more of my friends were like that. Some pretend not to be, but you know under the façade of well-wishing there's insincerity and jealousy. Hang onto them. They are definitely keepers."

The ride to the airport was uneventful. Traffic was light. The skies were clear, not a cloud in sight. They made small talk. Sara was nervous but refused to give in to her anxiety demons. Her "relaxing" pills should be taking effect momentarily.

"Aunt Sara, Alan and I will be traveling back to the coast today and our flight leaves around noon. We'll make sure you get to your gate and then head back to Parliament Square to gather up our things and the other rental car. We'd love to stay and wave as you depart, but time doesn't permit it. We want to hear all about your week, though. The censored version, of course. We'll discuss a trip out west for you sometime over the summer months, after you've settled into married life. I know Joseph wants to visit his daughters out west too, so you can visit all of us during your stay. Alan and I have many sights that we want to show you. It'll be so much fun."

"Thank you, Michael. I'm very thankful you were able to take time out from your schedule to walk your old Aunt Sara down the aisle. It meant the world to me. Alan, it was wonderful meeting you and we look forward to visiting you in California."

Michael and Alan assisted them with their bags, exchanged

hugs, said their goodbyes, and departed. This would certainly be a day to remember, one that Sara never expected. She was on her honeymoon with the love of her life. How lucky could one girl get?

The airport was relatively quiet. It was early. Some folks like to schedule their departure closer to lunch so they don't have to set the alarm too early. Sara was a morning person. Joseph not as much, but he wasn't a night owl either. Mixing an early-bird-gets-the-worm person with a burn-the-midnight-oil person could be risky. Penelope may have to learn to eat breakfast a bit later.

The ticket clerk was very upbeat and friendly. "Good morning. Please place your bags on the carousel in front of you and hand me your tickets. Your flight is on time. There are no delays or weather-related issues. Your boarding area will be at Gate 8. They'll announce when boarding may begin. Have a wonderful flight."

Sara's stomach rolled as she smiled at the clerk. She felt a bit calmer but also a bit queasy. *Oh, please don't get sick,* she kept repeating in her head. That would not be a good start to the trip.

They had about an hour before departure time. Joseph said, "Let's walk around the airport a bit to kill some time. I know you're nervous. Maybe it'll take your mind off the flight. I always felt safe flying. If my number is up, then I guess my number is up, no matter what I'm doing. My concern is if the pilot's number is up and he takes me with him." Sara's face turned white. "That's a joke, young lady."

"I would laugh but I'm too nervous. I understand that flying is safer than any other mode of transportation, but my mind just won't accept the facts. My medication should take effect soon and I'll be fine. If I sleep through the flight, don't awaken me. I remember on an old television program they used to drug the one character before flying. Otherwise, he refused to fly."

To take her mind off the impending flight, Sara suggested they play the people game like she and Michael used to do. There were plenty of other travelers walking around the airport waiting for their departures. Joseph said, "You have to tell me the details of this game. You mentioned it once or twice, but I'm not sure I know how it's played."

"The rules are simple. You select a person from the crowd. Then you tell me what you think that person's name might be and what that person does for a living, all based on the person's appearance. Of course, we never know if what we choose is correct, but the fun is in the guessing. Ready?"

"Sure. I like this kind of game where there are no winners or losers. I'll go first." He looked around the terminal. "The young woman walking toward us with the red luggage is named Lucy. She's a sales representative for a pharmaceutical company and on her way to a conference in L.A. This is kind of fun. It would be even more fun if we could ask the people what their actual names are and what they do. But that might get us into trouble. They might think we're two seniors who wandered away from the home. How was that for my first turn?"

"That was very good. I almost believe you. My turn. The gentleman holding a folded trench coat over his arm and purchasing a copy of *The New York Times* is named Edward and he is a retired college professor on his way to visit his family on the West Coast. His appearance is very erudite, and his perfectly shined shoes and freshly starched shirt make me think he may possess an OCD gene or two. Any thoughts?"

"I like that one. I wonder what people would guess if they chose you or me? They'd probably guess your name is Star and you're a pole dancer in a men's club." Sara rolled her eyes.

"I'm such a jokester. I think that would be referred to as a knee-slapper."

"Very Funny, Joseph. I think someone would guess your name is Reginald and you're a once-famous movie star from the early days of Hollywood, retired now and traveling to a tropical island to celebrate your marriage to a much younger woman."

Just then their flight number was announced over the PA system. Boarding would begin in fifteen minutes. The flight would depart on schedule. It was time to go to Gate 8, get in line, and embark on their honeymoon adventure. Sara noticed that her anxiety levels seemed to be under control. Maybe the meds? Maybe the walk and the game? Maybe being with her new husband? Whatever it was, she was glad she didn't feel like running for the exit screaming "I don't want to die! I am not getting on that death trap!"

Sara noticed that many of the passengers were younger, but that was the case more often than not as she advanced in age. Many of the senior population limit activities as their internal clock ticks away the years. They don't feel comfortable in crowds or on public transportation or in loud restaurants, and the list goes on. That's unfortunate, because they miss out on many events and grow out of touch with the younger generation by sitting in their rocking chairs watching *Wheel of Fortune* each evening after dinner, then dozing off before waking up to go to bed.

There are different degrees of old. Some younger people grow old before their time. They mimic elderly behavior while still in their prime. Some older people limit their lifestyle because they feel they're too old to do what they used to feel comfortable doing. They don't challenge themselves to remain as active as possible, accepting that their senior status prohibits them. Others throw caution to the wind and accept every offer as long as their physical abilities support them. They don't allow their chronological years to diminish their choices. Hurray for them.

Flying again was certainly a challenge for Sara. It was outside her comfort zone, but if she refused it would restrict what she could experience in her marriage to Joseph. She didn't want to miss a seven-day honeymoon in a tropical paradise with Joseph because she had a fear of flying. There were no trains to Montego Bay. She felt a little buzz in her head as they approached the boarding gate. Thank goodness for the pharmaceutical companies.

Joseph insisted on purchasing first-class tickets even though Sara felt it wasn't necessary. Sara wasn't tight with her money, but was still rather frugal. She had never flown first class in her life, so she was still able to experience firsts, even at her advanced age.

The flight attendant escorted them to their seats while congratulating them on their recent nuptials. She assisted them in placing their carry-ons in the overhead compartments. "Looks like beautiful weather for today's flight. Please push the call button if you need anything. I'll be around with the beverage cart after we reach cruising altitude. Relax and enjoy your flight."

"Joseph, I feel rather relaxed and a bit light-headed. I guess that's better than anxious and nauseous. We'll be here for a little under four hours. Maybe they'll show a movie to distract us and pass the time. Or we could fold down the armrests, cuddle under a large blanket, and become members of the mile-high club. That would definitely be a first for me, but I fear we may draw attention to ourselves. We could meet in the lavatory, but I doubt there's enough room to carry out our mission. It would be like a game of Twister in there. I guess we'll just have to be content with hand-holding, snuggling, and sipping wine."

"My, I certainly am glad that you decided to medicate for the trip. I haven't seen this frisky side of you before. I must admit that I like it. I brought some of my own pharmaceutical products. I'm told they're very effective. Fasten your seat belt sweetie, the plane ride could get bumpy and provide a precursor to the action in our honeymoon suite tonight."

The flight attendant explained the floatation devices, emergency exits, and blah, blah, blah. It must get boring to do this day in and day out. The passengers feigned interest to be polite. If this airplane went down, no one would remember these instructions or emergency door locations. Panic does that to people.

The plane slowly started to move. The airport passed quickly as the plane's speed picked up and the nose pointed skyward. There was liftoff and the landing gear clicked into place as they ascended. Sara felt her stomach roll and squeezed Joseph's hand. He squeezed back and leaned over to give her a peck on the cheek.

The pilot spoke over the intercom. He thanked the passengers for flying with them, announced the weather conditions in Montego Bay, the expected arrival time, cruising altitude, etc. Before he ended his announcements, he sent out congratulations to all the newlyweds aboard, especially Joseph and Sara, a very special couple.

Sara leaned her head on Joseph's shoulder. "I wonder how the pilot knew we were on board. Did you mention our honeymoon to anyone at the airline? I bet you did, didn't you?"

"Do you think I would do something like that? Maybe one of the flight crew overheard your sexual proposition. Yes, I bet that's it. They're going to keep their eyes on you, you love-starved young bride."

They laughed out loud. While they talked, the plane reached its cruising altitude and the *fasten seatbelts* sign went dark. Time to settle in for a while. The attendant brought them headsets to use while watching the movie *Paddington 2*. Sara remembered going to see *Paddington* several years ago with a friend and they laughed through the entire film. This was a good choice as it was family-oriented, funny, and didn't include any devious plots or intense characters. Yes, they would enjoy this movie and it would make the trip go by faster.

The movie was entertaining, the food was delicious, and the service was superb. Maybe she could get used to flying first class. As they approached their destination, the captain announced that everyone should return to their seats, put the trays in the upright positions, and fasten their seatbelts. She poked Joseph's arm. "You need to put your tray up. Didn't you hear the announcement?"

"I have a problem. I think I may have taken the 'little blue pill' prematurely. If I push the tray up, someone's going to ask, 'Is that a banana in your pocket or are you just happy to see me?' Maybe we can stall for a while and the situation will resolve itself, although the advertisement does say it can possibly last up to four hours."

Just then the flight attendant reminded Joseph to raise his tray. Sara broke into loud, contagious laughter. She couldn't control herself. Although this was a VERY embarrassing moment for Joseph, her laughter just could not be contained. This might be a common occurrence for a younger man but not for someone in his eighties. This was definitely a diary-worthy event.

Thinking quickly, Sara handed Joseph her cardigan and he spread it across his lap before raising the tray. This was quite a dilemma. They could laugh about it later but right now Joseph's funny bone was not tickled.

Maybe he could tie the sweater around his waist and

allow the sleeves to dangle in front of him? Yes, he would try that. Hopefully the elephant trunk in the room would not be revealed. This was already a trip to remember.

As they prepared to exit, Joseph fumbled with the sweater as he attempted to wrap it around his torso. It was a lovely purple with embroidered flowers on the sleeves, obviously not his. Maybe no one would notice, or they'd think that, at his age, he grabbed his wife's sweater by mistake. Whatever the case, he wasn't going to take it off just yet. Next time he'd pay more attention to the small print on the bottle.

As they exited the plane, Sara was embraced by the warm, tropical air. The sun shone without a cloud in the sky. She tried not to look at Joseph, fearing that the sweater would fall off or that she'd start laughing again. Joseph looked straight ahead as they checked the area for the Sandals complimentary transportation vehicle. Someone from the resort was supposed to retrieve their luggage from the carousel. Hopefully their suitcases, especially the one with the honeymoon nightwear, would find their way to the resort.

As they boarded the shuttle, Joseph handed Sara her sweater. "Everything seems to be under control. Maybe it was the walk from the tarmac to the shuttle, or the embarrassment of the situation, or maybe just sheer luck. I can tell you this, I *will* read the fine print from now on. I know you thought it was hilarious, but from my vantagepoint it wasn't the least bit funny. And . . . this is one honeymoon memory you are forbidden to share. There will be others, but this is the first."

"I felt so badly for you and I apologize for my behavior. Not sure if the medication, the airplane wine, the stress of flying, or some combination of all three made me react the way I did. I just couldn't control myself. I think I may have peed my pants a bit. The flight attendant looked at me as if she thought I was having a seizure."

The resort was as beautiful in reality as it was in the brochures and the video. Most of the guests were tanned, young, and wearing beachwear that left little to the imagination. "Eyes forward, Joseph. Most of these people could be our grandchildren. But not to worry. They don't have the wisdom that comes from experiencing life. Of course, when you look like they do, who cares what wisdom you possess? Let's head to our room where we can unpack, unwind, and carefully read that medication label. This is our honeymoon. Put the *Do Not Disturb* sign on our door."

# About the Author

ELAINE C. BAUMBACH was born in Whitestone, New York; transplanted in Camp Hill, Pennsylvania while in the fourth grade; and has lived in Central Pennsylvania ever since. After college she embarked on a forty-plus-year career in information technology. During that time, Elaine dabbled in writing, nurturing a gift she discovered during her early journalism classes in high school.

As the aging process became a personal reality, Elaine authored her initial manuscript in the Parliament Square Series, *You Can't Get There From Here*, published in 2018. This book introduced readers to Sara, the senior-citizen protagonist, in addition to other residents of her retirement community. The engaging characters and their adventures illuminate a part of life that is rarely celebrated in fiction, blending the stark reality of senior living with its inherent comic undertones.

This second book, *For Better . . . For Worse*, follows daily life for Sara and the other residents at Parliament Square. She says hello to new friends, says farewell to others, and prepares for a much-anticipated octogenarian wedding.

The series continues with *The Best Is Yet to Come*, currently in the making. The first chapter appears at the end of this book.

Elaine lives with her husband, James, and their furry family members, Andrew and Pippa, in New Cumberland, Pennsylvania.